FORBIDDEN SHORES

FORBIDDEN SHORES

JANE LOCKWOOD

A SIGNET ECLIPSE BOOK

SIGNET ECLIPSE
Published by New American Library, a division of
Penguin Group (USA) Inc., 375 Hudson Street,
New York, New York 10014, USA
Penguin Group (Canada), 90 Eglinton Avenue East, Suite 700, Toronto,
Ontario M4P 2Y3, Canada (a division of Pearson Penguin Canada Inc.)
Penguin Books Ltd., 80 Strand, London WC2R 0RL, England
Penguin Ireland, 25 St. Stephen's Green, Dublin 2,
Ireland (a division of Penguin Books Ltd.)
Penguin Group (Australia), 250 Camberwell Road, Camberwell, Victoria 3124,
Australia (a division of Pearson Australia Group Pty. Ltd.)
Penguin Books India Pvt. Ltd., 11 Community Centre, Panchsheel Park,
New Delhi - 110 017, India
Penguin Group (NZ), 67 Apollo Drive, Rosedale, North Shore 0632,
New Zealand (a division of Pearson New Zealand Ltd.)
Penguin Books (South Africa) (Pty.) Ltd., 24 Sturdee Avenue,
Rosebank, Johannesburg 2196, South Africa

Penguin Books Ltd., Registered Offices:
80 Strand, London WC2R 0RL, England

Copyright © Janet Mullany, 2007
All rights reserved

SIGNET ECLIPSE and logo are trademarks of Penguin Group (USA) Inc.

ISBN-13: 978-0-7394-8841-6

Printed in the United States of America

Even though it will make them roll in their graves,

this book is dedicated to the memory of the brave men and

women of the English abolitionist movement.

ACKNOWLEDGMENTS

Thanks to my agent, Lucienne Diver, and my editor, Laura Cifelli, who pointed out that although earnest Quakers collecting signatures for petitions in bad weather might do a lot for me, others might prefer a Caribbean island; writer friends Kiki Clark, Colleen Gleason aka Colette Gale, Robin L. Rotham and the ladies of the Passionate Ink Critique Group, and Pam Rosenthal; and thanks to Matron Lucy and the other inmates of the House of Corrections for diversions at work. Finally, grateful thanks to Maryland Romance Writers for the raging mob.

CHAPTER 1

Bristol, 1800

This was not the way Allen Pendale had intended his departure. He had anticipated a nostalgic, sentimental farewell to the city of his birth, which was dirty and noisy, bustling with life. Seagulls wheeled and cried overhead. The winter sky was a hazy smoky blue, with St. Mary Radcliffe's spire rising proudly among the terraced houses.

It was a pity that Lord Glenning, red-faced, cuckolded, and irate, drove his curricle in a chaos of spilled barrels and cursing seamen along the dock toward the *Daphne*. And an even greater pity that a ship could not be merely untethered and flicked forward with some sort of nautical whip, like a horse and carriage.

"Pendale, you whoreson!" Glenning's voice was audible, barely, as the *Daphne* meandered away from the quay.

The other passengers, standing in a knot on deck, surrounded by their luggage, paused and looked at Allen.

"Do your friends always bid you farewell so?" one of

them, a redheaded woman, asked, a cynical smile on her face.

"Only the ones I've cuckolded." Now Allen could see Glenning's bulbous face, and his arm rising, sighting, the glint of pale winter sun on metal.

"Get down!" Allen shouted and pushed the woman down, landing on top of her. Breathless he waited for the sound of the shot.

"What are you *doing*?" The woman struggled beneath him, her face red with fury, and flailed at him with a free arm. "Get off me immediately!"

"Beg your pardon, ma'am. I was merely saving your life."

"It would not have been in danger had you kept your breeches buttoned."

"I regret I didn't have such foresight." He raised himself from her, sorting out cloaks, her umbrella, and a reticule, and then he plucked her bonnet from under his knee.

"You've ruined it!" She swiped at her flattened bonnet.

"Beg your pardon," he said again, wondering if Glenning was reloading, or merely waiting for his head to appear within range once more.

The woman slithered out from under him, scooting herself across the deck, giving him a fine view of her ankles and one collapsed stocking, dull and gray, revealing a pale, slender calf.

Allen listened for the crack of a gunshot but heard only the stamp of feet and the hoarse chant of the crew as they worked the capstan.

The woman was the first to stand. "A telescope," she said in disgust.

A telescope?

He stood and peered at Glenning, who roared out inaudible curses, his fist waving in the air. Sure enough, his lordship had a telescope tucked under one arm.

"I thought—" Allen began in self-defense, his face reddening, but the woman turned away.

The gap between the sloop and the quay widened, as the sails overhead snapped and filled. The canvas belled, round and dazzlingly white, while familiar landmarks ashore slid by.

He followed the red-haired woman, prepared to make an apology for manhandling her. "I beg your pardon, ma'am. I acted unforgivably."

She shrugged. "I thought you were supposed to fight under these sort of circumstances."

"Only if the woman is worth dying for or marrying," he responded. "I don't believe we've been introduced. Allen Pendale, at your service, ma'am."

"I am Miss Clarissa Onslowe."

She glanced at him with a look he was used to seeing from his clients, when they had something to hide and hoped he would not notice the omission. *Not a very good liar,* he concluded, while wondering for a brief moment what this dowdy spinster—with admittedly attractive ankles—could possibly have to hide.

"Pendale? You are related perhaps to the Earl of Frensham?"

"My father."

Well, of course. What did she expect, on a ship bound for the Caribbean island where the earl owned one of the largest estates and was neighbor to her future employer? She gave Pendale an abrupt curtsy and turned away to follow the other woman passenger, Mrs. Blight, down to the cabin they were to share. Not only had Pendale been pursued by a jealous husband, but he had also been foolish enough to nearly miss the tide. She gave a sniff of annoyance, and gathered her cloak and skirts to descend the steep stairway, little more than a ladder, that led below.

She followed Mrs. Blight, ducking through a low doorway, and went into a small cabin the size of a closet.

"Where—" she began before realizing that what she took for two shelves were in fact their beds. Dim light filtered in through a small greenish glass window.

"Well, this is fancy, I must say!" Mrs. Blight smiled, obviously impressed with their accommodation. "Mind your head on the lamp, my dear. This is a far cry from the last ship I was on."

"You have sailed before?"

"Not exactly." Mrs. Blight, her back to Clarissa, dug into her possessions. "I was visiting a gentleman on a man-o'-war—some years ago, when I was young and foolish." She sighed, and produced a substantial traveling medicine chest, from which she took a tiny mirror, a rouge pot, and a length of gaudy ribbon. "The captain will expect us to show our best finery at dinner. Take this ribbon, my dear Miss Onslowe. Your cap may be finely worked, but it's not at all becoming."

Clarissa took the ribbon, a tawdry piece of stuff she'd normally turn up her nose at and give to a chambermaid. However, in these close quarters, it would be diplomatic to accept. "Thank you, Mrs. Blight."

"A woman should always appear at her best. I know these things, my dear, from my line of business."

"Your line of business?" Mr. Blight was Lemarchand's overseer—she knew that much. She tried to imagine what possible trade Mrs. Blight might have practiced—a servant, she would have guessed, or possibly the proprietor of a small shop. Not at all the sort of woman she would have imagined herself traveling with.

Mrs. Blight, mirror in hand, looked up from patting rouge on her cheeks. "I kept a house. I tell you, I was hard put to make the choice when Blight asked for my hand. When a woman does as well as I did, she must make sure she does the right thing in giving it all up for love." She sighed, produced a small vial, and shook a little of its contents onto the palm of her hand; then she dabbed liberally at her neck and bosom. A strong scent of roses filled the cabin.

"I was a housekeeper, too," Clarissa said, although wondering whether they had indeed shared the same profession.

Mrs. Blight squinted at herself in the mirror, and watched Clarissa lace the ribbon through her hair. "Better," she said. "Why, you might pass for thirty if you'd use a little rouge."

"I'm eight-and-twenty," Clarissa said. "Thank you for the ribbon."

She grabbed her spinster's cap and placed it on her head, covering the gaudy ribbon. Then she squeezed past Mrs. Blight and made her way onto the deck again.

To Clarissa's surprise she enjoyed dinner, which took place in the captain's stateroom, a relatively large space spanning the width of the ship, with the last of the afternoon light streaming in through many-paned windows on both sides. Captain Trent, a genial weather-beaten man in his forties, sat at the head of the table with Mr. Johnson, his first lieutenant, sharing the duties of host. Although Clarissa had heard Mr. Johnson bellow ferociously at the seamen on deck, he seemed struck dumb by the company of two women. He had taken some pains with his appearance; his hair was combed into a fashionable attempt at disorder, which was successful but for a wayward tuft at the back of his head.

The food was good—of course, at this stage in the long journey, everything was fresh—and the wine even better.

"Mr. Lemarchand enjoys his wine," Captain Trent said with a wink. "'Tis a pity indeed only eleven of the dozen casks of claret we carry will arrive safely. Your health, ladies and gentlemen."

Glasses clinked. Mrs. Blight shifted her considerable bosom onto the table and addressed Allen Pendale. "If I may be so bold, sir, what is your business with Lemarchand?"

Clarissa noticed he took a good look at the woman's breasts before replying.

"I'm something of an interloper, ma'am. My chief business is with his neighbor, the Earl of Frensham."

"An equally fine plantation, so I've heard," the captain said.

"Soft on his negroes," Blight said, removing a piece of gristle from his mouth.

"Blight is Lemarchand's overseer," Mrs. Blight explained to Clarissa. "And to think he came all the way back to England to marry me."

Pendale grinned. "You're on your honeymoon?" He turned to Clarissa. "We shall have to allow the lovebirds some time alone, Miss Onslowe."

"Indeed." What appeared to her an appallingly crude comment merely seemed to entertain the Blights. She attempted to change the subject. "I am to serve as governess and companion to Miss Lemarchand."

"Ah yes. A pretty young miss, she is. We carry a pianoforte for her, and all sorts of things young ladies like: books and lengths of cloth and fashion papers." The captain laughed. "He didn't want to risk the pianoforte on one of his slavers; besides, there wouldn't have been room."

"It would be a shame to take up a space that could hold twenty or so slaves with something so frivolous as a piano," Clarissa commented.

"Quite so, ma'am." The captain gave her an agreeable smile, her irony lost on him.

"They're not people, rightly speaking," Blight said. "You don't want to get sentimental over them, Miss Onslowe. You'll see what savages they are, when we get there."

"Why, shame on you, Miss Onslowe. You speak like one of those abolitionists," Mrs. Blight said. "We are all dependent on the trade, and on Mr. Lemarchand's generosity. Besides, business is business, my dear."

Clarissa bit her lip. "I've met negroes in Bristol. They are not savages, sir. They are as civilized as you or me."

Blight smirked. "You'll change your mind, Miss Onslowe." He ripped a wing off a chicken. "Lemarchand might be interested in knowing what sort of woman he hires to educate his daughter, that's all."

"And you will make it your business to let the gentleman know?" Clarissa asked.

Blight looked at her, his gaze stripping her naked. "It may be my duty."

Allen Pendale leaned forward, elbows on the table, one large hand around his wineglass, plate pushed aside. "Blackmail is against the law, Blight. Besides, I doubt Lemarchand cares what a woman thinks."

"And I am supposed to thank you for that astute observation, Mr. Pendale?"

"If you wish, Miss Onslowe." He addressed Blight again. "Lemarchand is well aware of sentiments in England. Feelings run strong. Why, the rope makers of Liverpool, whose livelihoods depend upon it, petition for the trade to end, and housewives boycott sugar, as well you know."

"We bought only sugar from India, where I was housekeeper," Clarissa said.

"So, if you have such scruples, Miss Onslowe, why are you here?" Blight tossed chicken bones onto his plate.

"That, sir, is my business."

"Ladies, gentlemen." Captain Trent shook his head. "We've several weeks ahead at close quarters. It's best if we try to get along, for I assure you, things will be most uncomfortable if we do not. I believe you'll find the island agreeable—Mr. Lemarchand lives like a king, the climate is like that of a fine English summer day, and so long as you do not get fever, you'll do well enough. There's plenty of hunting and shooting to be had there, too."

As the conversation turned to the topic of masculine pursuits, Clarissa studied Allen Pendale opposite her. He wasn't handsome, but there was something about his face she liked—the gleam of mischief in those dark eyes, his broad cheekbones, and his spill of fashionably unruly hair. He had, moreover, taken her side—somewhat—although she suspected it was because he enjoyed an argument, rather than caring about the subject itself.

Pendale cut a large slice of pie, oozing with blackberries, and deposited it on her plate. He winked. "Here, Miss Onslowe. To sweeten you up."

Her mouth watered.

With his own spoon he dug into the slice on her plate, and offered her the succulent, dripping mouthful as though he were feeding a baby.

Entranced, she parted her lips.

He whispered, "Full of sugar."

Of course. She was seduced, all the same.

Miss Onslowe had had a little too much to drink, Allen thought. Well, they all had, thanks to his lordship's claret and a bottle of rum Captain Trent had produced at the end of the meal. She ambled onto the deck, a slight smile on her face, her white spinster's cap glowing in the twilight. The garment aged her ten years, and made her plainer than she was. He'd yet to see her with her head uncovered, but why he should want to was a mystery.

He stood still against the mast and lowered his cheroot to his side so she wouldn't notice him too soon.

She looked around carefully, and removed the linen cap. To his surprise she wore a whorish sort of ribbon— red and silver—in her hair. She removed the ribbon and shook out her hair on to her shoulders, its brightness catching a spark of fire from the setting sun.

He clamped his cheroot between his teeth, sauntered forward, and bowed. "Miss Onslowe."

"Oh!" She grabbed a handful of hair and pulled the offending cap back onto her head. "Good evening, Mr. Pendale."

"Your servant, ma'am. Would you care to take a turn on the deck with me?" He offered his arm.

Her look was suspicious. Of course, it was the reaction of an aging spinster faced with a rake, and she had every right to think ill of his morals. On the other hand, what did she think he could do? Ram her up against the mast?

Not a bad idea. Remember those ankles? And where had that come from? He must be insane.

"Thank you, no. Good night, sir." She stepped away toward the hatch.

"Miss Onslowe, I must warn you. Mr. and Mrs. Blight are, er, in residence in one of the cabins for an hour or so. Blight asked, and I could not help but agree."

"Of course. Which cabin is it?"

"I'm not quite sure," he lied, liking the idea of keeping her on deck a little longer.

"Probably yours. Mrs. Blight said ours was smaller." She marched over to the hatch, and disappeared into the ship.

Allen drew on his cheroot, oddly disappointed that she had left, and he gazed upward, at the gentle billow of the sail, and the moon pale against the darkening sky. The leisurely meandering of the day had taken them far enough to escape the Bristol smoke; they had passed through the river's spectacular gorge some hours ago, and occasional small cluster of golden squares announced the location of farmhouses and villages.

He watched the lights move slowly out of sight and listened to the splash of water and the creak of the ship's wheel, blew out a puff of rich smoke, and wondered exactly how long it would take Blight to perform his marital duties.

Despite her confidence, Clarissa listened carefully, and tapped on the door of the cabin before entering. To her relief she found the cabin empty.

She considered Mrs. Blight vulgar, pretty, and in her

way kindhearted, although she tried far too hard to simulate gentility. Mr. Blight, lean, with dirty blond hair tied back in a queue, was almost handsome, but there was something about him Clarissa disliked—the set of his mouth, the cynicism in his deep-set dark eyes. He was, she felt, a man who would carry a grudge.

Once in her narrow shelf of a bed—it was just long enough for her, and she wondered how a taller person would fare—she lay for a time in a pleasantly tipsy state. The small space was full of unfamiliar sounds—creaks of huge timbers flexing and pushing against the water, small rustles (the housekeeper in her *tut-tut*ted at the blatant activities of mice and rats), the slap of water against the outside of the ship, only a few feet away. The ship had seemed large at first, with its two towering masts, and then smaller in comparison to the clippers and barques on the Avon; she wondered how it would feel when they were out of sight of land, and vulnerable on the vastness of the sea.

Warned by travelers' tales, she had brought her own sheets and quilt, and a plump feather pillow. She turned her face into the pillow and sniffed the faint odor of lavender—lavender she had picked, rubbing the wheatlike stems between her fingers for the pleasure of the rising scent. Did they grow lavender on the island?

The island—that was how they referred to their destination, as though it were the only one that mattered, giving it a mystique that reminded her of Prospero's island in *The Tempest*.

She'd have to ask someone, Captain Trent, maybe, about the lavender.

Or Allen Pendale.

Not that he'd know, but they'd have to talk about something for the next few weeks—a polite botanical discussion might last, oh, a few minutes.

She smiled and let herself think of what had been intruding on her thoughts for most of the day. Allen Pendale. The shock of finding herself beneath him, his warm heavy weight, his legs sprawled over hers. He had smelled of leather and wool slightly dampened with sweat, beer and tobacco, and some sort of scent—citrus, mixed with something earthier and more pungent—clung to him. And that voice, rich and warm, his large hands—he used them quite a lot when he talked, she'd noticed—and here she was, in a pathetic flutter because a man who wasn't at all interested in her had pushed her down, flat on her back, and landed on top of her.

A delicious shiver ran through her belly.

Because he thought his mistress' husband was trying to kill him, she reminded herself. He'd probably come aboard ship directly from her bed.

Her shift rode up, whispered against her calves.

You're a fool, Clarissa. The first time a man's touched you in five years and you're quivering like a silly virgin.

And here she was alone, with the luxury of being able to think and remember, and let her mind ramble where it would. First to her uncle Thelling's house, where she had picked the lavender on a warm summer's day abuzz with bees, the scents of crushed marjoram and thyme rising from under her feet. She had been happy then—or at least, she had had happiness of a sort; Lord Thelling's housekeeper was respected by the servants, her past forgotten and forgiven by them, at least. She had the pleasure of organizing an efficient and contented household, and the run of a good library.

All that had changed of course when Thelling decided not to get up from his bed one morning and was dead a week later. Her cousin Josiah, who had inherited the estate and title, took Thelling's deathbed instruction to look after Clarissa by accepting, on her behalf, this job as governess. She appealed to her father for permission to come home—surely after five years he could forgive her? She received a cold, brief letter stating that she had made her bed and must lie on it.

When she wished she had had the moral courage to starve instead, she was glad that she had the good sense not to. But the shame lingered deep inside, pricked at her conscience.

She thought instead about Mr. Pendale's voice—that beautiful resonant voice that reminded her of cream and silver, the richness of ordinary luxuries.

Mr. Pendale, dark and vivid and very much alive.

Back to Thelling's house, old-fashioned, dim, and creaky like this ship. Haunted, some of the maids said, until Clarissa shamed them out of their giggling terror. The only person who haunted that house was its housekeeper, wandering sleepless, late at night, restless with longing and desire.

Desire. Once she thought it a blessing; now she thought it a curse.

She shifted, restless, and her night rail twisted and

slid around her, the creases and seams of the worn cotton irritating her skin. She sat, pulled the garment over her head and tossed it aside, her breasts glimmering pale in the darkness. *Such a waste, such a waste,* she thought as she cupped them in her hands. Pretty breasts, or so she'd been told once: small, but shapely. Lovely to see them in the dark like this, glowing like mother-of-pearl, or opals, or some other precious substance.

If she half closed her eyes, she could imagine herself back in Thelling's house, the creaks and rustles of the ship transformed into the sounds of ancient wood and masonry, the sounds you only heard at night when you were alone.

She slid from the sheets and onto her quilt, the pieced cotton slightly scratchy under her buttocks and back. Her body stretched out startlingly white, except for the patch of hair between her thighs, and her nipples appeared dark and strange as though she were a different, bolder woman.

A bolder woman would slip out of bed and walk barefoot through Thelling's sleeping house, cold air brushing against her skin, caressing her breasts, her puckered nipples hard beneath her fingers. She might pause at the window and push back the tapestry curtain to receive a splash of moonlight on her belly; here. And here, running her hand down her body, stroking, parting her thighs, the thatch of hair mysterious and dark, springy. And now, as her finger dipped into her cleft—this bolder, wanton Clarissa haunting a house she had left forever, where was she? Drifting down passages hung with grave-eyed portraits, rush matting rough under her feet, and then a doorknob, smooth, shiny agate, turning in her hand.

The Blue Room, the pride of the household, where once kings had slept, and a great bed hung with embroidered satin stood. The slight creak of the door as it swung open, and the smell of the room, beeswax, the scorch of ironed cotton, woodsmoke, lavender, the faint hint of mildew in a room not often used. A log settled on the fire with a low crunch and the warm red glow, seen through the half-open bedchamber door, a beacon leading her onward.

Would he be asleep? Or waiting for her, his eyes bright and watchful, hot with desire?

I have dreamed of you coming. That beautiful voice was low and husky with sleep, his skin glowed warm and enticing as he raised himself on one elbow, and held out a hand to her.

How could I resist? She slid into his bed, opening herself to his touch and taste and weight, letting his hands go where hers were now, doing anything he wanted with her and to her. His touch would be different, harder and rougher. She'd follow his rhythm and open her thighs wide, wide, knees raising, so—

Like this. Like this. A pulse beating beneath her fingertip, her whole body wrenched into heat and light and all things wonderful and joyous.

CHAPTER 2

By the time Blight's call came from belowdecks, Allen was heartily sick of his vigil on deck, and regretted his spontaneous generosity. He blundered down the stairs in the dark, wondering when he would learn not to bash his head at every opportunity, and stumbled into the cabin. Blight lay snoring on the lower berth, already fast asleep, and the room stank of Mrs. Blight's cheap rose perfume, sweat, and the rankness of male and female secretions.

Allen opened the latch of the lantern, blew the candle out, and promptly had it swing back onto his head in the pitch-darkness. With only another minor blow to his head, he undressed, climbed aloft, and settled into the linens his sister had insisted he take with him for the voyage.

Allen's eyes, accustomed now to the darkness, picked out the small gray square of window. He thought about the day, the farewell to Bristol so rudely interrupted by Glenning, and his idiotic behavior with Miss Onslowe.

Miss Onslowe. He had enjoyed the prospect of her confronting that fellow Blight and was almost sorry that the captain had stepped in to soothe ruffled feathers. What a prickly, resentful sort of woman, an aging spinster who probably had missed the chance of marriage and had to fend for herself—a gentlewoman who now had nothing to lose by giving way to a certain sarcasm and bluntness in her address, although her voice was low-pitched and attractive. The combination of a spinster's cap and a whorish ribbon in her hair was interesting, too. He wondered if Mrs. Blight, who surely had a colorful past, had given the ribbon to her.

And what a fool he'd made of himself, knocking Miss Onslowe to the deck within minutes of their first meeting, and how irate she'd been—quite rightly, too, with some boor of a fellow landing on top of her and squashing her hat. He remembered the way she'd squirmed against him, and then the glimpse of the woolen stocking sagging around her calf, those finely turned ankles—her lips parting, eyes on his, as she had accepted his peace offering (or whatever he'd meant by it) of blackberry pie.

Damnation, he was getting aroused, his cock prodding against the sheet, and the stink in the cabin, an eloquent reminder of what had recently happened here, did not help at all.

Allen gave a loud cough and shifted to lie on his side with a thump.

Blight snored on.

There were distinct advantages to having a roommate who slept as soundly as this. Allen turned onto his back with a thud and accompanying creaks.

Blight grunted, smacked his lips, and resumed snoring.

Miss Onslowe. The image of her flashed into Allen's mind like an artist's sketch, of her scooting away from him, revealing her slender leg, the skirt lifting . . . and lifting . . . this time to her thighs. He was sure they were pale and slender, supple enough to wrap around him, strong enough to hold him while he arched and spurted. Soft skin on the insides, like velvet, fragrant, awaiting his tongue.

He imagined reaching to free her breasts into his palms and pinch her nipples. He guessed she had rather small breasts, but the Clarissa Onslowe of his imaginings had bigger breasts. And the rest of her body . . . He hoped that bright head of hair was reflected elsewhere, an invitation to lechery. And her mouth, those pretty lips parted for him—which should he choose?

Here, Miss Onslowe. To sweeten you up.

He had so many possibilities in the pages of his imagination and memory, and the power to summon and direct her as he chose. Why not? She was a vessel, a catalyst of his pleasure. *Take me in your mouth. Now.*

Her mouth . . . oh yes, taking and teasing him to the limit, closing warm and wet on his cock, soft yet insistent. Her eyes were raised to his for approval, for permission, her hands stroking his thighs and balls while his hand on her head guided her. Yes, turn her, enter deep into her silky firmness while she moaned and demanded more of him, twisting under him. That was how he wanted her, both of them greedy and fast, all tongues and hands and heat. And she'd welcome him with the tug and grip of her orgasm, her cry of delight as he spilled in a warmly glorious rush.

Yes. Like this. Like this.

Clarissa was on deck early the next morning, woken by the ship's bell followed by shouts and the thud of sailors' feet as they ran on deck overhead. Her breath steamed in the frosty air. She stood aside as the crew jumped from the shrouds, a few touching their forelocks to her, and smiled a greeting to Mr. Johnson and Captain Trent, who stood poring over charts.

Apart from the man at the wheel, the crew disappeared below. The odors of frying bacon, bread, and coffee hung in the air from the galley, a wooden structure perched on the deck. The door opened, and a crewman, swathed in a linen apron, came on deck and whisked a piece of canvas from atop a large wooden cage. A chorus of clucks arose. He saw Clarissa watching and touched his forelock. "Hens, ma'am, brought aboard last night."

She drew closer, interested to see how chickens fared aboard ship. A dozen plump bundles of silver-and-gray feathers rose from a thick layer of straw, fluffing themselves, wings flapping. The sailor unlatched the cover and tossed in a bowlful of table scraps.

He bent to rummage in the straw, looking for eggs, and Clarissa joined him. "You're the cook? Dinner was very good last night."

"Thank you, ma'am. They call me Lardy Jack, on account of I'm so fat."

The man was as thin as a rake, his hair tied back in an old-fashioned queue. He held out the pottery bowl for the eggs Clarissa plucked from smooth hollows in the straw, still warm from the hens' bodies.

"Breakfast with the captain in twenty minutes, ma'am." He left with the bowlful of eggs.

The air brightened and the mist lifted, revealing the Welsh mountains to the starboard side and the occasional thin trickle of smoke against a pearly sky. They were apparently making good time. Captain Trent had said it might be two or three days before they would make the open sea.

Sailors appeared on deck and busied themselves scouring the boards and polishing brass fittings, while others seated themselves cross-legged like tailors and stitched diligently at huge piles of canvas under the direction of a grizzled elderly man.

Allen Pendale, in shirtsleeves and breeches, hoisted himself from the hatch leading to the cabins. Scowling and rubbing at his curly black hair, he tossed his coat and waistcoat onto the hatch cover. He yawned and bent over one knee, hands on one thigh, stretching the other leg behind him, heel pressed to the deck, then repeated the action with the opposite leg.

He launched into a one-sided duel with an invisible rapier, lunging and feinting, light on his feet for such a solid man, as agile and graceful as a dancer, darting forward and back on the deck. Clarissa watched in fascination as his breath puffed into the air, and damp patches appeared on the back of his shirt, molding it to his body.

When he stopped, he saw her, started, and bowed to her. "Beg your pardon, ma'am. I'm hardly decent."

She shook her head, embarrassed that he had caught her watching. "It's a pity you don't have an opponent. Doesn't Mr. Blight know how to fence?"

Pendale shrugged. "He's not a gentleman."

A simple, contemptuous remark made at the moment that Blight stepped from the hatch. Clarissa saw his expression, one of fury and humiliation, and looked away, not wanting to embarrass him further.

Pendale, either oblivious or indifferent that his comment had been overheard, bent to retrieve his outer clothes, pulled a neckcloth from a pocket, and finished dressing. Clarissa noted that both men seemed to have shaved, and determined that if they could have hot water delivered to their cabin, then so could she and Mrs. Blight. She would talk to Lardy Jack about it after what promised to be an excellent breakfast.

That day and the next passed pleasantly, with a holiday-like atmosphere aboard. The ship's boat made frequent trips ashore for fresh meat, milk, and cream, joining the *Daphne* as she meandered slowly toward the sea, the scent of salt becoming stronger each day. In the evenings they gathered on deck in the chill air, warmly dressed, and danced to music provided by one of the seamen, who played the fiddle, and Mr. Johnson, who proved adept on the flute.

Miss Onslowe, to Allen's surprise, thrived. She lost

her look of wary cynicism and her skin and hair acquired a slight glow in the winter sunshine. She had befriended the cook—Allen met her once on deck cradling a large bowl in the crook of one arm, and beating its contents. "Egg whites," she explained. "They won't thicken in the heat of the kitchen."

Mr. Johnson seemed enchanted by her, escorting her around the ship and explaining how the rigging worked, while Allen tagged along behind, feeling like a resentful child. The sight of one slim, gloved hand tucked into Mr. Johnson's arm annoyed him even more.

Any day now he would feel jealous of those damned hens she had taken charge of. She'd even persuaded one of the sailors going ashore to pull whatever he could find in the way of greenery, groundsel, late thistles, and grass to encourage the hens to lay even better. Sailors with nothing better to do now hung over the chicken pen, discussing possible names for them with Miss Onslowe, and asking her advice about their sweethearts.

It infuriated him, and he couldn't work out why.

Late the next night, Captain Trent said if the wind held they would sail from the mouth of the estuary and into the open sea. He warned that they might find the movement of the ship a little more lively, but hoped no one would suffer ill effects. After a quantity of punch, the Blights excused themselves to go below, and Allen went on deck to stand vigil. Sure enough, there was a slight rock and dip to the ship's barely perceptible forward momentum.

He had thought Miss Onslowe had gone below, but she was on deck, lurking around the henhouse, doubtless tucking in the wretched birds for the night. She wore, as usual, the unbecoming spinster's cap and a long cloak. He drew his own cloak around himself, seeking a dark corner, and wondered if she had some sort of assignation with Johnson, who had gazed foolishly at her all through dinner.

She looked around cautiously and raised one hand to her head.

Allen burst from his hiding place, grabbed the cap from her head, and tossed it overboard.

"Why did you do that?" she shrieked, much as she'd done when he'd knocked her to the deck -within minutes of meeting her.

"Because it's bloody ugly, and—"

The ship gave a decided lurch. She bumped up against him, grasped his coat for balance and shouted, "*I* wanted to do that!"

He burst into laughter. Together they watched the white cap bob on the waves—yes, definitely waves, here— and then sink from sight.

"Damn you, Pendale." She bent forward to unlace her boots, kicked them off, and reached under her skirts.

"What—" He watched transfixed as her garters, pink ribbons, fell to the deck, and those same dingy gray woolen stockings slid down her ankles.

She hopped on one foot, and tugged the stocking off, then the other, with a swish of skirts, and maybe—or did he imagine it?—a flash of white thigh.

Barefoot, she tossed her stockings overboard, where they floated for a brief moment before disappearing from sight.

"Well!" She laid her hand on his sleeve for balance, grinning broadly.

He'd never seen her—or any woman, come to that—smile with so much abandon, her whole face lit up. She must be drunk—that was it. She'd had quite a few glasses of punch.

"I hated those stockings. I have been praying for them to wear out. I'm glad to see them go. Now I shall be forced to wear silk ones, like a lady."

"Miss Onslowe, do you imply you are not a lady?"

She ran her fingers through her loosened hair. "I do not wish to shock you, Pendale. You seem like a very respectable sort of gentleman."

"Oh, please, Miss Onslowe, do shock me." He grinned back. The atmosphere was becoming pleasantly erotic—a woman, who if not exactly pretty, was certainly interesting, and had shown no shyness in stripping off her stockings, stood before him, her hips swaying with the motion of the ship.

The deck gave a sort of sideways swoop.

She lost her balance, laughed, and fell against him, and they tumbled down against the hen coop, she with her legs splayed on either side of him.

He assessed the situation quickly. It was dark, but a nearby lantern threw enough light so he could see what he was doing. The helmsman was at the far end of the ship, facing the other way, and they were out of sight. If Allen could keep Miss Onslowe quiet, and if a swarm of sailors didn't rush onto the deck to do something with the sails—he should probably pray the wind kept steady—then he suspected the not so proper Miss Onslowe would let him do just about anything he wanted.

Thank God. I would never have worked out how to seduce him.

The suddenness of his response alarmed and delighted her. He was under her skirts almost as soon as she landed—as she bumped against his erection, one hand gripped her bottom, and the other snaked its way up the inside of her thigh, warm and rough and foreign.

"Miss Onslowe, Clarissa, you're a miracle," he said, his fingers probing. If he hadn't been so enthusiastic about the wetness he encountered, she would have been horribly embarrassed by her state. "I wanted to do this to you as soon as I saw you. I wish to God I had more hands."

"So do I," she said with a silly giggle she regretted. Didn't men hate gigglers?

"Unbutton me. Show me your breasts. Take this damned scarf off." His voice became muffled as he pushed the lawn scarf at her bodice aside with his lips and kissed her collarbone, wet and hot.

"Now I need more hands," she said, honestly confused as to which he wanted her to do first.

"Be quiet, woman. Enough talking." He reared up against her, the hand on her bottom leaving to grasp the back of her head and pull her head to him, kissing and kissing, his tongue doing things to hers as extraordinary and shocking as his fingers below—good God, what was he about, two fingers, three inside her, and his thumb, oh God, his thumb, there, *there, don't stop, keep doing that, please, please.*

He stopped, his mouth wet and puffy, eyes bright. "Christ, you have a big tickler."

"A big *what*?"

"Your clitoris. It's big. Hard. Shows you're a lecherous woman. Insatiable. You like this, don't you?"

"I—"

"Look," he murmured, and tipped her back into the circle of one arm, pulling her skirts back with the other. He parted the folds of her quim. "Look, like coral. Hard as coral, too. Like a little cock. Pretty."

Sure enough, there was sufficient light for her to see her clitoris erect and glistening between his thumb and forefinger. Her tickler. She'd never heard it called that before; but then how often did she have conversations about her genitalia?

He stroked her and laughed as she quivered. "You know why it's so big, don't you, Clarissa?"

"I'm sure you're going to say something obscene."

He put his mouth to her ear and licked, a lascivious slurp. "Playing with yourself, my love."

"I don't—" she said as her face heated.

"Liar," he said with extreme cheerfulness. "I'll show you something else big now."

His hand dropped to the fall of his breeches, and she tried not to show too much interest, but in reality she was intensely curious. Her only experience with an erect male member had been unsatisfactory, a glimpse of a white shirt distended by what lay underneath and then something surprisingly large and springy bumping against her in the dark. The ensuing tight shove and squeeze was surprising and disappointing at the same time, because the rest of it, the kissing and stroking, she'd very much enjoyed.

Oh, heavens. She regarded the blatant, dark red rearing thing with trepidation. Like the rest of him, it was broad and thick—powerful, rising blue veined from a mass of tight black curls, a drop of liquid welling at the tip. She ran her tongue over her lips. "And how did that get to be so big? You must have been playing with it for years."

He grinned, regarded his cock with pride, and gave it a friendly little shake. "Yes. And I've let others do so, too. I'm a generous man. Touch it. It won't bite."

She ran a finger up its length and to her immense gratification saw him bite his lip and swallow.

"Very nice," he murmured. "Now show me your breasts, and I'll frig you again. You're going to come for me."

Oh God. She could swear her clitoris twitched at the thought. With shaking hands she undid the drawstring fastening of her gown, holding the neckline open as he fished her breasts out from her stays. Her nipples hardened in the cool air.

"Ah," he groaned. "Very pretty. I couldn't quite decide how they were to look the other night."

"Which night?"

He lowered his mouth to her breast and sucked while

she squirmed in shocked delight, her hands on his head, fingers buried in his hair.

"Now, pay attention, Miss Onslowe." He shifted under her, returning one hand to her quim, the other to her aching nipples, twisting and pinching, a hairbreadth from pain, while she gasped and heard herself make strange whimpering sounds. His fingers inside her did magic things, finding a spot that made her jump like a startled horse, while his thumb circled her clitoris, her tickler—*Oh God, I can't, I can't*—and then she could, oh yes, and he captured her mouth with his while she shook and spasmed.

He laughed into her mouth as she moaned into his—*Why wasn't it like this before? I'm not even in love with this man. I think he's quite a dreadful rogue, and crude, too*—and he stilled his hand and then his tongue. He kissed the side of her mouth.

"Oh," she said.

"*Oh,*" he mimicked her, but took the sting from his mockery by stroking the side of her face.

His hand, she couldn't help noticing, was very wet—she had produced that, somehow, with his attentions—and she could smell it, too. She drew back, startled, and he grinned at her, mischievously, and touched his hand to her mouth.

"Taste it."

"No!" She tried to sound outraged but another giggle spoiled it.

"Come, I expected better from the fearless woman who strips off her stockings for strangers."

"Only for you, and you're not a stranger."

"What am I then?"

"I don't know." And she didn't. He was someone she now knew intimately and yet not at all.

His damp finger stroked her lips. "I'm the sort of stranger who is going to make you come again. I'm going to make you scream, you can try to make me scream, and in short, I shall fuck you silly, Miss Onslowe."

She giggled again. "We don't want to disturb the chickens, Mr. Pendale."

"God forbid. I'll have to stop your mouth."

Her lips parted and his finger slid inside her mouth, slow and foreign, tasting of her, strange and salty yet familiar, and he moaned. *He liked having his finger sucked? How extraordinary.*

She reached for his cock, wrapping her fingers around him, feeling the skin beneath slide smooth over the impossibly hard surface.

He sucked in his breath as if in pain, suddenly vulnerable.

He groaned again. "Don't. Don't make me . . . I'll . . ." But he didn't move, staring at her hand on his cock, his lips parted, legs flexing beneath hers. Then, as if a sudden decision had been made, he grasped her bottom again and slid her atop, first bumping against her, and then with one smooth, heart-stopping slide, inside her.

She gasped and grabbed his shoulder—too much, too fast, she'd forgotten—or had she ever known? All of this—his scent, his hands rough on her skin—and now he kissed her again, his mouth clever and searching against hers, and she was confused and dazed by the intensity, the shock of what they did. It was nothing like her first seduction, and even further from the elaborate fantasy she had choreographed last night. Mr. Pendale in the flesh—in her flesh, and she tried not to giggle aloud at the thought— was so much more vital and immediate, absorbing and consuming her. He was there. Here. Inside her.

"Oh." *You imbecile, Clarissa.*

"Oh." Only this time he wasn't laughing at her; it was a long, drawn-out exclamation, half sigh, half groan, his eyes half closed, as though he were making a discovery in a dream.

She moved her weight forward to brace her knee against the chicken coop, craving more of the wonderful slide and tug of his entry, as the ship rocked and swayed. He moved beneath her, thighs tense as he thrust, his hands at her breasts, then pulling her face to his as he groaned into her mouth.

So unashamed, so generous, so—and then he pulled out of her, panting.

"You're not prepared." His cock, wet and swollen, rubbed against her cunny, her thighs. He trembled.

Not prepared? Well, he was there, wasn't he? How more prepared could she be?

"Clarissa!" He shook her arm. "I can't come in you, can I?"

"I—I don't . . ."

He swore, grasped her hand, and wrapped it around his cock. His face had lost its innocent dreaminess; now he grimaced, fierce and frantic, cursing, arched his back and spilled warm over her hand and belly.

He sagged back against the henhouse with such sudden abandon she wondered for one dreadful moment if he was dead until he opened his eyes and laughed.

She stared at him, confused.

He patted her on the bottom, looking lazy and pleased with himself. "My apologies, Miss Onslowe."

"For what?"

"My excessive haste and the, ah, mess."

She peered down at herself, at her sticky hand, his sticky hand, his cock slumped wet amid a tangle of shirt-tail and petticoat. "No matter."

He reached into his coat pocket, and produced a handkerchief, wiping her fingers with an easy practicality, and then pushed her back—gently, but a push nonetheless—from his lap.

She stood, straightened her skirts and petticoats, irritated with him, and with herself—well, what had she expected? A proposal or a passionate declaration of love?

He stood, too, and regarded her in silence for a moment. "I should congratulate you, ma'am."

"What do you mean?"

"Miss Onslowe, you may choose to masquerade as— as some sort of Quakerish spinster, but you fuck like an emperor's concubine. I don't believe I've been so professionally seduced before in my life, and you certainly have the courtesan's art of bringing a man off as fast as she can. Who the devil are you?"

CHAPTER 3

The words tumbled, senseless and hurried, out of her mouth before she could stop herself. "You know who I am. I'm no one. I'm ruined."

"Not by me," he said, scowling.

"I never said—" She stopped before she made a greater fool of herself, wondering why he was so angry. *I never said I was a virgin. I didn't say I was unwilling.* . . . She cleared her throat. "Obviously not by you. It happened five years ago, plenty of time to reflect on my fate and to regret that I have no place in society. So I was housekeeper to a distant relative, and when he died, I found myself penniless, and my family in agreement that I should take this position or starve."

"He left you nothing in his will?" He looked interested now, as a dog might prick its ears. "It's customary to leave upper servants well provided for."

"No. I had hoped—"

"Too bad you didn't know me then, Miss Onslowe. A good lawyer could have squeezed something out of the estate."

She shrugged, and wound her chilly hands together beneath her cloak, staring out at the white crests of waves. "I had decided that my body might be a way out of a life of tedious servitude."

"In for a penny, in for a pound?"

"Something like that. My choices are celibacy, which I consider overrated, or a fall into deeper ruin. I gave the matter some thought and decided that should I have the opportunity, I should set myself up as a courtesan."

"Ah." He rested his hands on the rail, his shoulder bumping against hers as the ship dipped and swayed. "I regret I can't offer to be your protector, Miss Onslowe."

"I doubt you could afford me."

He whistled. "You set your sights high. Why not marriage? You could probably get away with it on the island."

"It would not be honest." She paused. "Besides, marriage, for women, is a kind of servitude, whereas a properly drawn-up contract allows freedom of a sort."

He laughed. "I'll draw up a contract for you when you find the right gentleman, Miss Onslowe. You will pay me, of course."

"Of course."

He smiled. "There is, of course, only one problem with your plan."

"Indeed?"

"An overabundance of black female flesh as competition."

"Then an English gentlewoman of some wit and learning may appear as an exotic."

He gave a cynical grunt. "A man with his breeches around his ankles doesn't care overmuch for wit and learning, Miss Onslowe."

There was a short, uncomfortable silence.

"Why are you going to the island? You've never said," Clarissa said.

"To visit my father." He hesitated as though about to add something, but had then decided to change the subject. "I suggest you ask Mrs. Blight for some advice."

"Mrs. Blight? Why?"

"She was obviously a lightskirt before she married Blight. I'm sure she'll have some advice for you of a practical nature."

Clarissa nodded, made uncomfortable by his clipped tone, his reluctance to meet her gaze. She held out her hand. "This is somewhat awkward. We have a long voyage ahead, and I should like to think we could be friends. Maybe we should forget what has passed between us tonight?"

After a moment's hesitation, he took her hand. "Ma'am." He dropped her hand and reached into his coat for a cheroot. "If you'll excuse me, Miss Onslowe, I'll visit your friend Lardy Jack for a hot coal."

She nodded, and made her way to the hatch. She glanced back. He had made no move toward the galley, but stood staring into the darkness of the night.

Nor had he accepted her offer of friendship.

She clambered down the ladder and knocked on the

door of her cabin, relieved to hear Mrs. Blight's voice bid her enter. Mrs. Blight, hair in curling papers beneath a frilly nightcap, was already in bed.

"I'm sorry. I didn't mean to wake you," Clarissa said as she undressed.

"I'm feeling a trifle out of sorts, my dear." Mrs. Blight gave a wan smile. "You look very flushed."

"Yes, it's quite cold tonight." Now down to her shift, Clarissa drew her brush through her hair. "Mrs. Blight, I was wondering. . . . I've heard women say . . . well, I believe it is possible not to become pregnant, if a woman does not wish it."

"What a wicked suggestion, Miss Onslowe. 'Tis flying in the face of nature."

"So it is," Clarissa said, calmly running her brush through her hair. "Will you tell me how to do it?"

"Oh, Lord," Mrs. Blight grumbled. "I suppose it's that Mr. Pendale. Or is it Mr. Johnson? Pass me my medicine chest—there's a good girl." She lurched onto one elbow and drew a small linen bag from inside. "Here."

Clarissa looked at the small object that landed on her palm. "A sponge?"

"Yes. Soak it in wine, or rum, or vinegar, or some such, and put it up your cunny. Or this—it's tansy oil and I have an extra vial."

"Before I—he—"

"Yes. Before. 'Twon't do you much good after."

Clarissa flushed. "But how do I get it out?"

"Tie a piece of silk thread to it, but make sure you leave it in a good time after to catch all his spunk. You needn't look at me like that, miss. I've not used this one, so you've nothing to fear."

"Thank you, Mrs. Blight. I'm most grateful, truly. I hope you feel well soon." Clutching her new treasure, Clarissa clambered into her berth, wondering why something so simple should be such a dark secret among women—and only among a certain sort of women, of whom she, apparently, was now one. She rubbed the sponge against her cheek, still confused by Allen Pendale's swings between playfulness and wounded arrogance. She thought about his hands and cock and tongue, hot and bewildering against her chilled skin, and smiled, falling into sleep with the gentle rock of the ship.

She woke early the next morning, hearing the thud of feet overhead on deck, various creaks, and the slap of waves from outside. She could smell salt, coffee, and frying bacon and was suddenly ravenous. She slid to the floor, careful not to wake Mrs. Blight, who was still fast asleep. Then she dressed and made her way to the deck.

The air was bright, fresh, and cold, there was no land in sight, and slate gray waves tipped with cream broke and sparkled. The deck shifted under her feet, sending her careening into Mr. Johnson.

"What a splendid morning!" she exclaimed, grasping his arm for balance.

"Yes, ma'am." His face, she noticed was pale, with a few beads of sweat on his forehead.

"Are you not well? Maybe some breakfast will put you to rights?"

He broke away from her and headed to the side.

Oh, poor man. He was seasick, and by some miracle, she was not.

She found Captain Trent and Allen Pendale at breakfast. They rose as she entered, and the captain congratulated her on having found her sea legs so easily.

"Yes, something's certainly given Miss Onslowe an appetite," Pendale murmured. "Would you care for a sausage, ma'am?"

"Thank you, no." She took some bacon and eggs from a platter on the table, and spread a piece of fresh bread with butter.

"I was telling Mr. Pendale we'll make good time if the wind holds," the captain said. "Congratulations again on your good health, ma'am, sir. Some of the crew do not fare so well, and I'm afraid Mr. Johnson is in a poor way. If you'll excuse me, I must see how things do on deck."

He bowed and left, leaving Clarissa alone with Allen, who reached into his pocket and unfolded a letter.

She really didn't mind his silence or his lack of manners in not attempting a conversation. While she ate, she examined him as unobtrusively as she could. She couldn't decide if he were handsome or not. His cheekbones were high and sharp, his eyes a dark coffee brown, and his hair—she'd had her hand buried in those curls last night—dark, lustrous, and slightly too long. His nose was snub and blunt—no aristocratic profile there—and his full mouth a little too wide.

She liked his hands, broad and capable, black fuzzed,

and remembered how much she had liked what they had done to her last night.

"Do you like what you see, Miss Onslowe?" he murmured, eyes still fixed on the letter.

"I was trying to decide if you were handsome."

He looked up. "And?"

"I don't think you are."

"It's not the first time I've been told I'm plain, Miss Onslowe." He smiled. "You should congratulate me. This letter came late last night as we left land to tell me that I'm an uncle once more."

"My felicitations."

"My sister had a daughter the day we sailed. She sent me this, too." He reached into his pocket and produced a miniature painting of a woman.

"She's very pretty." It was hard to believe the delicate, pale beauty could be related to Pendale. "Is she older or younger than you?"

"Older by two years. I'm the youngest of the family."

Lardy Jack entered with fresh coffee, balancing as adeptly as a tightrope dancer, wished them a good morning, and withdrew.

Allen once more paid great attention to the letter as though embarrassed that he had talked about his family. Clarissa pushed aside a pang of sadness. She had no family who cared enough for her to make sure a letter was delivered before she left England, possibly forever. She had not seen her own nephews and nieces for five years now, because she was a bad moral influence; would they find out they'd had an aunt, ever, and wonder about her?

She finished eating, gathered her cloak, and went back onto the deck, pondering how she would spend the day. She could always sew—she had pieces for two dresses already cut, light muslins—or she could read the one, precious book she had brought, poems by Cowper. It was really too chilly to spend any time on deck, and certainly, if she tried to sew, the wind would snatch the fabric from her hands.

Two figures, clutching at each other, staggered toward her—Mr. and Mrs. Blight, both looking extremely unwell.

"Miss Onslowe," Mrs. Blight gasped, "this is dreadful, indeed. I think I shall die."

"You look very ill," Clarissa said. "I can speak with Lardy Jack and see if there's anything he can prepare for you. I think ginger tea might help."

"Oh, do not speak to me of tea." Mrs. Blight sagged against her husband, who looked scarcely capable of supporting her. "My dear, I must lie down again."

"Maybe the fresh air will do you some good," Clarissa suggested.

A heartfelt groan met her suggestion. The two turned and zigzagged across the deck to the hatch.

Clarissa stopped by the hen coop on her way to the galley, and was pleased to see that the hens seemed to be unaffected by the ship's motion and approached the sides of their enclosure, heads cocked, as though expecting treats from her. She remembered what had happened here last night and a flush—of excitement, not embarrassment—rose in her face.

In the small galley, Lardy Jack manipulated pans and hot coals like a juggler at a fair and poured hot water over dried ginger root. "It may help," he said with a shrug. "Folks usually feel better after a few days."

Clarissa shuddered at the thought of having to spend days in such misery. With great care, the lidded mug swathed in an old piece of canvas, she managed to get across the deck to the hatch without spilling any.

"Allow me." Allen Pendale took the container from her. "What is this?"

"Ginger tea. Mr. and Mrs. Blight are unwell." She backed down the ladderlike steps and reached for the tea.

"I'll come to see if there's anything I can do."

He clambered down so close behind her he almost touched her. She went ahead, bumping off one wall of the narrow passage as the ship rolled, and opened the door to the cabin she shared with Mrs. Blight.

No one was there.

Meanwhile, Allen opened the door to the other cabin and recoiled. "I'll fetch a bigger bucket."

She peered over his shoulder at the stench and misery inside. "And a mop and bucket, if you please."

Allen watched Clarissa with admiration as she mopped the floor and handled the wretched situation with calm efficiency and kindness. She waved away his bungling efforts at helping, at first—there was hardly room for her to move in the enclosed space—and then handed him a reeking bucket to dispose of. He navigated the steep steps to the deck one-handed, emptied the bucket over the side, and wondered what on earth they would do if the Blights could or would not be separated.

Fuck her silly. Absolutely not. Hadn't he agreed with her that last night's activities were best forgotten?

Someone skidded into him and clasped his arm for balance. "Thank you for helping," Clarissa said. "Oh, God, they are so ill. I am quite worried. Thank goodness they have both gone to sleep."

"You were magnificent," he said.

She shrugged, assuming her usual cynical stance. "Someone had to look after them. I hope they would do the same for me. They may yet. The captain says it's a random thing. I feel remarkably well, however."

"You look well." It was true. Her hair, uncovered, blew in the wind, and her cheeks had an attractive pinkness. She had hitched up her skirts to mop the floor, and he noticed some of the sailors staring at her silk-clad ankles.

As though conscious of their gaze, she pulled at her skirts, releasing them to whip around her ankles. He noticed now she wore no gloves and her hands were reddened with cold.

"Here." He took off his gloves and drew them over her hands.

She laughed, wriggling her fingers. "You have such big hands. Thank you. I have gloves, but they are downstairs."

"Below," he said absently, thinking of her slender fingers burrowing into the silk lining of his gloves, taking his warmth. His cock stirred. He took a step away from her and wrapped his cloak around himself more securely.

Below, where the two of them might very well be spending more time and in closer quarters than they'd bargained for.

"I'm going to talk to Lardy Jack about some gruel for the Blights." She stared at the sea, then glanced at him and smiled. "Thank you for the loan of the gloves."

It was the first time she'd smiled at him without irony, a smile of pure happiness, and she almost looked pretty. Something tugged and stirred in him. This time it wasn't his cock.

Clarissa retired belowdecks to keep an eye on the Blights, tired from the constant effort to keep her balance. She started sewing, with little enthusiasm. Allen had joined some sailors in fishing—a shoal of herring had been spotted, and the men threw lines baited with bacon fat over the side, hauling in wriggling silvery fish. She wished she had joined them.

After a while someone rapped on her door. It was one of the ship's boys, whom the captain had told to help Miss Onslowe look after the Blights, and she was glad to hand over the messier part of the job to him. She shut the door, yawned, and stretched out on her berth. She was so used to working, to having things to do, that being able to lie down and close her eyes seemed a shockingly decadent act—and the very fact of being alone, with no one to call on her, made it doubly pleasant. She hoped that the Blights, or at least Mrs. Blight, would be well enough to move, although the thought of sharing this tiny space with a vomiting, wailing woman was unpleasant.

She let her mind wander to Allen Pendale, who might very well soon be disturbing her solitude as much as he did her peace of mind. When she had taken charge, mopping and cleaning up that morning, his willingness to help had been unexpected and welcome, not what she would have expected from an earl's son.

All the same, she didn't want to share a cabin with him. Did she?

"I'm afraid the Blights will not budge." Allen spoke as they stood at the rail after dinner. It was a clear, cold night—the sort of night that on land would produce a white frost by morning. Here the shrouds glistened silver, the deck had a frosty sheen, and overhead the sails belled against the night sky, the Milky Way flung across the heavens like a gauze scarf.

"Well, then, we shall have to make do."

They were both being very careful not to look at each other. She had tried to avoid doing so at dinner, but with only the three of them—Mr. Johnson had declined to dine—it had been difficult. And she had wanted to look at him, to watch the play of lamplight on his skin, which was darkened by a day of sun and wind. She couldn't help thinking how his hands had looked against her pale skin, probing her secret places while he made her watch.

He and the captain had been in fine spirits, doing their best to charm and entertain her, as they dined on herring fried in bacon fat. Allen had a lively wit and was a good storyteller, and she had amused them both with stories of mishaps belowstairs when she was a housekeeper.

But he was not laughing now.

"Would you care to retire first, ma'am?"

"Thank you. I shall wish you a good night, then. I fall asleep quite fast."

"Of course."

CHAPTER 4

I'm not an animal, he wanted to yell at her as she walked away from him. *I can exercise some self-control. I am not totally depraved.*

What was he thinking? She was a woman whose ambition was to be a courtesan. She had played the innocent: how seductive she'd been, with that girlish giggle, and her feigned orgasm—although he really wasn't sure about that, remembering the clutch of her cunt on his fingers. Well, even the most hardened courtesan might allow herself a moment of pleasure, and she'd used him, appealing to his pride in his sexual expertise. And then he'd spouted like a schoolboy in her hand—in his hand, too, to be honest, while she pretended she didn't know what to do with a cock. He didn't believe for one moment that she had been only a respectable housekeeper for the past five years. More likely she'd been old Thelling's mistress, and that was why the new lord had tossed her out of the house and across the ocean.

Her aspirations as a courtesan certainly explained why the men on the ship—with the possible exception of Blight, who was an unpleasant, low sort of fellow—seemed to adore her. That was what a courtesan did: demanded adoration, preferably in conjunction with bottomless pockets. Aboard ship, where pockets were empty, or full of holes, she charmed just to keep her hand in, as he lunged and sparred alone without a fencing partner.

Even he had been inspired to ask Captain Trent to send the boy, Peter, to help clean up the Blights' puke, and paid for the privilege.

If she showed any interest in Allen at all, it was because he was an earl's son, and might possibly be the means to find a rich protector.

She'd probably target Lemarchand, the richest man on the island, and under the same roof. He felt sorry for Lemarchand's daughter, whose lessons would be neglected while her governess concentrated on Papa's education.

Not that it was any of his business.

Mr. Johnson, pale and not looking at all well, standing beside the helmsman, blew a whistle, and a cluster of sailors stampeded onto the deck and up the rigging. Allen watched them swarm up the shrouds and determined he'd do that, once, up to the top of one of the masts, just to show Miss Onslowe he could. No, she had nothing to do with it.

Surely she'd had enough time to primp and priss and put her hair in papers, or whatever it was she did at night. It was time to go below.

In for a penny, in for a pound.

Clarissa took the lower berth previously occupied by Mrs. Blight, having determined that offering Mr. Pendale her own sheets seemed less indelicate. She knew her logic was convoluted, but did not want to explore her theory further. She left the lamp burning and decided she would go to sleep immediately, or feign sleep to avoid any more awkward conversation.

After a while, sleep evading her, she heard the clump of boots coming down the steps, and a light tap on the door. Eyes almost shut, she slowed her breathing and decided to enjoy the sight of Mr. Pendale preparing for bed.

He sat on his box of belongings, which Clarissa had asked Peter to move into the cabin along with the boot-jack, and gave her a quick glance as if surprised at her foresight. He eased off his boots and tossed them onto the upper berth, stood, stretched, and hit one hand against a beam. He swore softly under his breath, and stripped off his coat and waistcoat. In his shirtsleeves, he paused, face thoughtful, and untied his neckcloth, drawing the creamy length of cotton from his shirt. Then he lifted one hand to unfasten the placket. A curl of black hair became visible, similar to the dusting of hair on his hands and forearms, revealed when he unbuttoned the cuffs.

She wondered if he intended to sleep in his shirt and her question was answered when he stripped the garment off over his head, hunching his back, arms outstretched. With a shiver of delight, she saw his chest, as dark pelted as that first curl of hair had promised, the slick of hair under one arm as he stood over her to throw his shirt onto his berth. His stockings were good but serviceable gray wool, gartered with plain black ribbon, and she shut her eyes again, expecting him to bend to remove them.

Instead he moved away—she felt his warmth retreat—and through half-closed eyes, she watched him rest one foot on his box of belongings, lean over, and pull at the black ribbon, drawing the knot untied with great care. He shook the ribbon out, stuffed it into his breeches pocket, then bent again to roll the stocking down and off. He stumbled a little as the ship dipped, and stood, knees slightly bent, swaying with the movement, the bone of his bared shin sharp in the lamplight. She'd never seen a gentleman's foot before, and it was somewhat disappointing that his was like anyone else's, but broad and strong like the rest of him. His skin glowed gold; he sighed and scratched his chest while his other hand lowered to the fall of his breeches. His hand lingered, resting as though pointing the way to the noticeable masculine bulge before he unbuttoned the top button on each side, and his breeches slid a little onto his hips. More golden skin, the dark eye of his navel revealed as the flap fell forward.

Did he know she watched? Was he performing for her? She squeezed her thighs together, tingling and aroused.

He lifted the other leg, bent, repeated the untying and rolling down, and tossed both stockings onto his bed.

His breeches now, another button loosened, a further slide down his hips, and he paused.

He reached for the lantern as the fingers of his other

hand worked the next button. The cabin plunged into pitch-darkness, and his breeches slithered down—she heard the rasp of wool on skin. There was a warm gust of air from his body, scented with his musk and sweat as he hoisted himself onto the upper berth—and she took a much-needed breath.

She hadn't been sleeping, he knew. He could feel her gaze—she'd been quite convincing, but there was something in the chilly air: a watchfulness, a stirring, tight-wound like a strand of a spiderweb thrumming in a breeze. He could have challenged her, but decided not to after his initial surprise. He wanted her to watch him; he wanted to tease her. He liked the idea of a woman looking at him with admiration and desire while he pretended oblivion. So he had slowed down, taking his time, making each movement, each gesture—unbuttoning, rolling down or off—deliberate, significant.

And he'd denied her the final prize, which at the time had seemed like a good idea, although he wasn't quite sure why now. He'd been half erect by that time, she would probably have pretended to awake, and he could have bent her over and . . . and instead, here he was with a horn like a ship's mast while she lay a couple of feet beneath him, far too close for comfort.

He turned and shoved his face into the pillow. That was a mistake. It smelled of her, sweet, earthy, female. His cock shoved against the sheets that also held her scent. He was surrounded by her essence, drowning in it. He reached beneath the sheet and grasped his cock. Maybe . . . maybe if he were very quiet, she wouldn't know.

He squeezed. The berth creaked.

Another squeeze, another creak, and he groaned. He couldn't help it. *Go to sleep, Miss Onslowe, for Christ's sake.*

She turned over, rustled, sighed.

He should stop. Doubtless he'd have an erotic dream anyway and come all over her nice lavender-scented sheets. And she'd see the stain and know what it was, know he'd pleasured himself while she was blissfully unaware.

Clarissa Onslowe, raising her eyebrows at the sight of her polluted sheets, wondering, and then realizing. Yes. Excited by the thought of a man frigging himself while she slept, inflamed by her nearness. She'd think of him with his hand on his cock, small efficient tugs, that was all it would take now, thinking of him thinking of her—yes. Oh God, yes. The devil with any sounds, too late now— *Oh Christ*—

"Oh, Christ!" He let out a yelp of pure fear, spunk shooting from his cock, as something with small tickly claws ran over his feet.

"What's wrong?" There was a loud crack from below, her head probably, as she sat up. "Ouch!"

"A mouse, a damned mouse, something!" He leaped stark naked from the berth. "Right over my foot. Oh, Christ."

"You're frightened of mice?"

Damn her, she sounded as though she wanted to laugh. "No. Yes. I was surprised, that's all." He was out of breath for several reasons.

"It was probably much more frightened of you."

"Of course, since I wasn't frightened of it." His breathing steadied. He wondered if there was light enough for her to see his cock, now at half mast, still oozing seed, and the thought embarrassed him. "I beg your pardon. I woke you."

"No matter. I'll ask the sailors if they'll lend us one of their cats tomorrow. That should take care of it." She yawned and turned over. "Go to sleep, Allen."

Allen? She'd used his Christian name, without his permission, as though they were equals, and he was taken aback by her impertinence. On the other hand, she hadn't been surreptitiously frigging herself and then shrieking with fear at a mouse.

All too conscious that once again he'd made a fool of himself, Allen slumped back into his berth. He landed straight on the wet patch he'd made, covered himself up, and fell asleep.

Damn him. As though the ship wasn't bad enough in keeping her awake, tipping her around in her berth and bumping her against the raised edge, while all the while timbers creaked and groaned, and waves slapped and crashed. Allen Pendale was not a restful presence. She'd thought Mrs. Blight a noisy sleeper, grunting and snoring, but he was worse, thumping around—well, he was a large man, of course, and she didn't realize how disturbing it was to lie in the lower berth beneath someone—then jumping out and shrieking, and now he was . . .

surely not. She listened. Another wet snuffle, an intake of breath.

Allen Pendale, weeping?

She slid from her berth and stood. He lay on his back, broad enough to be wedged into his berth, although it surely couldn't be very comfortable. It was light enough now for her to see the tears that ran down his face. One hand lay loosely curled on the pillow next to his head.

"Allen. Mr. Pendale. Wake up."

He gasped and mumbled something.

"Allen!" This time she shook his shoulder.

"What the devil?" He came awake then, staring at her dumbfounded, and wiped his hand over his face. "Sorry. Bad dream. Didn't . . ." He wiped his face on the sheet, somewhat to her annoyance, and groped for her hand. "On a ship."

"Yes, you're on the *Daphne*. On a ship."

"No, the dream." He stared at her. "Why am I always such a fool with you, Clarissa?"

She'd wondered about that, too. Of course, she was pretty much a fool with him, too, but hoped she hid it better. Or was that just another instance of her cowardice? Didn't it take a certain courage to admit anything—interest, desire, love—to someone, not knowing whether your feelings were returned? Or a certain stupidity, and once she'd been stupid. She snatched back her other hand, which, like an independent being, had crept forward to smooth the tumble of rough hair from Allen's brow.

His fingers loosened and slid from hers, his eyes closed, and he fell back asleep.

Clarissa pulled her stays on, grateful that they laced on the side and she didn't have to ask for anyone else's help. She could only imagine Allen Pendale's reaction—or could she? Was he spying on her? No, his back was turned to her, and he appeared to be asleep. Naturally, as soon as she had abandoned the idea of sleep herself, he became as quiet as a lamb. There was a different movement to the ship now, a deeper swing and rock, and it was colder. Sleet rattled against the small window, followed by the splash of a wave against the glass.

She drew on her much-darned silk stockings, regretting now that she had thrown away her workaday wool ones, her back turned to Pendale in case some powerful male instinct alerted him to what she was doing. She would have liked to wash, but it was too rough. She imagined water slopping all over the cabin, even if she or Peter, the ship's boy, managed to get a bucket down the stairs. Finally dressed, shoes, gloves and cloak on, she tapped on the Blights' door and was greeted with silence. Cautiously she opened the door and peered inside. They were both asleep, but the necessary bucket had overturned and spilled onto the floor. Wrinkling her nose, she decided to seek out Peter, closed the door, and climbed up the stairs in darkness—the hatch was closed. With some difficulty, she threw it open, and was met with a spray of freezing salt water.

She clambered out, slammed the hatch shut, and stepped into another world, gray and fierce. A wave broke onto the steep slope of the deck, the water draining off as the ship righted.

"Best to stay below today, ma'am," Mr. Johnson bawled at her above the wind, apparently recovered from his seasickness. "Peter will be below in a while, so tell him what you need."

"Thank you," she shouted back.

"Mind yourself, ma'am!" He grasped her hand and closed it around a rope. "Hold on tight, and keep out of the way, if you please."

Water broke over her feet, soaking and chilling them, but she didn't care, exhilarated by the danger, the wild elements. She skidded and stumbled to the galley, where Lardy Jack, face red from heat and steam, controlled wildly swinging pots over the fire.

"Good morning, miss. A bit of weather today, but we're making good speed."

"Indeed, yes. How are the chickens?"

"Two overboard, the rest probably not laying for the moment. I'll send Peter down with breakfast, ma'am. You shouldn't be out in this."

"I'm most grateful. Make sure he brings the mop, if you please."

"You're not sick, are you, miss? We have bets on you and Mr. Pendale."

"Not yet." She grinned back at him. "I trust you won't lose any money on my account. Can you give me an ember for the lantern?"

"Surely, miss." He deftly shoveled hot coals into a small pot and handed it to her. "Careful, now."

She would have liked to stay on deck to watch the waves crest and break, but with the amount of activity going on, she knew she would only be in the way. She timed her entry into the hatch when there was little water on deck, slamming it closed behind her. Below, it felt relatively quiet and warm, away from the roar of wind and sails. She blew on the embers and watched the red glow, warming her hands on the pot.

She lit the lantern while Allen slept on. Oh yes, she and Mr. Pendale were going to be on very intimate terms, one way or the other, if this weather held.

He awoke to the vision of Clarissa Onslowe undressing. She sat on his box, one ankle resting on a knee as she peeled off a wet stocking. She wrinkled her nose, smiled, and wriggled her reddened toes to warm them. She smelled of salt, clean and wild, her face flushed.

"Here." He spoke before he realized the implications of what he was doing, spying on her while she undressed. "Borrow some stockings—there's a clean pair inside my box."

"Oh. Thank you."

It was strange to see a woman he didn't know poking around among his clothes, books, and papers.

She gave a small cry of triumph and waved a book at him. "A novel!"

"You may borrow the book, too, ma'am."

He would have liked to watch her put on the dry stockings, but he was having trouble enough with yet another erection, cramming it inside his breeches, rearranging his shirt so hopefully it wouldn't show, while flat on his back.

Time to take a piss—he wondered how she'd managed, but of course a cloaked woman could do a lot under skirts and petticoats with no one the wiser.

He really should stop thinking about what lay beneath her skirts.

"I expect you . . . I believe Peter is with the Blights. I should . . ." With great tact she left the cabin as he swung himself down from the berth, as usual bashing his head on a beam.

"If we were gypsies, we'd be married now," he said as she returned. Presumably she had fastened the stockings outside the door.

"I beg your pardon?" She gave him a frosty glare.

He swung himself onto his bed—her bed—and propped one hand under his head. "It's how gypsies marry. They both piss into the same pot, or so I was told once." The erotic charge of it had not escaped him, and he wondered if he was turning into some sort of pervert. At the same time, the intimacy of marriage, as something other than a series of legal arrangements, for the first time somehow seemed strangely attractive.

"How delightful," she muttered, digging into her own box of possessions. She drew out a long length of pale fabric and sat, searching for, and finding, a needle and thread in its folds. She looked up. "Do you have nothing better to do than lie there and stare at me?"

Miss Onslowe, it seemed, was not in a mood to charm today.

"Apparently not. I should go and see about some breakfast, if Lardy Jack can cook anything at all in this."

"I already have." She stabbed her needle into the fabric. "Peter will bring us something. Mr. Johnson said we should stay below."

"The devil with that." He swung himself down, annoyed by her bad temper. Maybe she was getting seasick, although he hoped not. He didn't want to see her wretched and undignified, like the sufferers in the next cabin.

He squeezed by her to put on his boots, noticing that she sat with one hand on her stomach, her face creased. "Clarissa, are you sick?" he barked, looking around for a receptacle for her to puke into.

"No, I am not. Thank you, Mr. Pendale. The crew, by the way, have bets on us, so you'd best go show your face."

When he returned, soaked and chilled, and awed by the force of wind and water, he found the reason for her bad temper. She straightened up, her face flushing red with embarrassment, cloths dangling from her hand—rags that held an unmistakable pale brown stain despite their bleached-out state.

"It's my woman's condition," she said, and he realized she was close to tears. "And I can't find the rest of my pins, and . . ."

"Let me look." He knelt at her side and poked through her possessions, as she had done his. He found her pins, fastened to a scrap of paper, by pricking himself on them, buried among petticoats or some such. She certainly owned very little—a few pairs of stockings, silk but much darned, neatly folded garments of linen and cotton, a small box that might contain jewelry, a hairbrush and toothbrush, a pair of half-boots, a straw bonnet. There were no letters or papers, nothing that hinted of family or friends.

He handed the pins to her and left the cabin.

Poor girl, he thought as he lurked outside. Far from home, stuck with a boor of a fellow whom she'd let get under her skirts and would far sooner ignore, and now having to deal with female matters with no privacy at all.

Wait, this was not some pathetic waif of a woman; this was Clarissa Onslowe, the woman who had used him and planned to sell herself to the highest bidder.

He tapped on the Blights' door, and asked cheerily about their health.

He was answered by heartfelt groans.

A spray of cold water and light from above, accompanied by the scent of bacon, revealed Peter coming down the stairs, agile as a monkey, a large bundle tucked under one arm. "Bacon and cheese, sir, and bread, and a cask of cider and a flask of his lordship's wine."

Allen thanked him and made his way onto the deck. When he returned, chilled and windswept to the cabin, Clarissa sat sewing, head bent.

"Thank you," she said, without looking up. "You've been very kind."

"It's a damnable situation," he said. "As you said, we must make the best of it." He paused, while concentrating very hard on opening the cask of cider with the minimum of spillage, and pouring some into the two cups Lardy Jack had provided. It was remarkable how difficult everything was when liquids wanted to move in unexpected ways and you didn't seem to have enough hands—something he'd discovered earlier aiming, with only a fair amount of success, into the chamber pot.

He handed a cup to her. She drank but refused food.

He was worried, now. She was getting seasick, he was sure. She didn't look well, pale and with dark shadows under her eyes.

"Would you like to lie down?" He asked her. "If you're getting sick, it might help."

She shook her head. "As I told you before, I'm not seasick."

"Good. I put a guinea on you in the stakes with the crew."

"You—" To his relief, she laughed. "I am flung about in all directions when I lie down. I have barely slept, and my back hurts."

Of course. She was so slender, whereas he filled his shelf—he really couldn't dignify it by calling it a bed—and could wedge himself in.

He stood and grabbed her quilt, folding it. "Lie down, Miss Onslowe. I'll put this beside you to keep you in place."

"But you'll be cold . . ." Despite her words, she lay down with a sigh.

"Don't worry about me. I'll use my cloak when it's dried out." He knelt by her. "Turn over. I'll rub your back."

She made a sound as though about to protest, but shifted, and let him put his thumbs on her lower back, where he kneaded and rubbed. A former mistress, who suffered greatly at such times, had shown him what to do.

Clarissa was lithe and taut beneath his hands, at first resisting—he could feel how she tensed, mistrusting—but then relaxed, her breathing deep and slow, as she fell into sleep.

He covered her up, tucking the covers around her, and knelt watching her sleep, her hair spilling over the pillow. Her lips were slightly parted as though awaiting a lover's kiss.

CHAPTER 5

Three days of rough weather—not rough enough for the hatches to be battened down, trapping them below, a possibility Clarissa dreaded—but bad enough for them to want to stay dry and relatively warm in the cabin. It was as though her courses dictated the weather, and she understood why sailors traditionally were wary of women aboard ships. Occasionally she or Allen ventured onto the deck, to return shivering and drenched, or visited the unhappy Blights. Finally in desperation she dosed them with brandy and laudanum from Mrs. Blight's medicine box, and hoped she did not kill them.

She found, after the initial embarrassments of bodily functions were dealt with, that she was surprisingly comfortable in Allen Pendale's presence. They spoke occasionally, and learned to tell the time of day from the changing light and the clang of the ship's bells. Allen's watch had stopped some time ago, either suffering from some sort of mechanical seasickness or a dousing with seawater.

They read, dozed, and ate occasionally. Allen produced a bottle of lime juice and insisted she take some, even though it made her mouth pucker. It was, as he pointed out, better than losing her teeth.

She didn't know when they started to use each other's Christian names—not often—there was little need for names in a small world where they were the only human inhabitants. She still smiled when she thought of Allen, stark naked, with a musky, salty scent about him, panicked over a mouse. And that particular scent, she realized, was semen. It excited her to think of his surreptitious pleasure; how did he look, had he wanted her to know what he did, or was he ashamed and frantic?

She stopped bleeding; the weather calmed.

"Clarissa?" Allen's fingers brushed her arm. "Are you awake?"

"Mmm." She caught his fingers in the dark, thick and strong, slightly rough.

"Shall we take a turn on deck?"

They both began the usual awkward scramble of getting dressed in the dark in the small space. She stood to lace her stays and found that now she could sway with the motion of the ship for the most part, as the sailors did, keeping her balance. She pulled her gown over her head and bumped into Allen as he descended from his berth, a brief, clumsy slide, his breath, sweet with cider, warm against her face, the rasp of his cheek on hers.

If they had turned their faces a fraction, they would

have kissed. She would have liked that, very much, and imagined his lips on hers—not the wet, openmouthed, carnal greed of their first encounter, but a gentle greeting between strangers who had grown to like each other. She did like him, she realized, for his practicality and kindness, the grace with which he accepted their forced intimacy. He had rubbed her back that first day of her courses as gently as another woman might, soothing her into sleep as she released a few tears of humiliation into her pillow.

"Ready?" His voice interrupted her thoughts.

"My gloves . . ." She patted her bed.

"Try your cloak pocket."

Like an old married couple, or brother and sister—neither comparison sat comfortably with her. She eased her cloak onto her shoulders and found her gloves. She bumped into Allen again as he moved to open the door for her, and she looked up to see a square of black studded with pinpricks of light—the night sky. The hatch was open, which meant calmer weather and no chance of heavy seas crashing onto the deck.

The air was freezing, the twinkle of the stars brilliant against the night sky. Behind them a slight lightening and a pinkish tinge to the sky at the horizon indicated that sunrise was not far off.

"It's like a miracle," he said softly into her ear.

Miss Onslowe, Clarissa, you're a miracle. Unsettled by the vivid memory of his hand up her skirts she moved away and took a deep breath of cold, fresh air.

"It smells so clean," she said.

He laughed. "Probably because I smell so bad."

"No, you don't. No worse than me. Besides, I ..." *I like your smell.* "Oh, I'd love to wash."

"Miss Onslowe, I'm devastated. I've brought you up to see the sunrise, and far from appreciating the poetic moment, you talk of hot water and soap." He grinned and rubbed a hand over the stubble on his face. "I should shave. I think I can do it now without cutting my throat."

She turned to watch streaks of pink and gray appear in the sky. A gleam of bright copper edged the horizon.

"What happens now?" she asked, hating herself for asking yet not having the courage to say what she really meant: *What is it between us? I wish I was in love with you—it would make everything so much easier. Instead I like you—I think, sometimes—and lust after you, oh, definitely lust after you, Allen Pendale, and now I don't know what to do.*

"We have breakfast, you'll charm hot water from Lardy Jack and charm Peter into carrying it below, and I'll shave." He, too, stared at the sunrise. "The sun rises every day of our lives, yet consider how we take it for granted."

Her cheeks and nose were pink with cold, and although he told himself a dozen times she was no beauty, nothing out of the ordinary, he couldn't stop looking at her. Maybe it was the shock of cold air, the splintering brightness of the sunrise, and colors—they had lived in a monochromatic world below, in half darkness, like moles. And the scent of coffee from the galley fired him with an appetite like lust, his mouth watering.

He hardly noticed the pitching of the ship now, could walk as easily as a sailor—Clarissa, too, her hips swaying as she prattled on to Lardy Jack, who grumbled but put on a large kettle of water for her.

"You're too early for breakfast with the captain, miss. You can have porridge—poor stuff, it's what the men eat—but you're welcome to it if you want to fill your belly."

"Oh, something hot! Wonderful. You are wonderful, Jack."

"Get on with you, miss." Lardy Jack dolloped a large spoonful of grayish gluey stuff from a large pot over the fire, looked at her and Allen, hesitated, and then put two spoons in it. "Save Peter time washing the plates, miss, sir." He winked, poured coffee into a mug, and handed it to Allen. "You don't mind sharing, I hope."

"Christ," Allen muttered, after they'd thanked him and moved out of the constricted space of the galley. "Does everyone know? I'd thought to save your reputation."

"Of course they know. And I have no reputation." She took a spoonful of the porridge and sighed with pleasure.

"But they—the sailors—don't know that."

"I'm sure Blight knows from talking to his wife. He doesn't like me or you."

"Who gives a damn whether he likes you? I'm concerned about whether he shows you proper respect." He dug his spoon into the porridge and offered her the coffee.

She handed him the plate of porridge and took the coffee, wrapping her hands around the mug. "Allen?"

He paused halfway through a sticky, chewy mouthful and gave an encouraging nod.

"About my ruin. I've been meaning to speak to you of it."

Where the devil was this leading? Obviously she was after something. He nodded again, having learned from his legal experience that silent encouragement produced a confession better than words.

"Well." She stared into the coffee. "I'm not *that* ruined."

Not that *ruined?* What on earth could she mean? "Miss Onslowe, either you are ruined or not. I believe you are, for you've told me as such. You're exceedingly metaphysical for so early in the morning."

"I mean that, yes, I am ruined, but I . . . I know very little."

He gave a snort of disbelief.

"You don't understand." Her voice was pitched a little higher than usual, and she handed him the coffee, fast, so some slopped over the rim of the mug. "I—I spent only one night with my lover. I understood little of what— I felt there must be more, and what he did seemed nothing to do with me—and then what you and I did behind the hen coop seemed entirely different, and—"

"You flatter me, Miss Onslowe." Once again he felt like a fool, hands occupied with the plate and mug, while she spun a series of preposterous riddles. "Have a word with Mrs. Blight when she recovers. I'm sure she'll provide the lurid details of which you claim to lack knowledge."

"I'd rather you—"

"What?" His cock hardened so fast he swore he could

feel the blood rush from his head. Did she mean . . . ? Oh good God, what was she suggesting?

She, however, seemed ready for a good argument, bright-eyed, alert, and with hands unencumbered by breakfast. "You were of course unspeakably vulgar, but I trust in the future—"

"Unspeakably vulgar? Come, now, Clarissa, that was fucking, not an afternoon call with the vicar—"

"Sssh. You'll shock the sailors."

Sure enough a couple of men dropped from the shrouds, touching their forelocks. "Good morning, Miss Onslowe."

"Good morning, Tom. Good morning, Ebenezer. Is your toothache better?"

"Much, thank you, miss. Good morning, sir. Still in good health, sir? I have my money on you."

"Good morning." Sometimes the haughty demeanor of an earl's son was useful, even if he stood with a mostly empty plate, a gob of porridge hanging on the edge and threatening to drop onto his coat. He thrust the plate and mug at one of the sailors. "Take these to the galley, if you please."

She smiled. "You're not indifferent to the idea, then, Mr. Pendale."

"I'm only human. Of course I'm not indifferent, but I won't be toyed with."

"Of course not." She swallowed. "You really would be doing me a great favor."

He burst into laughter. "Miss Onslowe, what do you wish to find out?"

She swayed toward him, a seductress, as the rising sun behind her illuminated her bright hair and bathed her in fire. "Everything. Everything you know, Allen."

"Water's ready, Miss Onslowe," Peter said from behind him. The boy staggered under the weight of a wooden tub that his arms barely reached around. Inside the tub a large kettle poured steam into the air.

"Thank you, Peter." She smiled at Allen and followed the boy belowdecks.

Allen fingered his bristly chin and decided it was definitely time for a shave.

He hadn't said yes. He didn't need to, and she knew it.

✦

Allen borrowed Mr. Johnson's razor and shaved on deck, using some ugly gray soap that smelled of pigs and barely raised a lather, and a basin of rapidly cooling hot water, his fingers numb with cold. It was the best he could do. He hoped that Clarissa would appreciate the effort and that she would be equally appreciative of the rasp of his bristles against her skin. All over her. His hand shook and he came near to cutting his throat as he'd predicted.

Belowdecks he rapped at the cabin door and heard Clarissa bid him enter.

Clad only in her shift, Clarissa stood in the tub of water, combing out her wet hair. He suspected she'd only just put on the shift, as it clung damply to her, her nipples poking out against the worn cotton. She should wear silk on that fine skin. Well, of course she knew that; that was why she wanted a rich lover.

"You look . . . you look very clean," he said.

"I'll call Peter to take the tub," she said, smiling shyly at him.

"No. Let me wash. I shaved but I'm dirty." God, he was turning into a pervert—first the same chamber pot, now an erotic thrill from sharing her bathwater.

"Certainly." She stepped away, sat on a box, and reached for a towel to dry her feet.

He stripped with little finesse, not like the other time he'd undressed for her, and she handed him a lump of soap flecked with some herb—lavender, like her sheets. He stepped into the tub, the few inches of water slightly warm and cloudy. He sank to one knee and poured water onto his head with a pewter bowl.

"Wait." She stepped close to him, cotton brushing his shoulder, and poured something cold and fragrant onto his hair.

"I can do that," he said, embarrassed that she was washing him, and then gave himself up to the pleasure of her fingers working through his hair, rubbing his scalp. More lavender, something else . . .

"Rosemary and sage," she said as he sniffed. "And lemon verbena in vinegar. I distilled it last summer."

She helped him rinse his hair and then sat on the box, still close enough to touch him if she wished, while he stood and soaped himself. She watched with open interest, particularly when he soaped his balls, and pulled back his foreskin to wash his cock.

"Does that give you pleasure?" Her voice was a throaty murmur as she watched his cock harden in his hand.

"Yes. And particularly knowing you watch me." He stroked himself, just to see her reaction.

She paused in combing her hair, her tongue flicking out to lick her lips.

And this woman thought she needed tutoring in the amorous arts? He grinned with delight and finished washing, arse, legs, feet, then squatted to rinse himself.

She took the bowl and poured water down his back, following the stream with her cool hand, running her hand over his shoulder blade, down his spine. She knelt next to him, her face close to his. She'd tied her hair back with a ribbon; it fell between her shoulder blades in a wet club.

"Clarissa." He took her chin in his hand, tilting her mouth to his. He wanted to kiss her properly, tease her with his lips. Her mouth was cool beneath his; she tasted of herbs and salt spray; he had a sudden urgent desire to taste his semen on her lips.

"We'll concentrate on your pleasure this first time. I trust that is agreeable, Miss Onslowe?" he whispered into her mouth. He wanted to be formal with her, a prelude to the reversal of formality when they would obey a different set of rules.

Her small gasp parted her lips to the tip of his tongue—just the tip, no more, give her a taste, make her want him as much as he wanted her.

He moved his mouth to her neck—good, she was sensitive there, flinching a little, but only a little, as his bristles rasped against the tender skin, his tongue and teeth giving her a small taste of what might follow.

"Your pleasure?" he repeated.

She shivered against him in a satisfying way. "Quite. And the next time? Or do we take turns?"

"Oh, we'll think of something, I'm sure. We could do some very . . . indecent acts of an advanced nature." His fingers crept into her shift and closed over her hard nipple. He pinched, not intending to hurt her, but not too gently. "Do you have any preferences, Miss Onslowe?"

"I . . . I don't know."

"I trust you're prepared this time, Miss Onslowe?"

"Yes, Mr. Pendale."

He liked the thought of her, shift raised, one slim hand reaching between her legs, inserting a sponge for his pleasure. He'd watch her do it when she was less shy with him.

"Good. I intend to come inside you. Several times."

When she stood, and he stood, too, drops of water falling against her shift, dampening it against her, she thought her legs might collapse with pleasure and nervousness. His erection pushed blatantly against her, his hand was still at her breast, and she wanted to touch him everywhere, barely knowing where to start. She reached her hands behind him and touched his back, the wet, cool skin.

"You're wet," she gasped idiotically.

"Am I?" He nipped at her ear. "Probably not as wet as you are for me."

Oh God, he's crude. Wonderfully crude.

He stepped from the tub in a shower of tepid drops so

he stood behind her. "Part your legs for me, darling. Pull your shift up."

"What about my pleasure?" As his cock bumped against her naked buttocks, she was afraid he'd take her there and then, when she wanted his delicious teasing to continue.

"Hold your shift up. That's right. Now watch." His hand, dark and square against her belly, slid between her thighs, parting her, touching her exactly where she yearned to be touched. His other hand pinched and stroked her nipple. He murmured that he wanted to frig her all the time when he wasn't fucking her, he wanted her to come and come, he wanted her lovely quim squeezing his cock, he wanted her wet and soaking him, milking his ballocks— crude, shocking things in his beautiful, resonant voice, words that made her pant and moan with excitement.

Then he stopped as her thighs tensed for her orgasm.

"But first, we'll take off this shift." He stripped it from her and turned her around to face him, cupping her breasts in his hands. "You're a pretty woman, Miss Clarissa Onslowe. And I'll do all of that for sure to you. But first . . ."

His cock reared dark and hard against her belly. She stroked one finger down its length and smiled as it jumped, a drop of fluid stretching and dripping onto her hand.

He caught her wrist to stop her. "Later." His voice was rough, and she realized then his excitement matched hers. "Sit down. On my box, I think."

She sat.

"Open your legs for me."

"What—"

He knelt before her, put a hand on each knee, and pushed her thighs wide apart, quite firmly, as though not brooking any argument. Her secret parts were exposed, vulnerable to his gaze—he was looking between her legs, at her cunny. She was wet and swollen, embarrassed, vulnerable, excited.

He raised his gaze to her. "You want to come, don't you?"

"Yes." Her voice was a whisper.

"Oh, you'll come, Clarissa." He stroked one finger slowly, too slowly, down the ridge of her clitoris—she shook with pleasure—down between her swollen labia, pushing just inside her for one moment, and then back up, circling. "I'm told women like this way the best."

Before she could protest, he dipped his mouth to where his fingers had played and replaced them with his tongue. She'd heard maids at Thelling's whisper of it, *tipping the velvet,* giggling to one another that it was the best thing a man could do, although they thought so highly of their cocks . . . and, oh yes, what a strange and wonderful thing it was. Who would have thought a tongue—tempting and wicked in her mouth—could be used so, and his lips and even a hint of his teeth. His hands stroked up her sides, closed on her breasts, and pulled her nipples hard, and she gripped the edge of the box tightly, torn between wanting to watch what he did and flinging herself back to enjoy his touch. She caressed his head, the springing curl of his black hair, pushed against him—*Yes, Allen, please*—then grabbed with both hands to steady a world flying apart. Coming, oh, not nearly enough of a word for what happened, for the glorious tumult of spiral, rolling, boiling over–ness—she laughed, still gripping his head, and repeated his name. *Allen. Allen. Allen.*

She slumped forward, her head on his shoulder, gasping for breath and still laughing. God, he'd never before had a woman who laughed when she came, and he wondered whether he should be insulted. But no, it was a splendid thing in its own way; he certainly preferred it to women who wept. At least this way he could be certain she'd enjoyed herself.

"Thank you," she said, which made him laugh, too.

"My pleasure. No, your pleasure. Our pleasure." He touched a finger to her open quim, wet with his saliva and her own excitement, stroked, watched her face. "Shall I do it again?"

"Oh." She looked quite thrilled, like a child at a fair being offered a second gingerbread man. Then she glanced at his erection and giggled.

"And what is so funny?" He tried to sound appropriately outraged.

"It's—would you like to—to fuck me?" Her voice had dropped to a whisper, and this extraordinary woman, who had avidly watched him finger and tongue her cunt and play with her breasts, actually blushed. "I thought you might be uncomfortable."

"Uncomfortable with lust for you? That's one way to put it." He grabbed her legs, locking them around his arse, his cock bumping up against her. "How do you like to do it best?"

"Best?" she echoed him.

He glanced around at their surroundings. If he took her on a berth, he'd get splinters in his arse, and there'd be nowhere for his knees and . . . God, he wanted a feather bed with bedposts to tie her to and big and soft enough to spread her out and fuck her and fuck her. . . . Somehow the fucking part would happen here, but he wasn't sure how.

He stood and opened the door, shoved the tub and bucket outside, and grabbed the quilt from Mrs. Blight's bed. "Come here." He tossed the quilt and pulled her down with him. "Tell me how you like it," he repeated.

She looked confused.

What the devil had her lover been about? Allen wondered.

"You know, on top, on your side, standing up, sitting, from behind . . . ? Let's try a few positions and you can tell me what works best." He positioned her on her back, spread her legs and thrust forward, making, to his great embarrassment, a small whimpering sound as he entered her.

He wanted to come. Oh Christ, he wanted to come.

"Well, this is quite pleasant," she said in a voice of cheerful determination that made him laugh again.

"If I were a more sensitive soul, I might slink away and kill myself. 'Quite pleasant,' indeed."

"I beg your pardon. Ecstatic, wondrous, like to make me swoon?" She frowned. "I did it this way before."

He sighed in mock dismay. "Miss Onslowe, please do not boast of your conquests to me. It is most unseemly. Unless"—he bent to nip her ear, and she squirmed beneath him in a most satisfactory manner—"unless you seek to arouse me unbearably by recounting an experience of absolute filth."

"I'm afraid I didn't find it particularly arousing then."

"No need for apologies. Let's try this." He turned on his back, hoisting her atop him, admiring the neat drop of her breasts into his hands.

She looked at him, confused, aroused.

"Move, darling," he said, thrusting upward.

"Like this?" She rose, slid, sank. And again.

"Oh yes." He gripped her hips, his balls and buttocks tightening. "Clarissa, I won't last like this. Let's try another way."

"Mmm," she said, swiveling her hips in a most distracting way. "Oh. Oh, I like this. I can rub myself against you."

He gritted his teeth. "We'll come back to this later, I promise."

"Promise?" She raised his hands to her breasts.

"Yes." With a heroic effort, he unbalanced her, tipping her off. "On your hands and knees, if you please."

She hesitated.

"You'll like it," he said.

"It's most vulgar," she said, presenting her backside to him. "Why do you want to look at my arse?"

"Because," he said, guiding himself in, entranced by

the sight of his cock disappearing into her quim, "your arse is 'ecstatic, wondrous, like to make me swoon.' "

She made a snorting sound of disbelief and rocked back against him.

"Also, I can do this." He slapped one creamy buttock.

"Ow! Don't!"

"Or this." He reached his hand round, seeking her clitoris, and found it swollen and hard. She was closer than he thought, or possibly than she knew herself. She moaned, moved with him, sighed. He moved his hand to her breast, leaning back to watch the wet slide of his cock, the tense and sway of her buttocks.

"Allen?"

"Yes, my love?"

"May I go on top again?"

He groaned. "In a moment."

"Please."

He'd promised to pleasure her, and so he would. Allen Pendale kept his word, so even though he thought it would kill him, he withdrew one more time, and flung himself on his back.

Damn her, the coquette took her time mounting him, rubbing shamelessly against his cock and leaning to kiss him—which he quite enjoyed, or would have enjoyed more if he had not been so eager to rush to the finish. She wriggled around, adjusting her position on him, while he tensed and moaned beneath her.

"Do you like this?" She pinched his nipples with her fingers.

"I—I don't know. Maybe." He thrust into her, impatient now.

"Stop!" Her face had an expression of intense concentration. She moved slowly, finding a rhythm to her liking, and he prayed he could hold out for her. He sought frantically in his mind for distraction: Latin declensions thrashed into him at school—no, too much effort; the catechism (forgotten, and surely he would rot in hell)—while she drove him on and on, kings of England and the dates of their reigns—William the Conqueror, 1066 to 1087 . . . William Rufus, 1087 to 1100, killed in the New Forest hunting, poor bastard . . . Stephen . . . no, Henry, can't remember . . . yes, Henry the First, 1100 to . . .

"Allen, can you feel that? Can you . . . ?" She clenched hard on him, her face alight with wonder, and he let go, soaring to the heavens.

Ecstatic, wondrous, like to make him swoon. Precisely.

CHAPTER 6

Afterward he held her, stroked her, and told her how beautiful she was. She didn't quite believe him—it sounded far too much like the sort of idiotic things a well-pleased man might say, and she knew she wasn't beautiful in any conventional sense. Once, in the only comparable circumstances she had experienced, another man had told her he loved her passionately and would never leave her—which he did the next day, abandoning her to the wrath of both an innkeeper demanding payment and her scandalized and tearful family. But she wouldn't think of her past folly now, not with Allen Pendale warm and large and very much present.

She sat, untangling herself from his arms.

"What are you doing? More, already?" he asked.

"I want to look at you."

She knelt beside him, skimming her hands over his body—too muscular and broad to truly be called beautiful, and densely furred on chest and groin, legs and arms covered with a fuzz of black hair. His cock stirred as she ran her hands down his chest and onto his flanks.

"You insatiable slut," he said, the affection in his voice taking the insult from his words.

"You are so very dark and hairy," she commented.

He grunted. "My mother used to call me her little changeling."

"That wasn't very kind."

"You saw the miniature of my sister. My brothers and sisters are, for the most part, tall and slender and very fair, like our father." He stopped, quite suddenly and she wondered what he had been about to say next. Did he suspect he had been fathered by a man other than the Earl of Frensham?

"I miss my family," she admitted. "I would do anything—anything—to be on good terms with them again."

"But you choose to become a courtesan."

She tried to keep her voice level. "When Lord Thelling died, I wrote to my family, suspecting I should soon be without a position. I begged them to forgive me. They would not."

"It's ridiculously illogical," he grumbled. He reached for her breasts, thumbs rubbing her nipples erect. "As though your seducer bore no part in the matter."

"So many things are ridiculously illogical."

Meanwhile, the man who had pledged to show her the pleasures of the flesh so she could honor an agreement with another, unknown lover showed distinct signs of carnal interest. She ran her hand through his bush of curly dark hair and grasped his cock.

"Push back my foreskin and lick the top," he murmured, hands in her hair, pushing her head down.

"I thought this was for my pleasure."

"It will be."

As his cock in her hand firmed and quickened, the head emerged from the foreskin like a questing creature. She bent her head to touch it with her tongue, inhaling the dark, earthy scent of him, their mingled fluids still beaded on the curling dark hair.

He gave a long sigh of satisfaction. "I'll teach you how to take me in your mouth tomorrow night. But at the moment, I'm feeling rather lazy. Kneel over my face and I'll tongue you."

She looked at him with some doubt. That sounded—well, vulgar. Arousing, too. But . . . "Would you like me to wash, first?"

"Whatever for? I know what I'll taste. Come on, Clarissa, don't be a silly prude."

"I am not a silly prude!" She scrambled astride him, grabbing one of the berths for support.

His hands clamped onto her bottom, and his tongue snaked right inside her—she wondered how she tasted, with the wine she had used as a preventative, and his seed and her own moisture—but then didn't care. His lips and mouth caressed her exposed clitoris, his chin scraped rough against her thighs, one hand tweaked her nipple, and the other . . . Oh, my God, the other stroked and caressed her buttocks, spreading them apart, with one finger playing . . .

"I'm sure that's unnatural," she managed to say.

"I should stop?" His voice was muffled.

"I didn't say that. I . . ."

"Does it hurt?"

"No. Don't stop." She couldn't help moving then, inviting more of that forbidden penetration, rubbing herself against his mouth and tongue as she tightened in anticipation. He showed no mercy, urging her onward, kept her hanging on the brink for an endless, breathless moment, and then brought her to release.

"Oh," she said as the long shudders subsided. "That was wicked, Allen."

"And you are an eager sinner." He helped her shuffle down his chest, his hands on her hips. "I'm at your disposal, Miss Onslowe, if you'd care to take advantage of me."

She moved farther down to kiss him, and something hard bumped against her buttocks. A moment before, she would have required no more, believing herself thoroughly pleasured, but his eagerness aroused her. She raised herself, positioned herself, and slid as slowly as she could onto his cock, watching his face.

His eyes narrowed as he sucked in breath. "You're so sweet, Clarissa."

"I thought I was an insatiable slut."

"You're a sweet, insatiable slut. Come down here. I want to kiss your breasts."

She lowered her breasts to his mouth, which had just given her such astonishing pleasure, and let him suckle and caress her as she moved, slow and with care, easing herself on that familiar journey into a place of heat and splendor.

Beneath her Allen moaned, flexed, gripped her hips.

She had power over him; he was at her mercy, and she could and would make him come when it pleased her, subject him to sweet agony as she brought him close, checked him, took him to the brink again, and then allowed him his release. He was, for the moment, hers.

"We missed breakfast," she said after they'd slept.

"We could miss dinner, too, if you like," he offered.

She shook her head. "We should eat. We need to keep our strength up."

Beneath her, he chuckled. They had retired to a berth, after finding the floor too hard. He had pulled her on top of him and ridiculed her fear that she might crush him.

"There's only one part of me you're afraid of crushing, Clarissa, and I assure you, you will not. Stay here."

So she had, lulled to sleep by the beat of his heart and the sway of the ship.

Beneath her, his cock quickened and firmed, growing against her belly.

His hands spanned her buttocks. "Such a sweet arse. Would you like my cock inside it, Clarissa?"

"Not now, I think," she said, hearing herself hopelessly prim, the housekeeper deciding when the silver should be polished.

He rumbled with laughter and nuzzled her neck. "Take me into that pretty cunt again, then."

"How?" She wriggled, tried to put a foot on the floor, and lost the angle.

"Stay where you are." He grasped her hips, slid her forward, tilted, and entered her.

She placed her hands on his shoulders, raising herself as much as she could to watch him. His eyes were half closed; he looked, she imagined, much as she did: greedy and sleepy and aroused all at once. "Tell me about your mistress."

"Which one?"

"How many have there been? To start with, the one whose husband chased you to the dock."

"Ah. Lady Ann. Voracious, greedy, demanding, shrill."

"Then why on earth—"

"This part of me"—he thrust upward—"did the thinking. And if her husband had sued for divorce, I would have been named and then obliged to marry her."

"But it doesn't seem fair. What will her husband do to her?"

Allen ran his hand over her neck, pushing hair aside. "Expect her to be more discreet next time. It's the way of the world."

His eyebrows drew together and his breathing became faster. Already she knew the signs; she had learned the lessons of his body quietly.

"Who else?"

"Who else what?"

"Who else have you been to bed with?"

"Hmm. You wish for the whole list?"

"List?" She put her lips to his ear and sang, *"Ma in Ispagna son già mille e tre . . . mille e tre."*

Beneath her, he rumbled with laughter. "Not in Spain, but in Bristol, maybe."

"A thousand and three in one city? You mean you outdo Don Giovanni himself?"

He shrugged. Inside her, she felt a softening, the looseness that occurred after his orgasm, except she knew he hadn't come.

Best to make light of the situation. "Is my singing that dreadful?"

He muttered, "I shouldn't—I had this bad habit of seducing merchants' wives. Silly boring rich women for whom I was a consolation, an entertainment. I didn't like any of them particularly. I don't think they liked me much, either. Each one presented a challenge, a mystery, but afterward I found I was lonelier—" He stopped and turned his face away.

"Allen—"

"Except," he added as his cock slid from her, "this never happened with them." He laughed, a dry, ironic chuckle. "You may tell me it doesn't matter. I believe that's the acceptable, sympathetic statement for a woman to make under these circumstances. God knows it's never happened before, so I'm not quite sure of the etiquette. But by all means coo something sweet while pitying me—and of course you secretly suspect it happens all the time."

"A moment." Clarissa eased herself onto her elbows. "May I borrow your writing desk? I must make note of this for future encounters."

He laughed and gripped her arms, turning his face to hers. "Don't move. Do you know, Clarissa, I think you might be the only woman I've fucked that I actually liked?"

"How appalling." She rubbed her nose against his. "Have you ever been in love?"

He shrugged. "Quite frequently, but it faded. I proposed to a couple of women, but fortunately they turned me down. I suspect I'm a little in love with you, Miss Onslowe, but I can promise you the condition will pass."

"I rejoice to hear it." She felt both disappointed and relieved. "Love might well be a complication for us both. You are quite right." She ran a finger over his lips. "Tell me about your family."

He groaned. "You won't stiffen my prick this way, Clarissa. Very well. I have lots of relatives, mostly annoying. There's a great uncle who collects useless items and never throws anything away, and there's an aunt who can drink anyone under the table—the usual assortment of embarrassments. I have a dozen or so nieces and nephews, whom I quite like. I don't think my brothers and sisters wholly approve of me. I'm the youngest and regarded as the feckless, irresponsible one. However, they decided I should be the one to travel to the island to break the news to my father that my mother died, and I'm an obedient brother."

"Your mother has died recently? How sad."

He grunted. His fingers played over her back. "I don't usually tell women this sort of thing."

"I'm honored. Do you like practicing the law?"

"I'm an obedient son, or I've tried to be. It's a perfectly respectable profession for a younger son with a little wit who likes arguments." He ran his fingers through her hair.

"You have the capacity to do good, to change things."

He laughed. "There are too many injustices crying out for my time, Miss Onslowe, and none of them have any money."

She put her lips to his neck, tasting slightly of soap, harsh with stubble left after his inadequate shave. Did he like this, too? She moved her mouth to the hollow above his collarbone and bit. He sighed. Between them, his cock shifted and firmed. She rubbed her belly against him and asked. "What shall I do?"

"Kiss me."

And this time it worked. She positioned herself so that his cock grew into her, as sweet an invasion as his tongue into her mouth. Soon they both groaned and sighed, straining against each other. The ship rocked and tugged them apart and together again.

"Don't come yet," she whispered. "I want you to think of me when you come, not of your one thousand and three."

"I am thinking of you."

"Tell me how it feels."

"Sweet, like my cock is in a silk-lined glove. Warm, plump." His voice caught. He tensed beneath her. "Wet so that I glide in you. It's like swimming in something warm and delicious. When you tighten on me—Oh yes, you're a quick learner. You know how to do that. I want you to suck the life from me, tumble me into oblivion, throw my soul to the stars."

"Pretty words, Allen Pendale. Pretty words for my pretty cunt."

He shuddered as she hoped he would.

"Did you know I was awake our first night? I think you did. You flaunted yourself at me. When you undressed for me I lay here and I squeezed my thighs together—like this."

He groaned.

"I was so wet for you, I could smell myself. I wondered if you could smell me, too. And I put my hand here, between my thighs, as you took off your clothes, so very slowly for me, and I put my finger here."

"Go on."

"I wondered if you'd know. But I had to do it." Her arm was pressed between their bodies. Her finger lay against the ridge of her clitoris, letting his tremors and the dip and sway of the ship dictate her orgasm.

"And then—"

"Yes. Like this." Heat burst and rippled.

Beneath her, inside her, he tensed, raising her, and pulsed in his own rhythmic release.

*

His taste was on her fingers and tongue; her chin and her thighs were rubbed raw by his stubble. All through dinner, neither she nor Allen could produce a coherent sentence. Their feet tangled beneath the table; their fingers brushed at any opportunity.

She reminded herself that this was not love—it was lust. A small, vague part of her mind reminded her in a fatigued way how unseemly her behavior was. Then she thought once again of Allen's hands and mouth, the feel of his cock, and stared at him across the dishes. Another indistinct voice noted that the fresh food was ended now, and the ship's biscuit and salt pork were uninteresting to say the least, but it didn't matter. It didn't matter at all. The only thing that mattered was getting Allen back into that dim, cramped space where they could be alone and she could . . .

Mrs. Blight said something to her. Poor Mrs. Blight, pale and diminished, picking at the food—it really was unpleasant, but food was unimportant—and waiting for her to reply.

"I beg your pardon. What did you say?"

"I said, Miss Onslowe, we are most grateful to you for looking after us. I thought we were going to die. And that boy Peter was kind, too."

"Oh, it was nothing," Clarissa said. "And it is Captain Trent you have to thank for Peter's help."

"Indeed, not, Miss Onslowe, Mrs. Blight," the Captain said. "You should thank Mr. Pendale, for it was he who offered to pay."

Blight looked at Allen with unconcealed dislike. Men were such very odd creatures. Why shouldn't Allen pay? Clarissa was fairly sure, from the condition of Allen's battered coats and boots, that he was not wealthy, but he probably had more money than anyone else there. She watched Allen's fingers close around the stem of his wineglass, listened to the buzz of voices around the table, and longed for dinner to be finished.

When they went back onto the deck, neither of them paused to look at the stars or bid the others more than a cursory good night. Under the cover of her cloak, he grabbed her hand and placed it against his groin.

"I want to fuck you," he growled.

He certainly did.

"Get below. And hurry." He pushed her toward the hatch, one hand loosening his neckcloth.

"Mr. Pendale, if the arrangement—" Blight stepped into their path.

"What arrangement?"

"Of the cabins, sir."

Clarissa noticed the flush of embarrassment on Blight's face.

"Don't be a fool, Blight." Allen pulled the neckcloth off and stuffed it into his pocket. "I'll wish you a good night."

He followed Clarissa down the steps so fast he almost trod on her fingers; then he pushed her into the cabin. "Get your skirts up."

"How—" *How do you intend to do this?* she wanted to ask, but her unspoken question was answered as Allen shoved her into the corner created by the wall and the end of the berths.

Cursing, he unbuttoned, hoisting one of her legs around his waist, and drove into her. She anticipated his urgency—what she didn't expect was her own readiness— the long, delicious wet slide of penetration, her cry of pleasure and alarm. She grabbed at his shoulder, his hair, to steady herself before gripping the edge of the berth with the nearest hand. The wall scraped her back; Allen panted, thudding into her like a battering ram, groaned, and then laughed.

"Thank you, Miss Onslowe." He broke his hold on her, withdrawing in a warm gush.

"You came?"

He grinned, stepped back, and buttoned his breeches. "Don't sound so outraged, my dear. I'm preparing you for your role as a courtesan, when you'll make your protector's pleasure your greatest priority."

"Indeed? So I can only assume you pleasure me from—what? A sense of duty? Because you said you would?"

He withdrew a cheroot from inside his coat. "It was my whim. It pleased me at the time."

She glared at him. "I trust you plan to smoke that on deck."

"Of course."

He left, with hardly the pretense of a bow. Clarissa dropped onto the lower berth, not pleased and somewhat astonished. This man, who had revealed his loneliness and vulnerability, now seemed determined to prove himself as boorish as any other male. And he'd made the decision, with his usual aristocratic high-handedness, about the future disposition of the cabins. He had not even thought to consult her. Not that she would have said differently—at least, not then—but she thought the indelicacy of his decision had possibly embarrassed the Blights.

She stepped outside and knocked at the door of the

Blights' cabin. There were some thumping, rustling sounds, and then Blight, a scowl on his face, opened it. He was half undressed, in shirtsleeves and breeches, revealing a lean, muscular body she'd never noticed before.

"What do you want?"

"I wanted to make sure Mrs. Blight and you are well and that the arrangement regarding the cabins is to your liking."

"Indeed." He leered at her, leaning against the doorway. "Quite the grand lady, aren't you, Miss Onslowe?"

"I meant no disrespect, sir."

"You're no better than me or Mrs. Blight, Miss Onslowe. Whatever you were before, or fancy yourself now, you're Lemarchand's servant. It makes no difference who fucks you."

"You—"

He leaned forward, close enough for her to catch a whiff of rum on his breath. "You're a pretty piece, Miss Onslowe, if a bit long in the tooth. When his lordship"—he jerked his head upward—"tires of you, I daresay you and I could entertain ourselves well enough. Mrs. Blight would have no objection."

"Yes, sir, but you forget I might. Indeed I am sure I would have not one, but many, objections." She backed away. "Good night, Mr. Blight."

God rot the whole male sex. She slammed her cabin door shut, absolutely determined that she would be asleep when Allen returned.

"Allen!"

He sought to free himself from the sorrow that dragged him down, the fathomless waves of despair.

"Allen!"

There was no way to hide the fact that he was weeping—blubbering, to tell the truth, his nose running, too. Making a fool of himself in front of Clarissa Onslowe, as usual.

"What troubles you so?"

"A bad dream, that is all." He resisted the temptation to clutch at her, drive his face into her shoulder for comfort. He rubbed his hands over his face, shamed by his weakness.

"Pray do not use the sheet." She shoved a handkerchief into his hand.

He blew his nose and mopped at the tears running down his face and soaking the pillow. "There's a ship. A monstrous ship. Huge. A ship for giants. And someone on it—someone I seek but can't find." He paused, remembering the steps he climbed with the greatest of difficulty. Each tread was at the height of his thigh. Miles of steps, it seemed, while he sought the unknown in growing despair and panic.

"And that is what makes you so sad."

"Yes." A wave of misery washed over him, fresh tears springing from his eyes. "I've dreamed this for as long as I remember. I realized it was of a ship only when I went to the Continent, but that was the first time I sailed, so how . . . ? I am sorry I woke you."

"No matter." She patted his arm and yawned. "Will you sleep again?"

He nodded.

She ducked out of sight and he heard the rustles of her settling back into her berth.

He rolled onto his side, dropping one arm down to touch her hair, craving the closeness he sought in his dream. Her fingers laced in his and he slept.

CHAPTER 7

"Do you think we will die?" Clarissa gripped Allen's hand.

"We'll die drunk." He passed her the bottle of rum.

She was thirsty, and knew the rum would make her more so, but she took a swig anyway.

After five weeks at sea, they had run into a storm. The ship bucketed and plunged. On the cabin floor, stinking water sloshed and gurgled, and she was glad she couldn't see what else swilled around in it. They'd been below three days—she thought it was three days, but she wasn't sure—with the hatch battened shut. Before entombing them, one of the crew had thrown down a sack containing two gallons of cider and some ship's biscuit, before nailing the hatch shut. Allen had produced the rum when they'd drunk their cider. He had grudgingly given the other gallon of cider to the Blights, grumbling that they might as well pour it straight onto the floor. This was a storm, a roaring, terrifying force; she knew the sails were tightly furled, the ship hurtling where it would.

They lay trapped in their berths as timbers creaked and groaned, and she feared the ship would split apart.

"What will you miss when you're dead?" It was an absurd question, childlike, and with anyone else, or any other time, she could not have asked it.

"Fucking. Fucking you. My sister. My land."

"Your land?"

"A few acres between Bristol and Bath. Small hills. Sheep. A little gray stone house." He hiccupped. "Pretty. I inherited it from my mother's side of the family. It's not entailed. Mine. The place I like best."

"My place is—was—the Blue Room at Thelling's. Queen Elizabeth slept there. I'd go in there and lie down, and look at the canopy all embroidered with stars and the moon. Solitude was very precious. And I'd dream of getting away."

He chuckled. "You did. To this. What will you miss?"

"The sky. Music. The smell of rain when it first falls." She gave a maudlin sniff that was only partly because of the rum. "That I could not make peace with my family."

"Ah, don't cry, Clarissa." She wished she could see him. His thumb stroked her wrist. "There's no one I'd rather die with, sweetheart, if it's any consolation to you."

When she woke next, everything had changed. Water still sloshed on the floor, but there was less movement, much less—and light. Blessed light. If only she were not so thirsty and her head did not ache so.

The cabin stank. She supposed she did, too, and Allen, whose hand hung on her shoulder. He gave a soft snore.

She was warm, and that was remarkable, since the candle, their only source of heat, had burned down hours, days ago. That must mean . . . Her befuddled brain fought to make sense of it.

Above her, the berth creaked, and Allen landed with a splash, and an expression of disgust, on the floor. He looked dreadful, eyes red-rimmed, face covered with stubble.

"Clarissa," he said in a hoarse voice, "it's calm. We can get on deck. Surely . . ."

She lifted her skirts to her knees and tumbled out, legs weak, into his arms.

"Oh, damn! My stockings!" Too late she realized she should have taken them off.

"Never mind about your stockings. What's important is that you don't puke," he said. "Remember, I have money on you."

She pushed past him, and took a deep breath of fresh air—the hatch was open.

Weak and clumsy after days mostly flat on her back, she was shaking by the time she got on deck, blinking in hazy morning light. And the smell—a wonderful green smell, heartbreakingly fresh. A seabird wheeled out of the brightness, and flew away.

When was the last time she'd seen a bird?

The crew, bedraggled and exhausted, was at work on

deck, mending sails, polishing, scrubbing, putting their ship to rights. They raised a ragged cheer at the sight of Clarissa.

"Any puking, Miss Onslowe? Mr. Pendale?" someone called out.

"Neither of us," she said with pride.

One of the men offered her a leather bottle and she tipped it back, and drained it—beer, slightly warm and sour, but wonderful. She felt as though she could never drink enough.

"You could have saved some for me," Allen said. "What's that smell?"

" 'Tis land, sir. We're not far off, now. A few days, maybe. The captain don't rightly know our position with the storm."

Allen, who had received a leather bottle from another sailor, wiped his mouth. He stared at Clarissa.

"Do I look so dreadful?" She knew her hair hung limp around her face, her clothes were rumpled and dirty, and her stockings—Well, she hoped they would wash. Oh, how she longed to wash, and if only she had some clean linen, but first they would have to swab out the cabins; she didn't know whether Peter could help them, with so much work to be done on the ship.

Allen shook his head. "No. It's . . . Shall we visit the galley?"

Stomachs full of coffee—lots of coffee—and ship's biscuits, with the promise of fresh food within the week, she and Allen repaired below to salvage what they could of their belongings and start baling out the filthy water that lapped around their calves. She didn't think it was the sort of work an earl's son might undertake, but he shrugged, and baled and mopped alongside her. Elizabeth Blight, pale and shaky, also helped, despite her air of fragility—and somehow managed to flirt mildly with Allen while she mopped.

" 'Tis not right, a gentleman doing such work," she murmured.

"I couldn't agree more, ma'am. Where is Blight?"

"Oh, he's talking to the captain, I believe. He went to ask if the boy could help us." Mrs. Blight gave a short scream as more debris was revealed. "Oh, God, is that a rat?"

"Quite dead, ma'am. You've nothing to fear." Allen picked the corpse up by its tail and tossed the rat up toward the hatch.

A cry of disgust and rage came from above.

"Beg your pardon, Blight. Didn't see you there," Allen said.

Mrs. Blight shrieked and giggled as the rat descended again, bouncing down the steps and landing with a damp thud at their feet.

Clarissa tightened her lips. Why was Allen behaving like a child? Why, for that matter, was he flirting with Mrs. Blight and ignoring her?

Allen ran up the steps, the last bucket of debris in his hand.

"A bucket of clean water and some soap, if you

please," Clarissa shouted after him, in the sort of voice she reserved for lazy servants.

She lifted her skirts and knotted them, in preparation for kneeling to scrub the floor. To her annoyance, Blight came down the stairs at that moment. He gave her knees and ankles a long, narrow-eyed stare.

"Very nice, Miss Onslowe." His comment was so fast and soft she almost might have imagined it. He turned to his wife. "My dear, you should come on deck for some fresh air. A ship is approaching—we believe it to be an English warship. I am sure Miss Onslowe can spare you."

They jostled awkwardly in the small space as the Blights went up on deck and Clarissa, scrubbing brush in hand, waited for Allen to appear with the water and soap.

He set the bucket down and looked at her.

She knew that look. After all these weeks of fucking—and, she had to admit it, their days and nights contemplating death—his closeness affected her more than she cared to admit. She cleared her throat. "I'm sorry Mrs. Blight isn't here to entertain you. I'm sure she would have appreciated your presence."

"And you don't?" Cocky, arrogant, he placed one hand on the timber near her head. "Oh, I think you appreciate it, just as much as I appreciate . . . this." With the other hand, he pulled the drawstring at the bosom of her gown. Her breast tumbled into his hand, the nipple tightening against his thumb. "Would you like me to fuck you now, Clarissa?"

"Certainly not. I have a floor that needs scrubbing, and you're in the way."

He leaned forward, his breath warming her hair. "You're in a very bad mood for one who has experienced death and resurrection. And speaking of rising from the dead . . ."

His cock stirred against her, pushing against her skirts, her thigh. Well, two could play that game. "Allen," she breathed, almost persuading herself that she was feigning surrender, "if only I did not have to get down on my hands and knees to scrub this floor."

She stroked one hand down his flank, wondering just how much she should tease him, while his hand on her nipple, pulling and circling, sent hot sweet darts to her quim.

His lips, cracked from their recent ordeal, brushed hers. "Woman's work is never done."

She glanced down at the sizable erection pushing against his breeches. "Very true. You know that as one rubs—so—there is just more to do." She slipped her tongue into his mouth, delighted at his groan, his thrust against her hand.

And she stopped, reached for the scrubbing brush, and pushed him away. She made her voice brisk and practical. "A passable attempt, Allen, but I'm busy."

"What?" He stared at her.

She tightened the drawstring on her gown. "Maybe you should find something useful to do."

He scowled. "You're lucky I'm a tolerant man, Clarissa."

"Of course." She dropped to her knees, and rubbed the lump of soap against the brush. No lather, of course, not with this soap and seawater, but she hoped the salt would cleanse and lessen the stink.

Allen stalked into the cabin and hit his head on the lantern as usual, while she didn't even bother to stifle a giggle. He muttered to himself as he picked through his posessions, complaining of damp and damage, lifting a shirt to sniff it. Of course it stank. At this point all their clothes did.

Clarissa scrubbed, regretting her teasing, but thinking, with a smile, that she would make it up to him later. And she could. She knew how to make him moan with pleasure, how to drive him wild with wanting, push him to the edge and then rein him in for her own gratification.

"You know," he said, "this is not how a courtesan behaves. You're here for my pleasure."

"You're not my protector."

"No, but you asked me to teach you. It's not just a question of bed. That's important, but . . . Oh, the devil with it." He produced a small knife and sharpened a pen. "This other ship is quite close. I expect it's going to England. Do you want to write a letter to anyone?"

"No. There is no one."

He grunted and began to write rapidly on a small sheet of paper from his portable writing desk. "As you will. I'm writing to my sister." He scribbled a few lines more. "What about your family?"

"I'll write to them when we arrive."

"Very well."

She scrubbed and listened to the small scratching sound of his pen.

"Captain Trent told me we'd probably be invited over to the ship. Since they're a few days out from the island, they'll have the better food." He folded the letter. "Just the gentlemen, of course, and I suppose Blight will come, too."

"Why don't you like him?"

"Like him? He's a jumped-up servant."

Clarissa sat back on her heels and wiped the back of her hand over her forehead. "So am I."

"You're different."

"Why?" She rubbed the block of soap onto the boards.

"Because you're a lady."

"No, I'm not. I'm ruined. But regarding Blight—do you really think it wise to make an enemy of him?"

Allen stood, tapping the letter against his thigh. "It's somewhat too late to worry about that, Clarissa. If I were you, I would not think about it. I assure you I barely think of Blight at all."

"Mr. Pendale?" Captain Trent's voice from on deck interrupted them. "We're taking the cutter over to the ship, if you'd care to accompany us."

Allen bowed. How ironic; the earl's son bowed to a woman who knelt at his feet with a scrubbing brush in her hand, and left dirty footprints over the freshly scrubbed floor as he left.

His head ached liked the devil and he wished there had not been quite so many toasts to the king, the Navy, and God knows what else last night. Clarissa was still cool with him—he'd somehow made it belowdecks without breaking his neck and fallen onto his berth with all his clothes on, although he'd fully intended to pay her some attention.

He blinked in the morning sun and looked at the very pleasant sight of Clarissa and Elizabeth Blight in their shifts, washing linen. Mrs. Blight's shift, trimmed with lace, showed off her unfettered bosom to great advantage. Clarissa's shift, however, was threadbare and almost transparent; he could see the outline of her slender body, the darkness of nipples and pubic hair through it. Although a piece of sailcloth had been strung across the deck to give the women some privacy, crew members drifted toward it frequently until Allen glared at them.

He had stripped down to a pair of cotton drawers and, dirty shirts, nceckcloths, and stockings in hand, hoped Clarissa would offer to wash them for him. She, however, had only smiled and returned to her own laundry. Beside her, Mrs. Blight, bosom jiggling, scrubbed industriously at one of Blight's shirts. She glanced at Allen, a quick, appraising look, before bending to her task.

Blight looked at him and smirked. "Now, if she were mine, I wouldn't stand for it."

"I beg your pardon?" Allen made his voice icily cool.

"Miss Onslowe. She's impertinent. She needs a good whipping."

"Indeed." He returned Blight's sneer. "She's not your

property, or mine, either. I think you confuse the lady with one of your slaves."

"There's a lot to be said for an obedient woman."

"I prefer a woman who can speak for herself." Allen called out to Peter, who lurked nearby. Whether the lad was trying to take a look at the women (at his age Allen would certainly have done so) or whether he was trying to help Allen keep the crew away wasn't quite clear. "Peter, bring me a tub of water and some soap if you please."

"Aye, that's right. Show her you'll take no nonsense," Blight said.

"I intend to," Allen said.

Peter appeared, red-faced and sweating, his face wreathed in steam from the hot water, and set the tub down. Allen thanked him, and tossed his soiled linen in the water.

"What . . . ?" Blight looked horrified.

Allen reached for the soap. Well, how hard could it be to wash linen? If women could do it, then it must be fairly simple.

Clarissa and Elizabeth glanced at each other and giggled.

The sailors, ever watchful, wandered closer, this time their attention on the sight of a gentleman about to do his own laundry.

" 'Tis women's work," Blight spluttered.

Ignoring them, Allen picked up the soap and a shirt, and smeared some—as much as he could with the smooth, shiny substance—onto the cuffs and collar of a shirt. He repeated it on another shirt, on a pair of stockings, and swished the water. It turned gray and cloudy with a greasy tinge to it. The soap slid from his fingers and disappeared in the murky depths. The devil with this. He remembered women in Italy gathered in the shallows of a river, beating creamy linen on rocks, and with skirts hiked up, treading garments in the water.

He stepped into the tub and trampled his linen, grinning broadly at the embarrassment and consternation on Blight's face, while the two women laughed and clapped their hands.

"Mrs. Blight would be ashamed to see me so," Blight said.

"Indeed? You think it's unmanly?"

"Since you say so, Mr. Pendale, then yes, I do."

"Very well." Allen paused in his stamping and splashing. "I challenge you, then. I'll race you to the top of the mainmast. We'll see who the better man is then."

Blight hesitated for a moment. "Done."

"But," Allen continued, hauling dripping armfuls from the tub, "you'll have to wait until I've rinsed my linen."

CHAPTER 8

Allen had seen the sailors swarm up the mast and inch out onto the yardarms dozens of times, watched them diminish to the size of his hand, and marveled at their dexterity and courage. Now it was his turn, and already he thought he must be insane. Around him the officers and crew placed bets.

"I'm putting a half crown on you, Mr. Pendale," Clarissa said. Her nose was slightly pink from the sun. He wondered if she'd freckle and if he'd live to see it. The irony of surviving an Atlantic crossing to plummet to his death on a whim was not lost on him.

"Only a half crown?"

"It's more than I can afford." She touched his arm and whispered, "Be careful."

The captain escorted Allen and Blight to the mainmast. "You shall draw for which side you are to take, gentlemen. The longer of the two takes starboard."

Of course, the port side would mean the climber could be dazzled by the sun. He'd not thought of that.

Captain Trent held out a handful of straws.

Allen gestured to Blight—it was after all, the gentlemanly thing to do, to let the other draw first—but it was he who pulled out the shorter straw.

"Mr. Blight shall take the starboard side," Captain Trent pronounced. "The best of luck, sirs."

Allen swung himself into the shrouds, the ropes insubstantial beneath his hands and digging into his bare feet. For the first part of the climb, at least, he would not have the sun in his face. Opposite him, Blight climbed and Allen wondered if he, too, looked as ungainly, like a spider in a swinging net of ropes. So far, so good—and then he came to the first arm, above the belled canvas and the sun struck him like a blow, dazzling and producing orange and red blotches in his vision when he looked away. His headache intensified—he really had been a fool to drink so much last night.

He'd never been so high in his life—he'd climbed trees as a boy, of course, and on his grand tour clambered up Mount Aetna, breathing in sulfurous fumes, slipping on ashes and rubble—as he remembered, a rope broke beneath one foot. He froze for a moment, clinging to the ropes, sweating. Then onward, and the first truly frightening part—swinging from the shrouds to the lower yard, hauling himself up and jeering at himself. *If you had to do so to get into Clarissa's bed, you wouldn't hesitate.* Opposite and slightly below him, Blight labored up the last of the shrouds, breathing heavily.

Don't look up. Don't look at that mast stretching up, swaying against the blue sky. Don't. . . . Get a move on. Blight may be better at this than you. The sea was calm, but the higher he went, the more motion there would be. More swaying shrouds billowing into the sky. Now he was well ahead of Blight, and his legs shook already with the strain of putting his weight on the balls of his feet. It was easier but slower, if he turned his feet out like those of a dancer, and then that hurt, too, but in a different way. The sun blazed down on him.

Something appeared in his peripheral vision. A seabird, dazzling white, close enough for him to see its impassive yellow eye and orange beak, floated out of sight and beyond as though tempting him to launch himself into the air. Instead he narrowed his eyes and saw the frigate where they'd dined last night, an elegant, painted model of a ship, sails white and full, on a turquoise and midnight blue sea. Farther up, his legs and hands felt the strain, his calf muscles, despite years of fencing and riding and walking, tight with pain. Past the middle arm. His mouth was dry. He should have had a drink before starting.

He risked a glance down and saw the crew foreshortened on a frighteningly small deck, faces turned up. One more yardarm to pass, and then onto the crow's nest, where he could stand normally and stretch his feet and legs out (something else he should have done first. He always did before fencing. What a fool he was.). He couldn't even see Blight—God knew he didn't want to look down directly, and the sway of the mast made him dizzy as it was.

Past the top yardarm, and resisting the impulse to stop

and rest, he hauled himself up the next six, eight feet—
Don't think of the height—and into the crow's nest, where
he collapsed in an undignified heap. Glad that no one
could see him at that particular moment, he rolled on his
back and stretched his legs, wriggling his bare toes with a
luxurious groan. Above him the top of the mast swayed in
lazy wide arcs against a perfect blue sky.

The top of the mast. A few, very few tortuous pieces
of wood to climb, roughly fastened to the mast. One dan-
gled from a single nail, shifting slightly as the mast moved.
He had another ten feet to go.

Where the devil was Blight? If he'd fallen, surely the
watching crowd would have made some sort of noise. *Up.
Get to the top.* He stood and waved to the onlookers far
below. The deck appeared too small to be real. If he fell
now, where would he land? Would he bounce from the
sails or burst through them, splat on the deck or disappear into the sea? Academic questions, since he would not
fall—absolutely not. He grasped a support and shimmied
up, using his knees as much as his hands now, and his feet
and calves feeling the strain immediately, despite the brief
rest.

And he was there, his hand groping and feeling the flat
surface, smoother than he'd expected. Far higher than a
man was meant to go, unless you counted such oddities as
hot-air balloons. Could they see him from the deck?

He grinned. He was there. He'd show them that a
male laundress was a man, nevertheless. He'd show Clarissa. He hoisted himself up and sat on top of the mast,
gripping tightly with his thighs as the thing swayed and

creaked, scribing vast circles in empty space. He raised his arms above his head and heard a cheer from below.

And now all he had to do was get down. He lowered his arms, gripped, and shuffled backward, letting himself drop, his feet finding purchase after one dreadful moment, and wondered how hideous the descent would be. There was still no sign of Blight. Slowly and with care he dropped into the crow's nest and stretched again. No hurry. But he didn't want them to think he was frightened of the descent— which he was; he wasn't that much of a fool—so he had best make haste. *Lower your foot, find support, balance, then the other foot, one hand, the other hand ... small, economical movements. Breathe. Don't think about the height, the pain. Think about Clarissa. What you'll do to her. What she'll do to you. Another step down.*

Her mouth first. Yes. Then make her strip, slowly. With care. Like this. Step by step. Down to her stockings. Another step, sliding his foot down into nothingness, toes searching. And another. Then her arse. They hadn't tried that yet. Needed goose grease, something. Ask Lardy Jack. Lard? No, not for Clarissa's sweet arse. Only the best. Goose grease, olive oil if Lardy Jack had it, which he doubted. Balance, stretch, grip. Of course Lardy Jack would know what he wanted it for. He might even withhold any suitable grease, appalled at the thought of Mr. Pendale plotting to invade Miss Onslowe's refined backside. But time was running out. They had—what?—a few days, a week at most before they landed. Probably she'd agree, impressed by Allen's bravery. He certainly wouldn't admit that he shook like a leaf the whole time.

Even if he had to delay that particular part of the plan, there were always the items he'd recently acquired from one of the crew, and which he'd been saving. Many possibilities there.

He stepped onto the yardarm, letting his feet stretch out, while the canvas roared and hummed below. From a distance the sails were pure and white, but here he could see how patched and weathered they were. Voices floated up from below.

"That's right, Mr. Blight. Take your time. No hurry, sir."

Peering down to the next yardarm he saw Blight, moving slowly, a sailor above and below him, guiding and encouraging. Poor bastard. Poor fool, rather. He followed them down, and then overtook them. He planned to make a victorious, dashing descent down the shrouds, into Clarissa's arms—not that she'd embrace him in public; she was very discreet—rather, into the promise of future pleasures.

He tried to find a compromise between unsafe speed and nonchalance. Not far to go. He had won fair and square; he had shown that poltroon Blight that challenging a gentleman was an exceedingly bad idea.

He jumped the last few feet, landing with a clumsy thump on the deck, every muscle in his body screaming with pain, while the sailors huzzahed and tossed their hats into the air.

Mr. Johnson reached him first, and clapped him on the shoulder. "Well done, sir. Some brandy?"

Allen took a deep gulp, and another, the liquor burning its way pleasantly into his gut.

Captain Trent shook his hand. "Very well done, sir, for a landlubber. You did not need to sit on the mast, you know."

"Aye, the biggest thing I've had hang between my legs—since last night," Allen replied, looking around to see how Clarissa would react.

"In harbor, the first time I send a boy up, I tell him to stand on it," Captain Trent said with a smile.

"Stand on it?" Oh, dear God. *Stand on the mast?*

"Well, it will move around a little, but not enough to throw a man off—not like it moved when you were there."

Stand on the mast? The brandy, a moment ago so welcome, now seemed to roil inside him.

"If you'll excuse me, sir." On legs that threatened to give way at any moment, and with as much dignity as he could muster, Allen pushed his way through the crowd of sailors, and vomited over the side.

"They're very disappointed," Clarissa said. "Mr. Johnson is still trying to work out the bets on his abacus." She stroked Allen's head, which was lying on her knee as she sat cross-legged on the deck. The sailors had rigged up a canvas for shade, under which she and Allen sat. Their washing flapped and waved on a line nearby. The Blights, he still pale faced and shivery, with Elizabeth cooing and fussing over him, sat a little distance off.

"Everything hurts," Allen groaned.

Clarissa dug her needle into the fabric of one of the

dresses. She hadn't realized how much Allen would interfere with her dressmaking plans. "I won the puking stakes, but you won the race up the mast, so there are quite a number of possibilities. I wish I had bet on myself for the seasickness."

"It's not amusing."

"Yes, it is." She drew her needle out, pulled the thread taut, and she wondered if she could persuade Allen to go belowdecks. She didn't have to look too hard to see his genitals through the thin fabric of the cotton drawers, and she wondered whether she should torment him a little. But no, she should finish this dress. A pity, though. She liked having him sprawl half naked on her lap, and after his triumph on climbing the mast, she knew he would be insufferable; an inconvenient erection, with the Blights watching on, might serve to humble him.

Or possibly not. He might enjoy displaying himself even more to Elizabeth Blight, and at the same time issue another challenge to Blight himself. She had a vision of the two of them strutting around like a pair of fighting cocks, erections aloft, and giggled.

He groaned again.

"Would you like some physic?" Clarissa asked.

"Oh, for God's sake." He turned his face into her knee. "A little sympathy, possibly even a little praise for my bravery, might suffice."

"Bravery? Foolhardiness, more like."

"I wouldn't expect a woman to understand."

"A woman would have more sense."

"Indeed." He shifted, lying more on his belly than his

side, and dropped his hand beneath the fabric she sewed. Oh, so casual, as though she'd hardly notice.

"Allen?"

He grunted, his hand now lifting the folds of her skirt, skimming her thighs. His breath was warm on her leg. "I think I'll make you come."

"Oh no, you won't. Not here."

"Well, if you get up and push me away with an outraged shriek, everyone will know what I'm about. Best to grit your teeth and bear it." His fingers tickled at the top of her parted thighs. "Wouldn't it be dreadful if people knew what was happening to you? Let's see, there are the Blights, most of the crew—yes, they're watching you. They're a little restless after all these weeks at sea and with land so close. You'd be doing them a favor, so they know what a woman looks like when she comes. They've probably forgotten, if they ever knew. And Elizabeth Blight knows, of course, though I'm sure not from bedding Blight—"

"Oh, you are so crude—"

"And I'm sure Mr. Johnson, who nurses a hopeless passion for you—"

"He does not—"

"I'm sure he'd like to see you come. Or they might all think you're giving an imitation of a cat yawning and think nothing of it. You may be able to get away with it."

"I do not look like a yawning cat!"

"You do." His finger tugged at the hair between her thighs. "Of course, you also make quite a lot of noise. I'm surprised you haven't learned to come quietly, given your five years of the solitary state. You're bound to betray yourself."

I shall ignore him. And then his finger searched, parted, circled, and she was very much aware of him, fine-tuned to every small movement. She dropped the needle and fumbled with clumsy fingers to find it in the folds of fabric.

Oh, he knew how to please her. He found a rhythm to her liking, his touch gentle but persistent.

"Did you miss me last night, Clarissa? Did you do this to yourself?"

"Don't be indecent." Good. Her voice was suitably stern while inside she fluttered and trembled. She kept her eyes on her sewing, and jabbed her needle into the seam. Her stitches were becoming very uneven.

"It's a pity I can't toy with your nipple while I do this. I know you like that. Maybe you could oblige."

"Certainly not." Her hand moved as of its own volition, her wrist brushing her hard nipple.

"I thought about you when I was climbing that big prick of a mast. Thought of what I'd do to you, particularly that lovely arse I've been too much of a gentleman to broach."

"A *gentleman*?" Her voice was unsteady.

"Maybe I should get my head under your skirts and lick you."

Oh God.

"I'd tell the Blights you had a splinter in your quim."

She choked with laughter, dropped her sewing, and dug her fingers into his hair as her orgasm ratcheted through her, horrifying, in front of everyone. Could they know? She couldn't help a strangled sound, a gasp of pleasure.

"That's better," he murmured. He withdrew his hand, slick with her moisture, and licked his fingers.

"Did that make you hard, Allen?"

"What do you think?" He yawned. "Although I can't make up my mind whether to get you belowdecks or sleep."

"Let me help." She shook her sewing out so that the swath of pale fabric billowed over them both, and reached beneath it to grasp his cock.

He grinned shamelessly.

"If I make you come, you'll have a big wet patch on your drawers, and everyone will see it."

"Not if I'm wearing a shirt."

"Oh, I don't think that would be very likely." She squeezed. "Your shirts are damp still. And, you know, you're not particularly quiet at such times. I think everyone will know."

His eyes narrowed as she stroked him. She untied the drawstring and slid her hand inside, cupping his balls and scratching them lightly with her nails.

"What should I do, Allen? Shall I make you come?"

"It would be a pity to stain your pretty dress before you've even finished making it," he murmured.

"True. I am really having a hard time making up my mind what to do. You are in a shocking state."

"A shockingly hard state," he agreed. "Maybe we could strike a bargain."

"Possibly."

"I propose"—he moved, swift and eyes alight with mischief, grabbing her—"that I shall not tickle you"—she thrashed and shrieked, helpless with laughter—"any more than I must if you let me escape."

She rolled on the deck in disarray and a tangle of fabric as Allen lunged for the hatch, one hand holding up his drawers.

"Tally ho, Miss Onslowe," one of the seamen called out.

She folded her sewing up into a neat bundle, sauntered over to the hatch, smiling for the onlookers' benefit, and lowered herself down. He must be hiding, waiting to jump out at her. It was very quiet. She pushed open the cabin door. His drawers lay on the floor; he was on his berth, his head propped on one hand, his cock in the other.

"Oh, please don't let me disturb you." She placed her sewing in her sea chest and watched his hand slide, the tug and pull of his foreskin.

"Come here."

"Whatever for? You seem to be managing quite well on your own."

"So you might think." He reached out with his other hand to stroke her hair. "Kiss me."

His mouth was warm and familiar, the hand on the back of her head gentle. He sighed, whether from the play of their tongues or from his own caress, she couldn't tell. She moved her mouth to bite into his neck, tasting salt, sea spray, and his own sweat as he pushed at her head, urging her to continue her traverse of his body.

She reached to take his hand from his cock, tangling

her fingers in his—warm, slightly damp—and sucked them briefly. She remembered the first time she'd sucked his fingers, his groan of pleasure, her surprise; she understood now that he foresaw it as a prelude to greater delights.

She rested her elbows on the edge of the berth and licked him, slowly, tantalizingly, from root to tip. A drop of liquid swelled onto her tongue. His hair tickled her nose as she engulfed his cock, taking him in deep as he'd taught her, then moving to mouth his balls, lick hard beyond them where his scent was strong and earthy.

He shifted, hand tightening in her hair, tensing, and muttered something. She identified the words "cock" and "mouth"—well, it was quite obvious what he wanted. She let him slide slowly into her mouth, but not allowing him all the control. He might have to strain and tense as she sucked and licked; it would be she who set the pace and rhythm. She moved her tongue over the rounded head of his penis and the sensitive flesh that anchored his foreskin.

"Oh God, I've taught you too well," he gasped. His hands clutched her head as he swelled and spurted warm and salty into her mouth.

She raised her head, out of breath, although not as badly as he, smiling at the sight of his depleted, slumped cock, his utter relaxation. He opened his eyes and ran a forefinger down her cheek to her mouth, swiping away a stray dribble of semen.

"It's a good thing I'm not in love with you," she said. "I'm afraid I'd find you quite irresistible at such a time."

"You'll find me even more irresistible quite soon. What would you like to do to arouse me again?"

"What would you like?"

"Undress for me."

Well, that was easy enough. "Very well."

As she bent to take off her stockings, he said, "No. The stockings last."

"Why?"

"Because men like it. And don't ask me why, Clarissa. I don't know. Men in only their stockings look ridiculous. Women in only their stockings look arousing. Slowly, girl. Don't pull your gown off over your head. Let it drop."

The cotton belled, slid, fluttered to her ankles. She understood what he wanted, now—a slow ritual of undressing like the one he'd performed for her, as though she were alone and oblivious of his presence. She pulled at the strings of her stays—usually she liked to give her ribs a gentle scratch as the canvas and whalebone slid away, but instead, for his benefit, she cupped her breasts through the thin fabric of her shift. "I wish I had a prettier shift."

"So do I. But you're pretty whatever you wear." He tugged at the neckline of her shift.

She let the cotton slide down one shoulder and then the other, her nipples still hidden.

He looked interested now, his cock firming against his thigh. Still holding her shift against her breast, she reached out to palm him, give him a gentle slap and a firmer squeeze. Her nipples poked against the shift, the cotton catching briefly on them before falling. Made of a coarser fabric than her gown, well-dried in the sun (on land she would have ironed it), her shift descended in stiff folds. She stood before him in her stockings and garters.

"Part your legs. One foot on your berth." His hand reached between her thighs. "Wet already." He leaned to kiss one nipple, then the other, while she shivered with delight.

There was the usual frantic scramble for the sponge and the vial of tansy oil, while he muttered in exasperation, "This time, we have something new to play with."

He produced a couple of thin braided strips of leather that he must have kept hidden in his berth. "Rat leather, made by one of the crew." Then, probably in response to her grimace, he said, "Feel how fine it is." He drew them over her breasts.

"And you intend to—" she yelped as he snapped one against her arse.

"That's one possibility. Hold out your wrists. Trust me."

"Trust you? You're a lawyer." But she presented her wrists to him anyway.

He chuckled and bound her wrists together with intricate knots. Of course, there was no better place than a ship to learn how to tie a good knot and find all sorts of places—a hook in the ceiling, in this case—to secure her wrists above her head, stretching her torso so she balanced on her toes, legs outspread.

"I know it's not particularly comfortable," he said. "But you won't care."

And she didn't, as he began a careful exploration of her body with tongue and teeth—her mouth first, deep, wet kisses while his erect cock brushed against her belly, both of them moaning, making the sounds they'd denied themselves earlier on deck. She wanted him inside her, now—*now*—but he continued, inching his mouth to her neck, her shoulders, pausing to bite and suck. Slowly. Very slowly.

"You bastard. I'll do this back to you," she gasped.

"I look forward to it." He resumed his careful exploration on the taut skin of her breast, his stubbled face teasing her nipples.

She moaned in frustration and lifted one leg to his waist, attempting to capture his cock.

He slapped her bottom. "No, that's not allowed."

"Please."

"When I say so." Having transformed her nipples into hard, aching points, he knelt before her, parting her sex with tongue and teeth, his tongue a hard lash driving her while her legs quivered and shook.

"Not yet." He withdrew, his face glistening with her moisture. "When I'm inside you."

He spun her around, held her hips, and oh yes, he was inside her. She hung, pinioned on his cock, toes scraping for purchase on the floor. And then she came, as he predicted, damn him, oh yes.

Damn him again, he laughed. "Feel better?"

He reached above her head and released her, catching her weight, and, her wrists still bound, positioned her so that she knelt on the floor against the lower berth.

Long, slow thrusts, their bodies slick together, his breath harsh in her ear, his hands tight on her hips. "Like this," he muttered. "Like this . . ."

And then he stopped.

"What's wrong?" Well pleased, a little drowsy, lulled by the pleasurable rhythm he set, she turned her head to face him.

"I wanted to tell you . . . I was so frightened on that damned mast I almost pissed myself."

She was torn between laughter and an odd sort of admiration at his candor. "But you weren't too frightened to do it—or to wash your own laundry, although that was done quite badly."

"Nonsense. My laundering was excellent."

"For a man."

He laughed, kissed her, and proved that there were other things, as a man, that he did very well indeed.

CHAPTER 9

Land.

What they first saw as a smudge on the horizon now defined itself in shades of green, other colors—white, brown, yellow—added in as they sailed closer, along with the misty blue of distant mountains. Although it was the island of their destination, it hardly looked inhabited to Allen. Only the sparse columns of smoke far inland indicated otherwise.

And this—the area, where, according to Captain Trent, sugar was loaded for the journey back to England—boasted only a modest wooden jetty. Allen had expected something like the Bristol docks. And then he realized there were slaves, lots of slaves, who would do the work of cranes and machinery. There was no need for anything more elaborate.

Clarissa chatted with the Blights, Captain Trent, and Mr. Johnson while Allen stood apart, staring at the land and feeling profoundly unsettled.

He was to leave Clarissa. In her plain, demure dress and unadorned straw bonnet, she looked every inch the governess—a cultured, respectable woman past the first bloom of youth.

But I know what you really are. I've tasted my spunk on your quim. I've made you scream and yell.

She'd made him scream and yell, too, but that was hardly the point. Their paths would separate now; she to her chosen career, and he to . . . Well, he wasn't quite sure. That was something else he hadn't really thought about properly, he who considered himself such a legal tactician.

Clarissa had guessed, of course. *Your father doesn't know you're arriving, does he?*

He'd laughed and denied it, and challenged her, in his bad French, to recite Racine to him, which she did in her beautifully accented French. She'd shown her accomplishments further by playing a Handel aria using his leg as the keyboard, with some fancy fingerwork in the upper octaves, until she couldn't sing for giggling.

Very odd, the things a man and a woman could get up to in an enclosed space with limited resources. He heaved a sigh, reached into his pocket, and fingered the small pot, well wrapped in a scrap of sailcloth, that he'd bought, with some embarrassment, from Lardy Jack. It might well be too late for escapades with goose grease.

Oh, good Lord. Young Peter was weeping at the prospect of Clarissa's departure, and she kissed him in a sisterly sort of way that made him blush. Several of the crew members pretended to burst into tears and Allen glared at them.

Captain Trent made an exclamation and raised his spyglass. Allen squinted against the glare of the sun and sea to see a trap, led by a mule, emerge from the greenery. The crew member who had been sent ahead to announce to Lemarchand that his ship had arrived waved from his seat beside the driver. A substantial ox-drawn cart followed, to take the piano and other precious items to Lemarchand's house.

There was a brief flurry of activity as the longboat was lowered and a final round of farewells said. Allen wrung the hands of the captain and Mr. Johnson, and swung himself down into the longboat, where Blight and the luggage waited. The two women were lowered down on ropes—Allen tried not to look at revealed ankles, but he was only human—and the arrival of Mrs. Blight, fragrant and pillowy, almost knocked him overboard. Clarissa landed with a long, sensual slither down his body that almost made him groan aloud with regret.

He planned to travel to Lemarchand's, pay his respects, and borrow a horse or some other conveyance to his father's estate. He knew it was quite possible Lemarchand might ask him to dine and stay overnight, and he was in two minds whether to accept such an offer. He should probably make a clean break with Clarissa. It annoyed him that she seemed so cheerful, excited even, at the prospect of her new life. He wondered, with a touch of sourness, what had happened to her abolitionist tendencies.

She clutched his sleeve. "Look, Mr. Pendale, palm trees. So many of them and so tall!"

He smiled, amused at her formality, and determined to

be cheerful for her sake. Besides, he was finding it difficult not to be cheerful under the bright sun and the prospect of once more being on dry land.

He was astonished to find that, when the longboat drew up onto the white sand and he jumped out into the shallows, the land rocked and moved as though he were still aboard.

Clarissa, skirts lifted—he couldn't help taking a look at her legs, and neither, he noticed, could Blight—clutched his arm and giggled. "You don't think we'll be seasick on land, do you?" She let go of Allen and darted away to pick something from the dazzlingly white sand. "Oh, look. What a beautiful shell."

Blight said, "Best get into the trap before the damn driver falls asleep, Miss Onslowe. You'll find they're naturally lazy."

Placing her shell into her reticule, Clarissa allowed Allen to hand her up into the trap, and they set off for Lemarchand's estate.

She was being driven by a slave, who was someone's property, like the mule and the trap. She wanted to touch his sleeve, to talk to him as she would a servant in England—ask him about his family, how long he had been on the estate—questions that here would have an entirely different meaning. An English servant would probably not be shy of initiating conversation with his betters, but this man stared resolutely ahead, concentrating on the mule and the road.

The air, so pleasant on the beach, became more humid as they traveled inland, passing from dazzling glare to moist shade. Vines cascaded from trees and unfamiliar birds darted and called. She loosened the fichu at her throat and wondered how the men, in their wool and cotton layers, fared.

"I expect you're anxious to meet your charge, Miss Onslowe."

"Yes, I am, Mr. Pendale. I hope she likes music. I'm looking forward to playing again."

While she appreciated his discretion—it would certainly not do for Lemarchand to know his governess had spent almost the entire voyage cavorting with a fellow passenger—she felt a pang of loneliness, missing the Allen Pendale she had come to know so well. To her relief— she had never quite trusted the sponge—her courses had started a few day before, and Allen had seemed equally relieved. It had meant, however, that they had not made love for a final time. They had never spoken of what would happen once ashore, but she was sure their association must end.

The trap rounded a corner and a vast expanse of emerald lawn dotted with old-fashioned formal flower beds lay before a substantial stone house with a long portico running its length. On the second floor, a balcony wrapped around the house, with long windows in the French style opening onto it. There were a huge amount of slaves—Clarissa assumed they must be so, dark-skinned and clothed in creamy undyed cotton—who worked in the garden and lingered on the portico. The thrifty housekeeper within her wondered exactly what so many found to do.

As the trap drew up in front of the house, the front

door opened and a young girl of about fifteen years of age, slender and with fair hair curling onto her shoulders, darted out.

Another woman, a slave, followed her, holding a book, a parasol, and a bonnet. "Miss Celia, de sun too hot—" She backed away as a tall man, Mr. Lemarchand himself, Clarissa guessed, stepped through the doorway.

"Papa, Papa, where de pianoforte?" To Clarissa's surprise, the girl spoke just like the slave, with the same lilt to her voice and distorted consonants.

He shook his head affectionately. "Try again, miss."

"Papa, where is the pianoforte?" She grinned and swung on his arm. "Dat better?"

Allen stepped down from the trap and offered Clarissa his hand to help her alight.

Lemarchand hesitated. "Mr. Pendale?"

"Mr. Lemarchand." Allen bowed, his tone a little cool. Of course, she remembered his comment about not looking like his family, and without a hat (lost overboard long ago) and in his rumpled state, he certainly didn't look like an earl's son.

"Delighted to meet you. You'll dine with us, I hope, and stay the night? Some of the other planters will be here." Lemarchand murmured a polite greeting to Mrs. Blight and turned to Clarissa. "Miss Onslowe, I trust you will teach my daughter some civilized ways. Celia, this is your governess."

Clarissa curtsied.

"Where dat lazy girl?" Celia demanded. "Rissa, you come here. Bring my parasol."

"Say 'please,' Celia," Clarissa said, before wondering if she'd be sacked from the job without ever having started it.

There was a short silence, broken by Lemarchand's laugh. "You'll see me in my study, Miss Onslowe, when you've had a chance to take off your bonnet. And, Celia, do as your governess bids."

Scowling, Celia muttered, "Give me de parasol. Please."

The slave sidled toward her, holding the parasol out at arm's length and ducking away as Celia aimed a slap at her.

"That's enough," Lemarchand said. "You will not be allowed to play the pianoforte if you do not behave."

Celia scowled and prodded at the floor with the tip of her parasol.

"Can't see much point in bringing a pianoforte," Blight said. "The ants'll eat it as fast as Miss Celia plays it."

"Thank you, Blight," Lemarchand said. "We'll talk later. Pendale, I expect you'd like some refreshment. Please come inside."

He led the way inside the house, leaving Clarissa alone with Celia.

"Is de pianoforte coming?"

"*The* pianoforte. Yes, it's coming. They have to unload it from the ship, along with the other things Mr. Lemarchand ordered."

"Miss Celia?" The slave, Rissa, said. "Miss, his lordship, 'im say I take de miss governess to her bedchamber."

"Of course." Celia, her former rancor toward the

slave apparently forgotten, took Clarissa's hand. "Rissa, you get hot water for Miss Onslowe. You come upstairs wid me, Miss Onslowe—if you please, that is. I picked your bedchamber for you."

Alone with Clarissa, Celia seemed to be more of a normal young woman, despite her outlandish speech. As they climbed the stairs together, Celia prattled of clothes and novels, and admired Clarissa's very plain bonnet.

"What lessons have you had?" Clarissa asked as they entered her bedchamber, a room simply furnished with a chest of drawers, a pier glass, and a bed swathed in a mosquito net as well as bed curtains. She crossed the room to doors that led to a balcony, and smiled with pleasure at the view of the sea.

"Mama taught me to read and write but she dead now."

"I see. How about geography? French? Drawing? Embroidery?"

"No." Celia hung her head. "Papa, 'im say you teach me to be a proper young lady."

"Of course," Clarissa said.

Clarissa curtsied as Lemarchand rose from his chair in the study.

"Miss Onslowe." He bowed and gestured to a chair.

She sat and waited to see if she still had a job. While she did so, she studied Lemarchand. He wasn't young— she thought he must be in his late forties, but he was lean and slender. His hair was long, tied back in a queue, still dark apart from that white streak; his eyes were gray and perceptive under finely arched brows, set in an angular face with an aristocrat slash of a thin, high-bridged nose.

"So, my daughter, whom I regret I have spoiled. She is fifteen years of age, behaves like an infant, and speaks like the slave nurses who raised her. It is your job to polish her and prepare her for polite society. I plan an entrée in London society for her. Are you up to the task, Miss Onslowe?"

"I believe so, sir." At least, she hoped so. "She seems sweet-natured enough when she chooses to be so."

"Hmm. Tell me about yourself, if you please." He leaned back in his chair, his hands—long and elegant, she couldn't help noticing—toying with a paperweight on the desk.

"I was housekeeper at Lord Thelling's for five years. My father is the Reverend Henry Onslowe of Cadminton in Somerset. I attended Miss Redding's Academy in Bath and taught there for a while. I—"

"The Reverend Henry Onslowe? Author of numerous pamphlets against the slave trade?"

"That is correct, sir." She paused. If she was going to be sacked, then let it be with a flourish. "To be strictly accurate, those pamphlets were not written by my father. They were written mostly by me."

"Well, well." He grinned. "And the irony is that you are here. Life is exceeding strange, Miss Onslowe."

"Lord Thelling—the present Lord Thelling, that is—persuaded my family that it was in everyone's best interests for me to take this position. You must be aware that a woman has little say in such matters."

He stood and strolled over to a sideboard. "You'll take some wine, Miss Onslowe? I can send for some lemonade, if you prefer."

"I should like some wine. Thank you."

He handed her a glass and stood leaning against the desk, his booted legs close to her skirts. "I'm quite used to people working for me against their inclination, Miss Onslowe, so your scruples do not worry me overmuch. I suspected you might well have connections with the Reverend Onslowe, who, I must admit, has been something of a thorn in the flesh of those who practice the trade. I need an intelligent and cultured woman to educate my daughter, and when old Thelling described you as such, I thought you were just the sort of woman I had in mind."

She smiled. "I was very fond of his lordship."

"And the present Lord Thelling?"

"A fool."

He laughed. "I think we shall do well, Miss Onslowe." He clinked his glass against hers. "To what shall we drink?"

"To liberty?" She glanced up at him to see his response.

"Worse and worse," he said. "A toast, then, to your fine eyes."

"You're flirting with me, Mr. Lemarchand."

"Call me March."

She cleared her throat. "I'm not so vain I can drink a toast to my own eyes, Mr. Lemarchand, and I don't think you should flirt with me. I'm your servant."

He looked at her with distinct approval, a measuring, carnal gaze.

She stood, and placed her untouched glass on the desk. It was time to let him know she was not easily caught. "I beg, sir, you'll remember that I am here to educate your daughter, which I shall do to the best of my ability— nothing more, nothing less."

"Ma'am." He straightened, placing his glass next to hers. "You are absolutely correct. And you, by the way, were also absolutely correct in reprimanding Celia for her treatment of Nerissa. Our house slaves are valuable investments and should be treated as such. Tonight I'm to dine in rough male company. I regret it is so, but tomorrow I expect you to dine with Celia and me."

"I look forward to it, sir. Thank you."

He bowed. "Your servant, ma'am."

***

"First time on the island, eh, Pendale?"

More claret sloshed into Allen's glass. He nodded and tried to remember the name of the man who addressed him,.

"You should've been here six months ago."

"Indeed?"

The man belched. "We had a burning."

"A burning?"

"A couple of Lemarchand's slaves escaped. Splendid sport, hunting them down. They made for the mountains, of course."

"Ran for days," another man, whose bulbous red nose

betrayed his interest in drink, interjected. "Blight took the dogs to find them. Lord, you should have heard 'em squeal."

"And then Lemarchand burned 'em."

"Took hours. Ever seen a man burn, Pendale?"

"A moment," Allen said. "You're telling me they were burned alive as punishment?"

The two men nodded drunkenly in unison.

"Works," one of them said. "That's why they don't run too often."

"Although"—one of them leaned toward Allen—"they're a sullen lot, now, Lemarchand's slaves, and none too happy, I'll wager, that Blight's returned."

"Mark my words," the other said. "March'll have trouble before long. And if it spreads to our estates, we'll all have trouble."

The other man, with the poor attention span caused by extreme drunkenness, stared into his glass and sighed. "March has some remarkably pretty girls. Quite light-skinned, a lot of them, almost look like white women. Think he'll give us one for the night?"

"One each."

"Two each," the other man responded with a chuckle.

The arrival of a large joint of mutton on the table halted the conversation among the three of them, and the guest on Allen's other side plucked his sleeve.

"Since you're new to the island, Pendale . . ."

Allen, having heard similar advice already, paid little attention as the man droned on. Always wear a hat. Always use a mosquito net and avoid the night humors. Don't let the Negroes get insolent. They respond only to beatings. They're not people, Pendale. Animals, really. It's our duty to protect them from their base natures. . . .

Others chimed in with discussions on the prices of sugar, ginger, tobacco. Complaints about prices, about abolitionists in England pecking away at the sugar lords' rights, causing seditious trouble with their pamphlets and petitions . . . spreading all sorts of sentimental rubbish about how the poor Africans were plucked from their hearths . . .

"Indeed. Something you'd never see in England," Allen said. His glass was empty again. A footman, bewigged and in elaborate livery—but with bare feet, which Allen really couldn't get used to—stepped forward to pour more wine.

"Of course not, sir. That is my point exactly. We are not savages. We are civilized men." The man opposite him, whose name Allen still couldn't remember, belched.

"Then I should inform you, sir, that the same does take place in England, in our port towns and cities. Men are captured against their will, plucked from their hearths."

A huge moth the size of Allen's hand fluttered in through the open window, evading the two footmen who stood with palm leaves to waft the flying insects away. The moth blundered into a flame and fell onto the table with destroyed wings, but tried to rise again.

"I suppose you talk of the press gang," Lemarchand—March, rather, he'd asked Allen to call him that—interjected. His smile was polite, but even as drunk as everyone was, Allen could tell his host was not pleased with the way the conversation was going.

"I do, sir."

"It is a necessity in times of war." Lemarchand shrugged. "Besides, the press gang provides employment for many, and the chance for prize money and advancement."

"Or more likely an untimely death, and makes widows and orphans of the men's families. Sir, those are Englishmen who are seized, who supposedly enjoy the rights of Magna Carta." There was a murmur of approval from the guests crowded around the table. "It is also their right, under that same institution, to petition as they will."

"You'd have the *tricouleur* fly in London?" someone demanded belligerently from farther down the table.

"No, sir, but some might argue that an ill such as the press gang exists because the slave trade has corrupted our consciences." Christ, that was a mouthful to enunciate after gallons of claret. Allen wasn't even sure it made much sense.

There was a short silence. The moth, its wings charred and ruined, lay struggling in a pool of wax and spilled wine. Allen reached forward and crushed it with a balled-up napkin.

"Damned moths," someone said with a laugh, and the drinking resumed.

Later, much later, Allen staggered up the stairs. *Careful, now. One step, and the next, and the next. One foot at a time, like climbing rigging. Don't rush. Don't look down.*

God, he was drunk.

And into his bedchamber, fumbling at buttons with clumsy fingers—*Boots off first, you fool*—and then, oh thank God, into bed. *Lie flat. Don't move. Room spinning. Puke? No, don't have the energy. Sleep.* That was it. Probably have the devil of a headache tomorrow. Today. Later.

Someone giggled. A female giggle. Cool air swept over him.

"Clarissa?"

"No, sir, Nerissa."

"Rhymes," he said with great satisfaction.

He opened his eyes. The pretty maid—the one who had accompanied Miss Lemarchand—stood at his bedside with a palm leaf in her hand. "Milord, 'im say I fan you."

"How thoughtful. Go away." He closed his eyes.

"Or anyt'in' else you want, sah."

"Anything else, eh?" How very hospitable.

"Yes, sah."

The palm leaf swept through the air and tickled his nose and chest. Some delightful possibilities here, but he really didn't want to move, and besides he'd far rather have Clarissa to do anything he wanted, and that she wanted, too. The palm frond caressed his erect cock. He opened his eyes, blinked, and focused. His erection lay against his belly—nothing to do with him, really. Just there, with no sort of urgency, only a possibility of pleasure should he choose.

Rather like Nerissa's offer that suddenly seemed a lot more interesting, as did the tickle of the palm frond.

"Stop that, girl," he said. He tried to cover himself with the sheet before realizing that he lay on it and moving was just too much effort. All too much effort. Far better to let Nerissa take over, replace the palm frond with her hand, and then kneel over him, musky and warm, her breasts brushing his chest and face. She tucked his cock inside her—his hands were too clumsy to be of much use—but they landed on her breasts, warm and solid. Meanwhile, below, far, far away she bounced and slid in a way that should have been enjoyable but seemed strangely detached.

She panted, rolled her eyes, and gave a fine imitation of a woman in the throes of ecstasy. She did it quite well. It might have convinced him if drink hadn't disengaged him from her efforts. He was reminded of times he'd bounced up and down on top of merchants' wives and bored aristocratic ladies, feigning passion, performing—one of the pleasures of Bristol: shopping, the waters, the play, and Allen Pendale's cock.

"Get off me!" He hadn't meant to shout and he certainly didn't intend to shove her off him, off the bed, and onto the floor.

She scrabbled away from him, pulling her shift down. She was afraid now, flinching as he sat up and dropped his legs over the side of the bed.

"I know you didn't want to come here. That you were told to—"

"De master, 'im said I should come to your bedchamber. I sorry, sah."

"I'll tell him you pleased me," Allen said.

She stood, curtsied, and cast a longing glance at the door.

"You may go," he said. "Look in my coat pocket. There's a shilling there."

She cast a sidelong, suspicious glance at him, and picked his coat from the floor. She shook it out, smoothed the fabric, and laid it over a chair before dipping one hand into the pocket. Her face lit up as she found the coin, and then she ran from the room as though afraid he might demand the money back from her.

CHAPTER 10

"But of course you must stay another day, Pendale." March smiled at Allen, who sat slumped and gloomy at the breakfast table. "Miss Onslowe, you must be my advocate here."

"Please do stay, Mr. Pendale," Clarissa said. She licked pineapple juice from her fingers. What luxury. Pineapple for breakfast—every day, if she wished it.

"My father expects me, sir."

You liar, Allen. He seemed in a dreadful mood, toying with a cup of coffee and glowering at the table—possibly he had drunk far too much last night.

"I'm sure his lordship can spare you another day. I'd like to show you the estate, and I'm sure the ladies will be disappointed if you don't eat dinner with us tonight."

"Well, then, I shall be honored to accept, sir." This with a brief smile.

"Mr. Pendale." Clarissa touched his hand.

He snatched it away as if she'd touched him with hot coals.

"Mr. Pendale, I'm very glad you are to stay. Miss Celia shall have her first dancing lesson and we'll have need of partners for her."

"You've plenty of possible partners for a dancing class loafing around here," Allen said, indicating the half dozen footmen waiting at the side of the room.

"Certainly not. This is my *daughter*." March sounded outraged.

"Beg your pardon," Allen murmured.

Celia, up until now yawning and sleepy, spoke. "I do so long to dance. 'Im play de fiddle for us." She nodded at one of the footmen.

"Again, if you please," Clarissa said.

Celia giggled. "Joshua could play the fiddle for us."

Allen heaved a martyred sigh. "And what if I do not dance, miss?"

"You do, Mr. Pendale." Clarissa wiped her fingers on her napkin.

"Or tread on your feet."

Celia giggled again while her father looked on with an indulgent smile.

"An' de mantua maker, 'er come today," Celia said.

"Pendale, I suggest we leave as soon as possible," March said. "We certainly don't want to interfere with women's business."

After the two men left, Clarissa gave a longing glance out of the window at the dazzling blue sky and then followed Celia to the drawing room, where the mantua maker, surrounded by lengths of shimmering fabrics, waited for them.

Allen had heard his father talk of his own sugar estate but was amazed at the crowds of slaves, who toiled in the square patches of cane under the blazing sun. Men slashed at the cane with murderous-looking machetes, while women and children carried the cut lengths away. As the long line moved forward, the slaves hummed, low and mournful. There were not many children, and he suspected, although he could not tell their ages, that most of the women were not old. He had heard complaints the previous night of how the slaves did not breed as their owners expected.

Blight, astride a mule, raised his hat to them. A whip was coiled over the pommel of his saddle. Two hulking, heavily muscled Negroes, also mounted on mules, rode behind him.

"He's a good man," March commented. "They respect him."

"Are the Negroes overseers also?" Allen asked. "What do they think of having to command their own kind?"

"Slavery is common among the Africans," March said. "Castor and Pollux obey Blight in all things. They're slaves, too, of course."

Patches of dark sweat broke out on the horses' flanks as the men rode on rough paths through a dry and inhospitable landscape, scattered with tamarind trees. March talked knowledgeably of the estate business, and Allen allowed himself to let down his guard and enjoy his host's company. He was impressed by the sheer scope of March's plantation, the large number of scattered outbuildings, mills to crush the liquid from the cane, carpenters' shops, and smithies that helped run the enterprise.

"What's that building?" Allen asked, pointing toward a low stone building that stood in isolation in the fields.

"The slave dungeon," March replied. "They all live in deadly fear of it. After a whipping and a day or so in the dark and heat without food and water, even the most rebellious among them will become as docile as lambs."

They rode by a line of slaves carrying huge bundles of dried cane on their shoulders toward a stone building about the size of a small church. Smoke poured from a chimney.

"How do you find the heat?" March asked.

"Tolerable."

"Excellent. I'll show you the boiling house."

They dismounted and entered a building that reminded Allen of descriptions of hell—terrible heat and stench, dark figures stirring huge cauldrons, reducing the liquid from the canes to crystals. The dried cane provided the fuel for the fires that burned day and night. March, seemingly impervious to the heat, strolled over to a tray of crystals, and chatted to an overseer while running the finished product through his fingers.

Allen, his shirt drenched, staggered outside, away from the suffocating heat, and March joined him.

"How the devil do they stand it?" Allen gasped. "Do they not swoon with the heat?"

"Quite frequently. There are others to take their places."

They stopped at the house of another of March's overseers for ale and simple food before returning to the house. Allen swung himself down from his horse; as he'd expected, he felt the muscles in his back and legs twinge after all those weeks at sea.

March laid a friendly arm on his shoulders. "What say you to a plunge bath? I have a bath here based on the Turkish model."

March's friendliness disarmed Allen, and he accepted. This was not the cynical despot who dispatched his female slaves to visitors' beds, but the charming, attentive host who yesterday had chatted of mutual acquaintances in Bristol and London over brandy in his study.

March gave orders to the slaves, setting them to work with the kindly indulgence of a father with charming, disobedient offspring, and dispatching others ahead to prepare the bath.

As March and Allen walked through the house, March made easy conversation with Allen. "Did you visit Constantinople on your grand tour? I based the design on the baths there—delightful places."

One of the barefooted footmen flung open a door to a room paneled with mahogany, a graceful curving staircase led down to a circular bath lined and surrounded by turquoise-and-scarlet tile.

"Magnificent," Allen said. "How does it work?"

March laughed. "It is remarkably simple. A cistern on the roof catches water, which is heated by a fire downstairs—the heat rises, you see—and the pressure of the water falling from above ensures a steady stream."

March nodded to a footman, who turned a dolphin-shaped faucet and steaming-hot water gushed into the bath.

"I found Constantinople remarkable," March continued as the footman helped him out of his coat. "I hoped to see the fabled harem, but of course I should likely have come home without my ballocks. The women I did see were like tents, hidden except for their eyes. And while there's a certain pleasure in a pair of dark, lively eyes, it's not all one looks for in a woman."

As he spoke, he stripped and the footman poured brandy, bowed, and left. Allen discarded his clothes and followed March into the steaming water. Two broad steps, one at water level and one below, formed seats in the bath, which was about three feet deep.

The two men settled into the water, each with a glass of brandy.

"Do you plan to practice law indefinitely?" March asked. "You should consider running for parliament."

"I've thought of it," Allen admitted.

"What do you make of Miss Onslowe?"

Allen immediately became alert, although he kept his relaxed posture. "She's a pretty woman. Easy to talk to. Accomplished." He added, since possibly March already knew, "One gets to know one's fellow travelers pretty well aboard ship."

March was interested in Clarissa? She'd been in his house less than one day. Surely not.

Allen stole a look at March, handsome and with only that streak of white in his hair revealing his age. He was lean and well muscled, and Allen knew how formidably fit he was. If March was interested in Clarissa, he'd keep her happy enough in bed, damn it, and thanks to Allen's tutelage and her quick appreciation, she'd service him well. Far too well.

Allen eased down farther into the water, his foot brushing against the other man's, apologized, and rested his head on a folded towel on the tiled surround. It would be most discourteous if he was to fall asleep, but that was what March appeared to be doing. Allen dozed off and dreamed pleasantly of Clarissa, her pale limbs entwining his, her tongue on his cock, and was woken by the sound of running water—March leaning over him to turn the faucet on and replenish the hot water.

"I beg your pardon. I fell asleep." And Allen now had a cockstand the size of a small tree to his embarrassment, waving merrily underwater as though demanding attention. He hoped March had not noticed.

"No matter. I generally do myself." March closed off the stream of water, but remained leaning across him, his hand now planted on the ledge close to Allen's hip. "You look quite peaceful when you're asleep."

"I do?"

"Yes. You seem to be enraged about one thing or another when you're awake."

Allen shrugged.

March continued. "I found it interesting. Arousing, even."

Oh, Christ. March had an impressive erection cradled in his other hand.

He had a choice. He could pretend ignorance of his own and March's state and talk of the weather. Eventually, he supposed, his would subside, he could leave, and March could deal with his own tumescence, hopefully when Allen was not there. He had an image of himself sitting in cooling water for hours, grimly willing his erection away. Or he could—

"I'll ride with you or drink with you, but I won't fuck you, sir." Allen got out of the water, dripping wet, his cock bobbing senselessly in front of him.

March grinned, seductive, terrifyingly beautiful, cock sliding in his hand, gazing at Allen's nakedness. "Allen—Pendale—calm yourself. I'm not asking anything of you."

"I'm not some pretty boy who'll roll over for you," Allen continued, backing away, nearly slipping on the wet tile. He grabbed a towel to cover himself.

"My dear, I'd never describe you as a pretty boy."

Despite himself Allen burst into laughter. "Ah, well, I suppose not."

"And," March added, "I haven't invited you to roll over—or anything—for me. Perhaps you flatter yourself."

"Go and frig yourself," Allen growled, conscious that March was doing just that, although in a lazy and frivolous sort of way, and his own cock remained resolutely hard and begging for attention.

He bent to retrieve his breeches.

"Mmm. Delightful," March murmured.

"You old lecher," Allen returned.

"Such a splendid arse."

"Which, believe me, you won't get up." Just to show the unnatural bastard he wasn't that much of a prude, Allen gave himself an ostentatious tug. And another. And—his hand slid, pumping.

Christ.

"Of course not." March lay back in the water, his hand moving a little more urgently. "Never. Not until you beg me, Allen. And I assure you, if I put my mind to it, you will."

Breeches half on, Allen grabbed the rest of his clothes and fled.

CHAPTER 11

Ladies, it appeared, rested in the afternoon, lest the heat of the sun should destroy their complexions. Clarissa, suffering from a surfeit of what she considered female silliness—much serious discussion of fabrics and fashion papers probably already out-of-date, trims, sleeves, buttons, ornaments, headdresses, hats—longed to walk in the garden. She wanted to explore the greenery, the vines and trees, that lay beyond the flowerbeds and graveled paths. On the horizon were blue-green hills, or perhaps she should call them mountains, as their rocky contours suggested. Celia didn't know if the mountains had a name, and nor did Nerissa.

Perhaps she should rest. Celia had warned her of fever and Clarissa knew many visitors became ill; settlers often did not survive their first year. She stripped to her shift and wandered around her room, opened and closed a few books and wondered if she'd ever get the opportunity to actually teach Celia anything.

She went over to the window and pulled up the linen shade to look at the inviting greenery outside, made wavy and greener yet by the glass. How could anyone believe all the theories about miasmas and such, when the sky was such a clear, glorious blue? She pushed the window up and took a deep breath of the air.

The bedchamber door flew open, crashing against the wall. Allen entered the room, kicked the door shut, and tossed his coat and waistcoat onto the bed.

"And good afternoon to you, too," Clarissa said. "I trust you had a pleasant ride."

His answer was a snort. He leaned back against the panels of the door, his arms folded. His hair was damp, curling wildly around his head.

"I've come to bid you farewell."

"So soon? I thought you were to dine with us."

"I've changed my mind." He took a step forward, launching himself from the door. He pulled a neckcloth from his pocket, hesitated, and threw it onto the bed.

"What's wrong?"

He really had been difficult ever since they'd reached land, surly and brooding. Of course, it must be his impending meeting with his father; he had decided to get it over with, and not linger.

She let the blind fall. "Allen, you speak in riddles and non sequiturs. If you've come to bid me farewell, that's one thing, but I will not bear the brunt of your bad humor."

With a startling change of mood, he smiled; even more surprisingly, his smile was of infinite sweetness without a trace of cynicism. "Ah, Miss Onslowe, I should like to have you as my governess. You're right. My manners are atrocious."

"Indeed." She spoke coolly, but her mind played over a few interesting possibilities. She imagined telling a man—or Allen, specifically—what to do. Making him obey her, serve her. Pleasure her.

He took a step closer.

Her nipples poked out against the thin cotton of her shift. The room was very quiet; a few birds whistled and chirped outside. A slight breeze set the linen blind tapping against the windowsill. They had never been together in such stillness; always they had had the accompaniment of wind and the roar of sails or sea, the creak of timbers.

"What are you thinking about, Clarissa?"

"I think you know."

Another step. "On the ship, all that time, I thought about having you in a real bed."

She took a step toward him, placing her hands on his chest. His heart beat rapidly against her palms. There was a scent about him new to her—some sort of expensive soap, she guessed.

"Don't forget me," he said with an urgency that surprised her.

She raised one hand to the drawstring of her shift. "I won't."

Cotton belled and fluttered as her shift slipped down her body to the floor. She fumbled for her sponge. Vinegar splashed onto the floor as she tipped the bottle, its cork rolling somewhere beneath the bed. She was made clumsy by lust—by anxiety and loneliness, too. *This may be the last time with Allen.*

His hands shook as he unbuttoned his breeches. It was unlike him to be so clumsy, so urgent. Rough, almost, though already well aroused, he tore off the rest of his clothes and bore her onto the bed, muttering nonsense about the beauty of her pale skin in the sunlight. He tasted of brandy. Was he drunk? She thought not—his mouth hot and greedy, moving over her face, her breasts—only avid for her as she was for him. And down to her quim—*Oh yes, there,* she almost shouted at him—and he twisted to kneel over her so she could take his cock into her mouth. So much of him, demanding and lengthening, while below his tongue flicked in exquisite torture. She was tempted to let her mouth go slack, and concentrate on the luxury of his lapping tongue while tremors ran through her thighs and belly. But she wouldn't—both of them had to maintain a certain sensual aloofness to concentrate on each other's pleasure.

She knew, from the swell of his cock in her mouth, the salty taste, how close he was, too. And how must they look, twined together. Ah, she turned her head to the mirror. There they were in the brightness of the reflection, her skin pale like milk, Allen dark and furred, both of them moving, slow surges against each other. More than a tremor now, a shudder, an urgency that tugged her greedily toward his mouth. And he felt it, too, she could tell, bumping over her mouth and chin as he withdrew, turned to position her, his knees pushing her legs apart, his mouth coming down hard onto hers. Her taste in his mouth, her mouth, wet heat. His cock in her, thrusting hard, their bodies slapping together.

He paused to raise himself on his hands and looked down at her.

Then at the mirror, smiling. He nodded in satisfaction, lifted her legs around his neck and resumed his thrusts.

She gasped and clutched at his arms, wanting to tell him it was too much, too hard, unable to find the words while he pinned her down, relentless, the muscles in his arms corded and taut.

"Wait—"

He slowed. "What's wrong?"

"It's not working."

"Am I hurting you?"

"No, but . . ."

"Well, tell me what to do." A bead of sweat trickled down his forehead. "What do you want, Clarissa?"

What did she want? She wasn't sure. As she hesitated, Allen resumed his hard thrusting. She tried to follow him, but the rhythm had gone awry. What they did was enjoyable enough, but not what she wanted.

His thrusts became fast, a liquid warmth spread inside her, and he collapsed onto her with a deep sigh.

"Allen?"

She moved under him, freeing an arm that had become trapped between them.

"Allen, there's something in my back."

"Sorry." He rolled off her. Sure enough, she'd ended

up on his coat, with a button pressed into her back. He lifted her, pushed the coat aside—the sponging and pressing now undone, but he didn't really care.

He'd failed her. She hadn't come. Worse, she hadn't complained, while he'd slammed away at her like a rutting beast.

Should he warn her about March? What was there to warn her about? That she should look elsewhere for a protector? He closed his eyes and laid his forehead against her shoulder, inhaling her scent. He trailed one hand down to her quim, but she moved away with a slight impatient sound.

"How was your gentlemen's dinner party last night?"

Odd how women became chatty after fucking, as though, once the act was completed, the real business could now begin.

"Oh . . . lots of drink and cheroots."

"Indecent stories?"

He grunted. "March gave me a woman."

"What do you mean?"

"One of the slaves."

She pushed him off and sat up, gathering her disordered hair into a clump at the back of her neck. "What do you mean?" she repeated.

"March sent this girl to my bedchamber and—"

"And what?"

He was a fool to have even started this. Now he'd have to tell her everything. "I was too drunk."

She reached for her shift, which was as wrinkled as his coat, and pulled it over her head. She didn't seem unduly put out—maybe she thought he hadn't done anything. She really knew little of men, despite his tutelage.

A good lawyer would have left it at that, let the evidence rest. But the strange thing was that often the accused, under oath, blurted out damning truths.

"I fucked her."

A long silence.

"Indeed? Why are you telling me this?" Her voice was definitely frosty now.

"I was drunk. I didn't want to, but—"

"You didn't want to?" She reached for her stays. He saw her hand shake. "So why did you? You raped her so that you could boast about her to the other men next time you dine with them—"

"It wasn't rape." *Was it?*

"And what would you call it? She could hardly refuse you, could she?" She yanked the laces of her stays tight.

"I know that. But I'm only human. She came to my bed when I was half asleep, and—"

"And if you hadn't, you'd be less of a man? Like risking your life climbing the mainmast?" She pulled her gown on and reached behind her neck to button it closed.

"Oh, for God's sake," he said. "I know now I'm sober I should have sent her away immediately. You don't understand, Clarissa."

"Oh, I think I do." She'd been reaching for a ribbon—that gaudy, metallic one, now somewhat tarnished from seawater—but it fell from her hand onto the floor. "Are you asking for forgiveness from me, Allen? Because what you did to that woman was unforgivable. I thought you . . . you weren't . . ."

There was a tap on the door. Nerissa came into the room with an armful of clean linen, and looked at Allen, standing, thank God, fully dressed, apart from the neckcloth in his hand. She gave him a knowing grin.

"You want I come back later, Miss Onslowe?"

"Yes." Clarissa sank onto a chair. When the girl was gone, she said, "So it was Nerissa."

Allen nodded. He didn't want to point out that Nerissa seemed in exceptionally good spirits—certainly in a better mood than Clarissa or he.

Her voice was quiet and cool when she spoke. "It's unavoidable that we shall meet while we are both here on the island. I have no wish for anything between us but common civility." She glanced down at her hands, knotted on her lap. "I was mistaken in thinking you a better man."

"My regrets that I did not live up to your high standards, ma'am." He bowed, furious with her but damned if he'd show it. "May I wish you the best of luck with March."

Sick at heart. She'd never appreciated the phrase before. Regret, sorrow, disillusion—she'd had plenty of those, five long years to regret her previous folly. But now, after the exchange of harsh words with Allen, she felt abandoned, empty. She was pretty sure she was not in love with him, but she had lost her only friend in this strange place.

She finished dressing and made her way downstairs to the drawing room, where the pianoforte stood, shining and elegant. When she raised the lid, she found it badly out of tune—no surprise there, considering the long journey and humidity, however well it was packed. Tuning the instrument would occupy her mind well enough; she craved something solitary and mindless that did not require her to maintain any sort of facade or conversation.

"Miss Onslowe?"

The tuning fork in her hand clattered to the floor.

"Oh, Mr. Lemarchand, you startled me."

"My apologies." He bent to retrieve the tuning fork and handed it to her. "I regret Pendale has left for his father's house, depriving us of his company tonight."

"A pity." Best not to mention she already knew— Lemarchand might be offended at Allen's precipitate departure, as it was. She gestured at the pianoforte. "I was about to tune the instrument." Good God, what an idiot she was. What else would she be about?

"Of course." He stepped back. "You need silence and solitude."

"Silence, but not necessarily solitude. I can hardly send you from your own drawing room."

He smiled. "If you do not object to my company . . ."

"Not at all." Dithering. That was what she was doing. Dithering. As though she were some silly girl. In a moment she'd blush and twist her hands. It was just as well she held the key and tuning fork to stop her making even more of an idiot of herself.

She wondered what he did—not watching her bottom

as she leaned over the keyboard, surely—while she pecked at notes, hummed, played chords—the fiddly business of tuning the modest four octaves of the pianoforte. To her relief, the instrument seemed to have weathered the long voyage well; she could only hope it would hold the tuning in the humid warmth.

She fingered an octave and listened beyond the ring of the notes. Yes, a crackling sound—he was reading a newspaper; she'd noticed it lying on a small table, months old of course and much creased. And he was watching her. She could feel his gaze as surely as if he stroked his hand down her back, cupped her bottom, continued a leisurely exploration down her thighs to her ankles. How much ankle was revealed by her posture? Quite a lot, considering she had one knee rested on a chair, her skirt, not overfull, hoisted up.

At least she was wearing good stockings.

Wasn't she?

Resisting the impulse to twist and inspect her stockings—something that would draw March's attention even more closely—she applied herself to the pianoforte.

Behind her, March cleared his throat and turned the page with a rustle.

The drawing room door creaked open. Celia had arrived; Clarissa heard the slight shushing sound of muslin and the pad of calfskin slippers on the wooden floor. The paper rustled again, and wood creaked as March stood.

Clarissa straightened and greeted her pupil. *"Bon soir, mademoiselle."*

Celia giggled. *"Bon soir, Madame Onslowe et Papa."*

"Most impressive," March murmured, "considering the main business of the day was with the dressmaker. I should congratulate you, Miss Onslowe."

"Your daughter learns fast, sir."

Celia tugged at her father's sleeve. "Can we eat dinner, Papa? Den Miss Onslowe, she play for us. An' she teach me."

March patted his daughter's hand. "Your French accent is superior to your English accent, still." He held out his other arm to Clarissa. "Come, ladies, I believe dinner is served."

Clarissa slipped her hand into the crook of his elbow determined to play the correct governess. But even the most respectable of governesses could not help but be aware of the tight-coiled strength of the man, the scent of bergamot that hung around him, the fine cloth of his coat.

Dinner was tremendously civilized, particularly if you ignored the fact that the furniture and footmen were the property of one man, who made charming, intelligent conversation. Despite her reservations, Clarissa found herself captivated, sharing with him which poets she liked, her desire as a young girl to learn Greek, and her attempts to learn Latin from her brothers. She told Celia, whose eyes were as wide as saucers, of how at boarding school the girls would rise and break the ice in pitchers of water so they could wash.

"No," Celia said. "Dat not true, Miss Onslowe."

"Indeed it is. In the winter—at this time of year, even, in early spring—snow falls. It's like rain, but colder and white and fluffy, and pretty to look at. And the rivers and ponds freeze over so you can skate on them. That's wonderful. It's like flying."

She hadn't skated in years but she remembered that effortless freedom. The power of gliding over ice, the wind in her hair.

"I don' believe it," Celia muttered.

"It's true, my dear," March said. "But don't worry. When you go to England, you'll be warm and snug. I can't have my little hothouse flower shivering in the cold."

"I don' wanna go," Celia said.

"Nonsense," March replied briskly. "A husband will keep you warm enough."

Celia made a face.

After dinner they returned to the drawing room, where Clarissa played the pianoforte, her fingers stumbling on the notes. Her clumsiness was from more than lack of practice; she was intensely aware of March's presence, agitated by her attraction to him.

You came here to be governess to his daughter.

Yes, but you also came here looking for a rich protector. Why look farther?

She had to be careful, very careful.

She finished the piece and took the music from the stand.

"Will I play like dat?" Celia, eyes dark with longing, gazed at her.

"Better, I hope. But I believe it is your bedtime now."

"Yes, Miss Onslowe." Celia dropped a curtsy to her and kissed her father.

"You instill great obedience in my unruly child," March said after his daughter had left the room. "I usually like to take a turn in the garden with a cheroot after dinner. The smoke keeps away the insects. Would you care to accompany me, Miss Onslowe?"

"Certainly." She rose and placed her fingertips on his forearm.

She remembered overheard fragments of conversation—things she, as an unmarried woman, a spinster past her prime, wasn't meant to hear. *Keep him guessing. . . . Let him think he is the one who pursues. . . . Behave as if you are displeased with him or indifferent. . . .*

Not that any of that had entered her mind when she had fallen in love and brazenly offered an unworthy man her heart and body. Matrimony had not been on her mind, and certainly not on his. And as for Allen Pendale . . . Well, it was probably best not to think of him at this moment.

Now she gave March a cool smile and unfurled her fan. If he thought he was about to tumble her between his neat flower beds, he was in for a rude shock.

March bent to light his cheroot at a candle, and a footman padded ahead on quiet, bare feet to open the door into the garden.

Outside the air was warm and fragrant, the stars blazing huge in a sky of dark blue velvet. Clarissa gave a gasp of pleasure and tightened her grasp on March's forearm.

"I wish I could claim credit for the moon and stars, Miss Onslowe, to see that look directed at me."

"Isn't that rather blasphemous, Mr. Lemarchand?"

"Call me March." There was a touch of impatience in his voice.

"I think not. It implies a certain level of intimacy that would not be proper."

He laughed. "I suspect you care little for propriety, Miss Onslowe."

She fanned herself with slow, luxurious sweeps. "Indeed."

"I believe a sensualist lurks beneath the proper demeanor you work so hard to maintain."

"What a fanciful imagination you have, sir."

"Not so much an issue of my imagination, Miss Onslowe, as my powers of observation."

She smiled, while wondering how on earth she had given herself away.

"The way you move," he said. "Your enjoyment of such simple things as food and wine, the night sky. Your voice. You are more than a governess, Miss Onslowe, although I think you may do very well as such. So what would you expect from a man who wishes to be your lover, Miss Onslowe? What is your price?"

"My price?" She looked over his shoulder at the deep indigo of the sky and the blaze of stars. "Oh, I expect very little, sir. The moon and stars in the sky—that is all."

CHAPTER 12

Allen borrowed a horse from March's stable to ride to his father's house, with one of the house slaves to run ahead and show him the way. Still smarting from Clarissa's high moral tone—she was right, of course, not that he'd ever admit it, and certainly not to her face—he had deliberately not bidden March farewell or thanked him for his hospitality.

Hospitality March had abused, in his opinion.

Of course, under the circumstances, and once the family news was shared, it was very unlikely he need see March or Clarissa again. He kicked the horse forward, appalled at the bad state of the road—the path, rather, heavily rutted and dusty—and ducked to avoid a creeper-covered branch overhead. Above the sky faded to rose and lavender, the shadows lengthening, the greenery on either side of the path becoming dark and mysterious.

The boy flitted ahead of him, turning occasionally to give him a wide grin. "Nearly dere, sah. Nearly dere."

And then the path opened up to a wide vista of carefully maintained grass, and a modest stone house—a house not much bigger than his farmhouse in Somerset, but flanked by wooden porticos, and with a covered wooden walkway that he knew, from his stay at March's house, led to the kitchen. Gravel crunched underfoot as he turned the horse onto the driveway and pulled it to a halt at the front door of the house.

He kicked his feet free of the stirrups and dismounted, wondering why no slaves rushed out to greet him. He removed the straw hat March had lent him—rather a battered piece of headwear that scratched the back of his neck—and tossed the reins to the boy.

"You, mon! Take dat horse round de back!" The voice issued from the shadows of the portico, stern and male, accompanied by the scuffle of bare feet on wooden planks.

Not a well-ordered household. He raised his voice. "Tell Lord Frensham Mr. Allen Pendale is here."

The scuffling ceased.

Lemarchand's boy, meanwhile, scrambled astride the horse. "I must go, sah. Dere be ghosts in de night."

"She'll look after you." Allen slapped the rump of the horse.

"Sah?" An elderly Negro man, clad in the Frensham livery, approached. His voice was no longer sharp, but frightened. Was he, too, afraid of ghosts in the dusk? "I—I beg your pardon, sah. I t'ought . . . I . . ."

"What the devil is going on?" The front door opened,

revealing Allen's father. He frowned at Allen as though he did not recognize him—or looked through him.

"Milord . . ." the slave quavered.

Allen couldn't understand why the man was so mortally afraid of him—he refused to think it was because slaves were notoriously superstitious—and stepped forward, addressing his father. "Sir, I'm—"

"Allen!"

His father descended the steps in a rush to Allen's surprise—the earl had never been particularly demonstrative—and gripped his son's arm. "For God's sake, wear a hat. Always. Look how dark you are," he muttered. "Well, come on, then. Never mind Reuben, my majordomo. He's a little cautious of strangers. Come into the house. I wish I'd known you were to visit."

Bewildered, Allen let his father push him inside the house. Had the earl really not recognized him? It had been two years since their last meeting and his father had not known his youngest son was to arrive. He should have sent word from March's house; it would have been less of a shock.

"You're looking well, sir," Allen said.

His father seemed very little changed, still with that arrogant tilt to his head and his mane of silver hair as thick as ever. For a man near seventy, he was in exceptional, vigorous health, despite complaints in his infrequent letters that the climate of the island sapped his strength.

His father led him into a book-lined study and gestured to a chair. "You'll take some wine? Tell me how the family does."

Allen accepted a glass of wine and waited until his father sat before breaking the news.

"My sister was brought to bed of a daughter the day I left England."

"A girl? A pity. What else?"

"Sir, I regret I must tell you there is bad news also. Lady Frensham is dead."

He didn't know how else to say it. There was no easy way to announce such news, even though his mother and father had lived apart, the earl on this island and his mother in the family's country seat, for much of their marriage.

"When?" his father asked.

"Three days before Christmas Day."

The earl nodded. A tear gleamed on his cheek. "Poor woman."

"We—my brothers and I—were there. She told us she was at peace and that we should not grieve." At his mother's deathbed, he had not been able to ask the question that had brought him to the island. Seeing his father's shocked face, he could not ask him now.

Who is my true father?

Instead he reached into his pocket. "We had this made for you, sir."

The earl opened the small, velvet-lined case and turned the mourning ring over in his hand before slipping it onto his finger. "I knew she was not well, but she wrote to me that I should not come back to England, some six months ago. I did not realize how ill she was."

"None of us did, sir. She kept the truth from us. I have letters from my brothers for you. And this one from my sister to me, announcing the birth of her child." He handed over the bundle of letters.

"Poor Kitty." The earl gazed at the ring on his finger.

⁂

After restless dreams Allen rose at dawn the next day with something of a headache from drinking late into the night with his bereaved father. As at March's house, there were slaves everywhere, offering to help him dress, bring him breakfast or coffee—he accepted the offer of coffee and dismissed them.

His father was not yet up, although a visitor had arrived early, while Allen shaved. He had heard the crunch of a horse's hooves on the gravel, and the jangle of the front door bell. *Probably someone on estate business,* he concluded, *to call so early.*

He wandered downstairs, stood on the portico, enjoying the fresh, cool air, and then continued down onto the flagstones that formed a patio. He removed his coat and waistcoat and began his usual early-morning routine, fencing with an invisible partner. A couple of small black boys lurked behind a pillar on the portico, giggling.

"Would you care for a bout, Pendale?"

At the sound of March's voice, Allen almost lost his footing. He turned to see March, followed by Reuben, standing on the portico.

"I didn't mean to startle you," March said. "I have offered my condolences to Frensham. We're old enough friends that I could come before the business of the day started." He stripped off his coat and handed it to Reuben. "What do you say?"

Allen could hardly refuse. "Of course."

"Reuben, your master has foils and masks, I believe? Excellent. Fetch them, then." March unbuttoned his waistcoat, rested one hand against a pillar, and stretched out his calf muscles.

More slaves appeared to watch the show, brooms or garden rakes dragging behind them. They made no attempt to hide their interest.

March had a better reach than Allen, and he was surprisingly fast on his feet for a man almost twenty years Allen's senior. March was a good opponent, a strategist, and Allen realized fairly early on that March aimed to tire him, playing him as though he were a horse on a lunging rein. Allen refused to circle him, backing away instead, and saw March grin through his mask. Having a balanced opponent was like participating in a dance or a courtship—each gesture and stroke rich with meaning and intent.

At one point they locked foils, meeting face-to-face, forearm to forearm, close enough for Allen to scent the other man's sweat, for the warmth of their bodies to mingle.

"Had enough, Pendale?"

"I think not." He restrained himself from kicking his opponent's ankle as he would have in a real fight—this was his former host and his father's friend, after all—and tried shifting his weight to rock him off balance.

March grinned, looking straight into Allen's eyes, and something—Allen wasn't sure what—disconcerted him, sending him off balance and crashing into a roll. There were a gust of laughter and squeals from the onlookers, who scattered out of the way, while March stepped back with the utmost courtesy to allow his opponent to rise.

Now Allen was really off his stroke, uncoordinated and fumbling like a beginner, with sweat running into his eyes—a good thing, indeed, he was not fighting for his life. March toyed with him now, teasing like a deadly coquette, and Allen was grateful the foil had a button as it flickered dangerously in the vicinity of his chest and belly.

All too soon he stood panting, with March's foil planted squarely on his heaving chest, to the applause of the onlookers.

"Touché," March murmured.

"Indeed, sir, you have me at a disadvantage. I fought exceedingly ill."

Lemarchand removed his mask. "Not that badly, Pendale. You kept me busy enough."

"It's kind of you to say so."

"Well fought, sirs!" Allen's father, wearing a dressing gown, stepped forward to clap March on the shoulder. "You're sure you won't stay for breakfast, March? No? Allen, I'll see you in the morning room shortly, then." He shook March's hand and returned to the house.

Reuben helped March on with his coat and waistcoat and sent the slaves back to work, muttering of lazy ingrates.

"Will you walk with me to the stables?" March asked.

Again, Allen, in a position where he could not refuse—as seemed to be the case around March—agreed.

"I fear we parted on less than friendly terms." March's voice was low, his attention apparently on the pair of leather gloves he held.

"No matter," Allen said, his suspicions raised by March's apparent humility. They turned into the stable yard, where a boy brushed one of the earl's horses, which was tethered to a ring on the wall.

March paused at the doorway of the stables, working his fingers into one glove, his whip tucked beneath one arm. "I should not like there to be impediments between my family and yours, even for so short a time as you are to visit."

"So short a time?" Allen echoed. He and his father had not discussed the duration of his stay.

"I understood from Frensham that you will return to England when his next ship is loaded, in a matter of a few weeks."

Trying to collect his thoughts, Allen headed for the stall where March's mare nibbled on a net of hay, and swung the saddle down from its perch on the wall divider. His father, for all his affection and pleasure at seeing Allen, intended to send his son away as soon as possible. He lifted the saddle onto the mare's withers and slid it back into position.

"I've often thought being a younger son has problems and responsibilities that often go unrewarded," March said.

Allen, settling the saddle on the mare's back, looked at him in surprise.

"Oh, yes. I was the youngest of my brothers. I had to make my own way in the world until I could buy my plantation and my independence. So I know what it is to be the one who is at the beck and call of the family."

"I was not unwilling to make the voyage," Allen said. "In truth, I needed to leave the city for a while."

"You enjoy the law, though?"

Allen ducked beneath the mare's belly to retrieve the girth. "I've never felt it was what I should truly do, but as you say, a younger son has no choice." He tugged the girth tight and buckled it.

"If you are willing," March said, "I could intercede for you with your father, should you care to change your profession."

"It's kind of you, but I'll stay with the law. It's interesting enough, and I'm quite good at it." He slapped the mare's neck.

March laid his hand on Allen's arm. "You'll visit my house again, I hope. I know you're in mourning, but I should like to see you."

"Of course. I thank you, sir."

They were surrounded by the quiet sounds of the stable—rustling and the occasional thud of a hoof on straw, or the steady munch of a feeding horse.

"I've rarely had an opponent who fights me with such passion. One would have thought it was to the death, not a friendly bout." March's voice was quiet.

"Sir, you must be aware that in one matter we are opponents."

"Miss Onslowe?" March smiled. "That is one part of the puzzle. As for the other . . . well, desire is a wondrous thing, striking where one would least expect it."

As he had when they fenced, Allen could feel the heat of March's body. The dim light of the stable, golden where a shaft came through the doorway, fading to dun and brown, created a small intimate world.

March raised one hand to touch Allen's shoulder. "My dear, I . . ." He shook his head.

This was not the seducer, the sensualist Allen had seen before, but a man uncertain of himself, whose eyes held promise and fear.

"I don't know what . . ." Allen began.

"Ssh. No words. Not now." March bent his head to Allen's—a rough, clumsy brush of lips, the rasp of shaven skin. He made a small sound in his throat—impatience or lust, maybe—and clasped Allen's chin with his gloved hand. "Give me . . ."

Urgency flared between them. Not like kissing a woman, no soft yield of breasts or the ribbed stretch of stays—this was masculine and harsh, Allen's erect cock pressing against March's; March's hand hard and possessive on his hip, driving him back against the mare, who shifted and turned her head to nose at them.

"Enough," March said. He broke away and glanced down with a rueful chuckle. "I'll have a devil of a ride home."

Allen found himself blushing like a virgin. Well, by March's standards he probably was—an even more appalling thought. He must be mad. Had the languid air and luxury of the island corrupted him already?

He stepped away from March. "I— Sir, I do not wish you to misconstrue—that is—" He stopped. He had no idea what he wanted to say. He could have pulled away and been the first to break the embrace, but he had chosen not to, giving March the control. Something—curiosity, lust—had muddled his wits.

March's voice was strangely gentle. "Don't fret. You need to consider what we do, here, Allen." He unfastened the halter that tethered his mare, letting it fall loose as he backed her out of the stall, one hand on the bridle. He leaned toward Allen and murmured, "I can wait. Think of me."

The mare's hooves clattered on the cobbles of the stables as March led her outside. The young groom moved forward, but Allen waved him away and grasped March's raised heel to hoist him into the saddle. March's whip stroked briefly over his face, a thin kiss of leather, a touch of his hand on Allen's shoulder, and then he cantered out of the stable and out of sight.

CHAPTER 13

Following her moonlight stroll with March, Clarissa was unsettled and ill at ease. He had been perfectly gentlemanly that night. He had smiled at her wild conceit of wanting the moon and stars, and then bowed and escorted her back into the house. He had made no further reference to the encounter, and she wondered whether she had misjudged him, as she had Allen Pendale. It was now two weeks since Allen had left the house, and she had stopped looking for him every time she heard a horse or vehicle approach.

She had also stopped looking for March, who rarely dined at home and spent much of the day outside the house. Occasionally he would turn up during lessons, to tease Celia and ruffle her hair, and make polite enquiries as to the governess' welfare. These short encounters left Clarissa uneasy and disappointed; she put it down to the general malaise, the headaches and lassitude, that newcomers suffered in the island's fierce heat.

She lay wide-awake for hours each night, yearning for what she could not have and desperately wishing she had a confidante. *Do you think he favors me? Do my looks suffer in the heat?* And, most important, *Am I in love with March?* How could she possibly be in love with someone she saw so little and knew less?

She sighed, turned over, and punched her pillow into shape. She knew the patterns and subtleties of the night sky now after so much sleeplessness. Soon it would be light, and for the moment, the air was cool.

She dressed and wandered downstairs and out of the house. Smoke rose from the kitchen chimney but nothing else stirred. Then she heard the sound of a horse's hooves on the gravel drive. Shading her eyes against the first rays of the sun, she saw the man on horseback approach: March. A shiver of wanton awareness ran through her.

"Miss Onslowe." March slowed the horse to a walk. "You're up early."

She shrugged. "I wished to take the cool air."

He dismounted. "You're not unwell, I hope? No fever?"

"No, sir. I'm perfectly well."

He stared down at her. "So you say, yet . . ." He put a fingertip beneath her chin. "Dark shadows. Do you have trouble sleeping? I trust you don't pine for our friend Pendale."

She shook her head, dislodging his finger. "Oh, I'm sure we'll see Pendale again." That was good—the right tone of lighthearted affection.

"Walk with me, Miss Onslowe." He swung himself down from the saddle, looping the reins over one arm.

She fell into step with him, disappointed that the smell of horse and leather masked his own scent. They passed from shade into a patch of bright early-morning sunlight.

"Your cool air dissipates rapidly now with the sun," March said. "And speaking of celestial bodies, I have thought frequently of your yearning for the moon and stars. Do you remember that evening?"

She shrugged. Oh yes, she remembered. "I have some recollection of it, sir. We were quite foolish, as I remember."

He stopped. The horse snorted and ducked its head toward March's hands. "We have unfinished business, ma'am, and I wish to open negotiations once more. What do you say to that?"

"I say, sir, that I should send for a lawyer."

"Very good." He took her hand, tugged gently. "Into the shade with you, Miss Clarissa Onslowe. I can't have a mistress with freckles. Send for Pendale. Name your terms."

Allen didn't recognize the writing on the letter that came from March's house. He'd never seen Clarissa's writing, yet in some respects, he'd never known anyone so intimately. At first he thought the letter was from March and tore it open with shaking hands, afraid that it would be either a declaration of passion or a suggestion that they consider their episode in the stable a fortnight ago as never having taken place.

But it was a note from Clarissa. A cold chill wandered down his back and he wondered if he were getting fever. Her writing was refined and flowing, pleasant to the eye.

Sir, I have need of a lawyer. I think you can guess why. Please call on me any afternoon when it is convenient for you.
Yours faithfully,
Clarissa Onslowe

He should make her wait. Make March wait, too, keep him itching to bed her. Or maybe he already had. The lawyer in him hoped she had not yielded to him, for she would have lost valuable negotiation points; but Clarissa was no fool. As affectionate as she had been with him, until recently at least, she had kept part of herself aloof and cool. A woman in her profession had to be so. Even a governess could not become too attached to the family she served.

At the time he had admired her for her detachment.

Now he wasn't so sure.

Whose heart was he worried about, anyway? His own, Clarissa's, or March's?

It had been a week since March had called, and there had been no word from him. Of course, the Frensham household was officially in mourning, although other than his father's habit of retiring to the library with a bottle in the afternoon, Allen suspected little had changed.

He ordered Reuben to have a horse saddled, knowing that the order would pass through the ranks, while he waited and waited, and that eventually he would have to go to the stable and shout at one of the stable boys. It would be far more efficient to saddle the horse himself; it was a ridiculous way of doing things, but as his father had explained, it was the way things were done here.

After a good fifteen minutes of pacing up and down, he left for the stables and found one of the boys dozing in a shady corner. In England a lad of his age would be working, too, Allen reasoned, or at school if he came from a good family. But he wouldn't be another man's property.

"Milord." The child rose to his feet, knuckling his eyes, fearful. He cringed from Allen.

"Oh, go back to sleep," Allen said, half exasperated, half amused. He had a nephew that age, not long out of his petticoats. He doubted if this boy had ever been an adored baby. If he were lucky, he'd stay in the stables, unless he were sent to work in the fields or the hell of the boiling house.

With the child stumbling behind him, he made his way into the stables and saddled one of the horses, letting the boy believe he was helping, but making sure he kept from under the horse's hooves.

March's house was quiet at this hottest part of the day, although smoke rose from the outside kitchen hidden behind a stand of trees. Miss Onslowe, the footman told Allen, was in the library, and he found her sitting at a table, sheets of paper and an inkwell at the ready.

"It was good of you to come." Her voice, although as attractive and musical as ever, held a note of hesitation.

"I told you I would, if the occasion arose." He reached into his coat and produced the braided strands of leather and the small pot of goose grease that he had acquired on the ship.

"Gifts?" Her mouth twisted.

"Tools of the trade, Clarissa."

"And this?" She tugged at the twine holding the scrap of canvas over the mouth of the crock. She sniffed the contents. "Goose grease?"

"Some activities require a certain slickness."

She nodded, a faint flush rising in her cheeks. "Shall we begin, then? You'll take some refreshment?"

He took off his coat and hung it over the back of a chair as she summoned the footman to bring ale for him, tea for her. He spent a little time sharpening a pen while she sat silent and ill at ease next to him.

More delays while tea was poured, and he swallowed half a mug of ale. She referred to a small scrap of paper on which she'd made notes, and cleared her throat.

"I beg your pardon, Allen. This is somewhat awkward, considering . . . well, what we have shared."

He didn't consider it his job to put her at ease. "So. I believe March is worth a good deal. What do you want from him?"

"I thought maybe an annuity." She didn't look at him, but at her notes.

"We'll ask for two hundred guineas a year, but chances are, he won't keep up the payments when you part. Ask him for property—he owns half of Bristol and a good deal of London, by all accounts. I'll specify houses of a modest freehold." His pen scratched. "I know he has a house on Queens Square, although I doubt he'll give that to you. It's still the most expensive part of Bristol. Do you intend to continue as his daughter's governess?"

"Yes. I—I like her, and she's lonely. She is becoming much attached to me."

He raised his eyebrows.

"I wish you to specify that my role as his mistress be discrete from that of my role as governess."

Despite his misgivings, this amused him, but he wrote down the terms. He suggested, among other items, that she should ask March to provide her passage home if she wished to return to England, and for a clothing allowance.

He took another swig of ale and wrote three fair copies of the contract—one for Clarissa and March and one for himself to keep.

Clarissa sighed and pushed back a lock of hair, dark with sweat, that clung to her forehead, elbows on the table.

Allen summoned the footman again, told him to take the papers to the master, and return when told to.

He and Clarissa were alone in the room. A bee buzzed and droned at one of the windows.

"I should pay you," she said.

"I'll send Lemarchand the bill."

After a while, the footman returned with the three copies of the contract—signed. At Allen's bidding, the slave laid them on the table, with a small, wrapped parcel about the size of a small book.

Clarissa picked up the pen and looked at the parcel.

"Are you not going to open it?" Allen asked.

"Why are you so angry?"

"Why am I— Oh, for God's sake, Clarissa, you know why. You must know."

"Allen—" The pen in her hand hovered above the creamy surface of the paper.

"Wait," he said. "Before you sign, there is something I must say."

She shook her head while he considered the enormity of what he was about to do, the foolishness to which he was reduced, and how much of it had to do with his feelings about March. It was damnably intertwined, and he barely understood it himself.

He took a deep breath and dropped to one knee. "Clarissa, you must be aware that I . . ." He heard the slight snap as the wax seal broke, the crackle of thick paper unfolded. "My prospects are modest at the moment, but I can use my family connections to acquire more clients when we return to England." He paused. "I can certainly provide for you although admittedly not to any extravagant degree. I offer you my name, my honor."

Her slim hands laid the paper aside and undid the clasp of the leather case.

"Marry me, Clarissa."

Against cream-colored silk, jewels blazed and glittered, a parure of precious stones. She gave a soft sigh.

He dared then to look at her face. She lifted the necklace from the case, gazing spellbound at the play of light on the jewels.

Had she not heard a word he'd said?

Her head turned; her expression was stunned. "No, I can't marry you, Allen."

He raised himself to his feet again, humiliated and angry. "Christ, you're no better than any other woman. I should have known. A man gives you jewels and you get wet for him. I was a fool to think you might be more than that. They're stones, Clarissa. Lumps of rock. I offer you my beating heart."

She clutched the jewels a little tighter in her hands. "I regret you misunderstood. There never was any question that our arrangement should last more than the duration of the voyage, or mean anything more than what it was."

"I told you things about myself I've never told anyone. I— How can you go to Lemarchand?" He wanted to leave his mark on her pale skin, grasp her slender shoulders and wrench sense into her, but he clenched his fists tight so he could not touch her. "You know he prefers boys?"

"You mean he might choose my mouth or arse?" She gave a chilly smile at his discomfiture. "And if he does prefer boys, why does he want a mistress?"

"Because he can't get what he really wants."

She laid the necklace back into the case, settling the jewels into their niches. "You assume—or invent—more than you could possibly know. I regret I cannot accept your offer, Mr. Pendale."

She took the pen and hastily signed her name, one copy after the other.

He could not believe this was the same woman who had lain in his arms and looked upon him with such trust and tenderness. If she had not loved him, it had certainly felt like something very similar.

She looked again at the jewels, lifting a shorter strand from the case, a bracelet, or—

"It's not for your wrist. Allow me to show you, ma'am." He took the fine cotton of her gown in both hands at the bodice and ripped. His hands shook—with anger, he supposed. He wasn't sure what he felt: lust, grief, jealousy, humiliation certainly. He wanted to hurt her, one way or another, yet he claimed—he knew—he loved her. "March can buy you other gowns. Allow me to complete your sensual education."

"Let me go!" She hit him then, her hand cracking against his face as he loosened her breasts from her stays. "How dare you—"

"Oh, you've allowed me greater liberties than this." He pinched her nipples, this time to hurt her, not arouse her. "I know you, Clarissa. I know the sounds you make, the expression on your face, when you come. I know—"

"I was mistaken in you. I hate you!" She struggled to her feet, aiming a barrage of blows at his face.

He trapped her against the table, thigh to thigh, shoving his erection against her as he reached for the jewels. "This is how it fits. Not on your wrist, but here, Clarissa. *Here.*" He fastened the strand to her nipples and was glad when she caught her breath, wincing at the pressure of the clips. He caught her wrists, pinning them behind her. "It hurts, doesn't it? But it's a pleasurable sort of pain I think you'll become accustomed to, and even enjoy. You'll like it when March shows you off like this, his plaything. His property." He pulled at the jewels. "He could put you on a leash as though you were his favorite bitch. You'll enjoy that, too—" He stopped as he sensed a change, her body slackening against his, her breathing quieted. *What the devil am I doing?*

"Allen." Her voice was very soft and tears shone in her eyes. "I thought once you were my friend. Please, do not poison what we have had. I must ask you to leave."

He released her wrists, wondering if he had bruised her and what other damage he might have inflicted on her, and on himself, too. As he stepped back, he became aware of his own hurts—a sting at his mouth, painful spots on his shins (he had not been aware at the time that she had kicked him)—and an overall ache and exhaustion, as though he had lost a bout in the boxing ring.

Without a word, Allen bowed and walked away, out of March's house, and, he hoped, out of Clarissa's life.

Clarissa took a deep breath as the door closed behind Allen, and sank to the floor, shaking and finally letting the tears flow. The intensity of his feelings, his violent anger had shocked and surprised her, fool that she was. Certainly she had not expected an offer of marriage—that had taken her entirely by surprise, and from his inarticulate proposal, she suspected it was not something he had intended, although it had not lessened his pain when she refused. She could not say that she was sorry. If she'd said she cared for him, but not in the way he wanted, it would have been like rubbing salt into an open wound. She wanted to tell him that she honored the confidences he had whispered to her and the extraordinary intimacies they had shared, that she would miss him.

Best to let him be angry, to hate her if he must, and she must accept the guilt and the chill he left in his wake.

The note from March had fallen to the floor and lay faceup next to her.

Madam,
You told me what you wanted from a lover. These poor
baubles are the best I can offer.
Be mine.
Lemarchand

She unclipped the cruel little clips from her breasts and ran the heavy stones over her hand. Light flashed in diamonds with the cold brilliance of stars, sapphires held the deep intensity of an evening sky, and moonstones glowed, subtle and sensuous.

"He remembered," she whispered as the stones warmed against her skin and she could not help smiling with absolute delight and anticipation. "He listened to what I said. He understood."

CHAPTER 14

Clarissa had once dreamed of walking naked by moonlight through an ancient house, to the arms of the lover of her imagination. That man existed only as a foolish abstraction; his earthly equivalent had failed and insulted her.

He had also offered her marriage and the protection of his name.

March had offered neither.

But it was to March's bedchamber that she made her way, perfumed and adorned, by the light of a full moon casting splashes of silver light through the tall windows of the house. Her bare feet were as silent on the floorboards as those of his slaves.

Did March own her, too, now?

Outside March's bedchamber, his valet, Finch, a taciturn Englishman who was one of the few servants in the household, moved forward to open the door.

She stepped inside.

The room held March's scent overlaid with the pungency of a scented candle alleged to keep mosquitoes away. The only other light in the room came from the moon, creating a dramatic interplay of silver and black. The moon was hidden and the room plunged into near darkness as with a swish the punkah descended—a canvas screen designed to create a breeze by its rise and fall, operated by a slave on the balcony outside. Moonlight flooded the room once more as the punkah rose, then fell again in a steady hypnotic rhythm.

Ahead of her, March's bed, draped in the filmy white of a mosquito net, awaited. And he—the hairs on her arms stirred beneath the wool of her cloak—he was present, hidden in the shadows. Watching her. Waiting for her.

Her constricted nipples tightened.

She heard the snap of fingers, and the punkah rose, stilled.

"An apparition." Silk whispered, rasped on male hair—she guessed he had discarded his dressing gown—and a dark shape moved between her and the window, a long shadow cast onto the floor; there was light enough to see that March was naked and fully erect. His loosened hair flowed onto his shoulders.

"Show yourself, spirit," March commanded.

She raised her hands to the fastening of her cloak and let it drop, releasing a slight gust of salt that clung to it still. For a moment the floor beneath her feet heaved and swayed like a deck and she heard Allen's voice again. *Oh, please, Miss Onslowe, do shock me.*

March moved his head, a lift of the chin, summoning her from her ghosts to his imperious presence, and she stepped from the dark puddle of her cloak toward him.

"Ah. The queen of the night." His gaze traveled over her, pausing at the jewels at her ears and neck and breasts, admiring his possessions, the beautiful things he had bought. "The jewels become you."

She bowed her head.

He gestured with his head again, a different command, accompanied by a slight gesture of one graceful hand.

Down.

She dropped to her knees and ran her hands up his thighs, long-muscled, cool, sleek with dark hair, to trail her fingertips up his cock. He was hot there, hot and eager, skin stretched taut. She explored him further with her fingertips, the dark weight of his ballocks, the tender skin of his inner thighs, the hair curling tight at the base of his cock.

He didn't move, but he was not indifferent. His breathing quickened.

She touched her tongue to the smooth, slick head, drew back, and licked him, around and down, exploring the bumps of veins, his shape and taste and scent for her own pleasure. *Let him wait.* Beneath her palm his ballocks tightened.

Not indifferent at all. How long would it be before he dropped the control, the pretense? Before he demanded and took, gripping her head with his hands, groaning as he gushed into her mouth?

She blew on his cock, damp from the attentions of

her mouth, and bit softly at the base. Why let him suffer further? She took him in her mouth, lasciviously sloppy and wet, her breasts pressed against his hard thighs as she sucked and licked. Her pinched nipples throbbed; wet heat pulsed between her thighs. If she squeezed her thighs together, she could come, she was sure, but restrained herself. This was for his pleasure, all her concentration centered on him.

He groaned, the first sound he'd made, and now his hands came up to cup her head, to guide her, tilting her face and throat, tremors in his legs and belly. His fingers dug in her hair. She raised her eyes to see him, head thrown back, jaw clenched, belly and arms and shoulders tight and sculpted—a man fighting to loose and spend. She took him deeper, breathing through her nose, working one finger to the very base of his cock, beyond his ballocks. Rubbing the ridge, a little roughly.

Rough enough to make him surge salty into her mouth—a quantity indeed, although he was deep enough to spend mostly into her throat, but she wanted to taste him, to share the moment. Her quim clenched, the clips on her nipples announcing their painful presence anew.

His hands moved to her shoulders. He sighed and toyed with a lock of her hair.

"You may stand."

She did so, excited by his formality, the indifferent tone of his voice. She knew better—she'd felt and tasted his excitement, his abandon.

She stood close enough for her jeweled nipples to brush against his chest.

He raised a hand to tug gently at the jeweled strand, creating more pressure on her oversensitive nipples. His mouth closed on hers, nipping, sucking; his tongue coiled against hers, sweet and arousing, drawing a soft moan from her. Slow, wet kisses on her throat, her jaw, her lips, her shoulders, returning to her mouth with an insistent thoroughness.

He pulled away. "Now make yourself come."

Dazed, wanting his mouth again, she stood and stared at him.

He put his mouth to hers. "Do it." His voice was low and seductive. His tongue licked her mouth. "Touch yourself." He lowered his mouth and licked a swollen nipple. "I expect to be obeyed. You know that, don't you, Clarissa?"

"Yes, sir," she managed to gasp.

He pushed her toward the bed, drawing the mosquito net aside. "Sit."

She sat and let him arrange her: legs raised and parted, her quim exposed to him as she lay back against the pillows. One quick, painful flick to her nipple.

"I'm waiting."

He retreated to the end of the bed to watch her. She was about to perform. Of course she should be shamed and horrified—she was, wasn't she?—but another part of her dared and urged her on.

Her breasts, first—tingling and swollen, the nipples hard under her fingertips. Maybe she could come if she stroked and flicked enough, but she knew March wanted more—to see her fingers dip into her quim, draw her swollen folds apart, and play with the erect ridge of her clitoris. First, a slow trail of her fingers down her belly, onto her thighs, a fleeting brush against the hair that, in her present position, concealed nothing, but framed her most intimate parts.

March watched, motionless apart from a stir in his cock.

Now her fingertip strayed to her clitoris. A slight touch, a little pressure—teasing herself, teasing him.

"A moment." March's voice was not as steady as previously. He took the candle and moved to a small cabinet, opened it, and removed a bundle, wrapped in some sort of fabric. The cloth—it had the gleam of silk by the light of the candle—he tossed aside, revealing a model of an erect cock, gleaming white in the moonlight.

"Ivory." He ran his hand up the length of the phallus in a slow, sensual caress. "From the Orient. Wondrously lifelike, is it not?" His own cock lengthened and swelled. "If I may?"

He brushed the head of the ivory cock in a slow sweep from clitoris to buttocks, then positioned, pushed, penetrated her. "Do what pleases you best, Miss Onslowe."

She grasped the base of the ivory cock in her other hand—cool at first, then warming as her body closed and took the length. Not quite like a man—too hard, without the flexibility, but enough to arouse her. Slow, even strokes while she teased her clitoris—*Keep it slow, extend the pleasure, it's what he wants.* Her captured nipples throbbed and ached.

March's cock rose. He stroked himself while gazing at

her. What did it look like, the white of the ivory against the pink of her quim?

Her quim made small, wet sounds as she eased the phallus in and out, releasing it entirely occasionally to rub it against her clitoris. Tension gathered in her thighs, her nipples, her belly as she began the delicious climb to an orgasm.

March's hand continued the slow, casual slide on his cock. "You like that, don't you, Clarissa?"

"Yes." Her voice was tight and breathless.

"You like me to watch you."

"Yes." She could barely speak now.

He leaned forward, looking not at her quim but directly into her eyes. "Come for me, then."

Finally. She let go, arched and cried out, her finger merciless on her clitoris, sliding the phallus ever faster as her orgasm took her, March's eyes the constant in a plunging universe.

She fell back, astonished and breathless, her hands falling away, and the ivory phallus sliding wetly between her thighs.

"Now lick it," March said. "Lick it clean."

He knelt between her outspread legs and pushed his cock into her, filling her—ah, that was better, the warmth and flex of a man—pushing slow, curving into her. He held the phallus to her mouth; she tasted herself, salty and with a touch of vinegar from the sponge as her tongue explored the carved veins and folds. He groaned, his mouth joining hers on the shaft, and his tongue meeting hers until they both abandoned the phallus and it tumbled away into the sheets. Now he thrust slowly inside her, the length and breadth of his cock stretching her, vital and alive. He rocked his weight back onto his knees to release the clasps that had so teased and pinched her nipples, and moved his mouth to lick her there. Both of them moaning now, lost in a drugged sweetness, the playacting abandoned, the slick of wet skin and tangled hair and the scent of sweat-drenched bodies all that existed.

He came with a tremor and a wet surge although she held herself off in a sort of detached daze, as though an orgasm would detract from the wonder. This was March, so lordly and demanding and fierce, now vanquished in her arms, his head fallen onto her shoulder, his back heaving as he sucked in air.

He kissed her shoulder as though too lazy, or too depleted, to reach for her mouth. "Well?"

How was she supposed to answer that? She searched her dazed mind for suitable compliments on his virility and stamina, failed, and mumbled, "Thank you, sir."

He laughed and propped himself up on one elbow. A lock of his hair swept over his arm and tickled hers. "I don't believe you have very much to thank me for that last time."

His admission surprised her, and embarrassed her, too. She was his mistress, the instrument of his pleasure. Did he want her to perform with the ivory phallus again?

He kissed the corner of her mouth. "What would you like?"

She remembered that first—no, second—time with Allen, when she was dumbfounded by his need to know how and what she liked. Then, of course, she had no idea, only overwhelming excitement. Now she knew.

She took his hand and guided it between her thighs. "Here." She pressed his fingers into the wet heat, against the swollen length of her clitoris, letting her knees fall apart. His face was serious, intent—a profile worthy of a Greek coin—his hand dark against her thighs as one finger dipped and played. She watched his hand dabble intimately between her thighs.

"We'll do this with more light and in front of a mirror," March remarked. "I think you'd like that, wouldn't you? You'd like to see my hand on your cunny."

She gave a small gasp of shock and excitement. How easily he read her.

"What else would you like me to do?" March asked, his voice calm as though offering her more claret at dinner.

"I'd like you to lick me," she gabbled in an embarrassed rush.

"Ah. Where, precisely?"

"My tickler." Her face heated—she really couldn't tell whether it was shame or desire, so linked were the two emotions.

"A capital idea." March bent his head and took her clitoris between his lips in a deceptively gentle kiss. But only gentle for a moment—his mouth engulfed her folds while his tongue beat a wicked rhythm. And his fingers, dear God, his fingers thrust inside her, hooking up to a surprisingly sensitive place—she gave up the idea of trying to trace the topography of her quim as his fingers and tongue and lips merged into one splendid instrument of pleasure. *Please please please.* She writhed under the intensity of his caress, almost hoping he'd stop—and then spasmed against him, amazed at the wetness and violence of her response.

He held her at the peak of her orgasm, as skillful as a musician sustaining a long note, while she thrashed and groaned and shook.

"Oh," she said in amazement as the seemingly endless tumult subsided. Her legs still quivered, and small shocks reverberated in her belly.

He raised his head, very wet around the mouth, and smiled. "You are quite extraordinary."

"So are you." She could barely move, quite limp and perfectly content.

He yawned. "I should sleep." He pulled the sheet up to his waist, leaned to kiss her lips, and closed his eyes.

She curled onto her side and watched him. He seemed to fall asleep quickly, his breathing slow and even. His skin was almost as pale as hers in the moonlight, with a sparse slick of hair on his chest, thinning to a narrow line that ran to his navel. Below the sheet, she knew the hair thickened and spread around the base of his cock, and his legs were covered with a fine sheen of hair, as were his exposed arms.

Beautiful. An odd word for a woman to use of a man, but beauty he had in abundance—a profile that belonged on an ancient coin, an elegance of bone and muscle, that spill of dark hair with the white streak.

Was she supposed to leave now? She regarded the sleeping man, sighed, and unfastened the jewels from her breasts. As she sat to place them on the bedside cabinet, he shifted and his hand landed on her shoulder.

"Where are you going?" he said.

"I'm sorry. I didn't mean to wake you." She turned to him.

"You don't look happy," he said quietly.

"I . . . I'm confused." His acuity served only to confuse her more.

"About what?"

"You."

"Ah." His hand slid to her breast, cupping it in his palm.

"I don't know you. I feel I see you with a series of masks—as master of your plantation, as a father, as a man who takes and gives pleasure—" She bit her lip. She remembered Allen grumbling at her for not behaving like an obedient vessel of male pleasure. For one absurd moment, she wished Allen were there so she could ask his advice.

"Our contract does not cover matters of the heart." The words could have stung, but from March, they had a certain kindness and gravity. He bent to kiss her breast and slid his hand to her hip. "I wish you to be happy, Clarissa. You are far from home and I suspect you have been lonely for much of your life. We can offer each other comfort and companionship as well as our bodies. I'm not an easy man to know and I think you, too, have your secrets. So be it. Let us start there and see what ensures."

She leaned to kiss his mouth. As her lips touched his, he tensed and then sighed, pulling her close.

"Sleep now," he said.

She woke later to gray light with March's cock rising against her spine, his hand at her breast. He rubbed against her, his intention perfectly clear.

"Fast," he murmured. "Not much time. Let's see who comes first."

She wriggled to take him in. His cock bumped lazily between her buttocks and lingered, prodding, at her arse. He groaned and laughed. "Another time."

And then he slid into her, perfect and smooth, while he whispered how wet she was, how sweet her cunt, and he knew how much she liked to frig herself at his command. Or did she like to do it on her own, too?

Oh yes, she said. *Oh yes, like this. But if I had a splendid big cock like yours, I'd want to play with it all the time.*

You can play with it all you want, Miss Onslowe. He nipped her ear, his chin rasping against her shoulder. His fingers spanned her breasts.

More indecent, playful murmurs. His thrusts became faster, more urgent and he released her breast to grip her hips and spend himself inside her soon after she clenched and cried out.

He withdrew in a gush of fluid. "Finch will escort you back to your bedchamber." He rolled over and rose from the bed. "It promises to be a busy day. I've much work to see to on the estate."

"Yes, of course." Confused, Clarissa reached for her cloak, puddled on the floor, where she had dropped it earlier. She dropped the jewels from the nightstand into the pocket.

"You'll come to my bedchamber tonight."

"Yes, sir." She wrapped the woolen cloak around herself—itchy and unpleasant in the cold light and coolness of early dawn.

"Clarissa?"

She turned. March stood naked before her, drawing his hair back into a queue. He smiled. "Forgive my abruptness. I mean no disrespect. You have given me a night of wonderful pleasure." He bent his head to kiss her lips. "I trust I pleased you, too."

"You did, sir."

"March."

"Yes, March, you pleased me greatly."

CHAPTER 15

When she became a housekeeper, Clarissa had inherited a book of recipes and useful household tips dating back at least a half century. She had added in more of the same as she learned the intricacies of the household.

Why wasn't there a similar volume for a mistress? She certainly would have found it useful in the confusion of this first week with March. Sometimes she thought she should create such a book for her successor, who would find herself bound by the same complicated, subtle web.

Finch, waiting with utmost respect outside her bedchamber, cleared his throat.

Clarissa glanced at him through the half-open door. What did he think, having to escort a mistress through the house at night? March liked the sense of ritual it conveyed, she supposed. She was quite capable of walking alone from one end of the house to the other.

"A moment." She ran her brush through her hair and

touched perfume between her breasts. March had handed the tiny crystal bottle to her quite casually that evening before dinner. She breathed in the scent—something exotic and carnal. She wondered where he had acquired it—March, the magician of his island, producing jewels and perfume for her, paid for with money from King Sugar.

She glanced at herself in the mirror one last time, adjusted an earring to hang straight, and blew out the candle. The scent of honeysuckle drifted in through the window, and the stars ablaze—would she ever become accustomed to their fierceness in these latitudes? She moved toward the circle of light cast by Finch's lantern.

Silently he led her through the darkened corridor of the house, tapped on March's door, and opened it.

To her surprise, March was already in bed, a book in his hand.

Once again she was struck by his beauty—the dark hair tumbling onto his shoulders, his grave stillness.

He raised his head. "You wear the perfume, then."

"Yes. Thank you." There had barely been time to thank him for the gift earlier—time only to slip it into the bosom of her gown before Celia noticed.

"The mantua maker calls tomorrow. She'll bring some fabrics for you to look at. Order whatever you like."

"Thank you, sir."

"Oh, I have some very specific ways you'll thank me, Clarissa." He gave a faint smile.

She waited, wondering if he enjoyed her apprehension, sensed the nervous desire that coiled in her belly.

He raised his eyebrows. "Aren't you going to come to bed, my dear?"

"If you would be so kind . . ." She moved to sit on the bed so he could unbutton her gown. Of course she could do it herself. All her gowns were fashioned so that she did not require assistance in dressing or undressing. They were the simple, hard-wearing gowns of a woman who worked for her living, not those of a courtesan. She didn't even really know what a courtesan should wear here, where there was so little society and fashions were bound to be months behind their London counterparts.

Meanwhile she enjoyed the touch of March's long fingers, the errant caresses on her spine and shoulders.

The buttons released, she stood to pull the gown over her head. Her stays were simple enough, made of canvas and whalebone, and she unlaced them herself.

March watched with great attention as she raised one foot to remove her stocking. Despite his carnal intentions there was an unnervingly domestic feel to the scene. She half expected him to yawn and turn over when she came to bed.

As she slipped between the sheets, he closed the book and laid it on the cabinet next to the bed.

"Your book proves tedious?"

"I fear so." He turned on his side, facing her, his head propped in his hand. "You shall be my storyteller tonight."

"What sort of story would you like?"

"Something arousing." His hand brushed her jaw, stroked a lock of hair back. "Tell me of your first lover."

He couldn't have chosen a worse subject for an erotic tale. She hesitated.

"You may begin." Very courteous but with a hint of a challenge.

"His name was Frederick. He was a little older than me, handsome and gentlemanly. He visited my family often, to talk with my father on business matters. I was fascinated but shy."

Long hours spent in her father's study, with her trimming the lamps and providing tea and refreshments, while Frederick and the Reverend Onslowe talked. And of course she talked, too, because five years ago things were different; the abolitionist cause was full of passion and energy.

"Although I had had my share of admirers, there was something about him that was different. When he looked at me, my hands shook and I felt a yearning here, in my heart. After his visits I would think of him. I would remember the touch of his hand on mine, the way hair grew on his fingers, so." She stroked March's knuckle. "I would wonder if the touch of his knee against mine beneath the table was deliberate. He seemed to watch me when he thought I was not looking. And I watched him, too."

That much was true.

"And alone, late at night, I would lie sleepless in my bed. I would close my eyes and imagine his touch—on my neck, my shoulders, my breasts, my quim. I discovered sensations that were unsettling and delicious, while I knew what I did was a sin."

That was true, too. Lonely and thrilled, touching herself, stifling her cries of pleasure in her pillow.

"Continue." March's eyes were bright. Beneath the sheets his hand moved.

"I would close my eyes and pretend it was Frederick who touched me, who brought me to climax. It was Frederick for whom my nipples hardened and my quim became wet."

Not strictly speaking true. Frederick might have been the initial inspiration, but her private pleasures galloped away with her like runaway horses.

"And then one day, when I had traveled into Bristol to visit an old schoolfriend, I met Frederick by chance in the street. He invited me to dine with him at the inn where he lodged, and naturally I accepted. We were shown into a private room, where we dined and I drank a quantity of wine."

Frederick was nervous and picked at his food. She, excited to finally be alone with him, talked and talked, drank too much and, emboldened by the wine and his presence, clasped his hand. Had she seduced him? she wondered. Had he bowed to the inevitable, finding himself alone with a garrulous spinster whose every gesture and word revealed her desperation, her availability?

"At length, he drew me onto his lap and kissed me."

Probably to stop her talking.

"I was most surprised at the sensation of his arousal beneath me. I longed to see his member, for although I knew what it was, I had not had the opportunity to view one at my leisure, and in a state of excitement."

And I told him I loved him.

"So we proceeded to the bedchamber, where he

stripped me of my clothes. I was ashamed that my nipples were hard."

"As they are now," March said.

"He took his clothes off and I gazed aghast at his member."

"Describe it." March's jaw was tight, his hand sliding on his cock.

"Thick and reddened and hard—although not as large as yours, sir—"

"Oh, of course not," March said, heavily ironic.

"I could not imagine how such a thing would get inside my tender flesh."

Of course all of this had taken place in the dark, with much fumbling and muttered protestations of love.

"He caressed that part of me I touched only alone."

If only he had. Frederick, for all his bravado, had no idea of how to please her and she was too embarrassed to let him know.

"He licked and kissed my breasts until I thought I should come from that alone."

She'd very much enjoyed that part of it.

"And he kissed me all the while."

She wished their dinner had not included so much onion.

"When I thought I could bear it no longer, I begged him to put his cock in my quim. He pushed it in, filling me so that I shrieked with mingled pain and pleasure."

Ouch, *she'd said in the dark, disappointed that he'd abandoned her breasts.* Is this right, Frederick?

No wonder he'd kissed her again at that point.

"And I—"

"Fetch the goose grease."

She reached out one hand, grasped the small pot, cool against her palm, and turned to him. He lay on his side, one knee raised, his cock fully erect, cradled in his hand. He dipped his fingers into the goose grease and smeared it on himself, his touch sure and deft, while his gaze met hers.

"Would you like me to do that?"

"No. Watch me. I want you to watch me."

He pleasured himself as though he offered her a gift with this most intimate of acts. His foreskin slid back repeatedly to expose the dark, engorged head, the moisture welling shiny in the firelight, forearm flexing as he tugged and stroked.

"Will you come?" she whispered, as though, incongruous though it might seem, they were in a church or some other holy place.

"Would you like me to?"

"Yes. Yes, I would." She raised her hand to her mouth, bit into a knuckle to control her excitement.

"On all fours, if you please." His eyes were hot, his breathing fast.

"I—" She hesitated, fearful yet curious.

"Do it."

She scrambled onto her hands and knees and waited, hearing the slight slap of his pleasure, the wet kiss of his foreskin, his fast breathing. The goose grease was cool between her buttocks, then warming and voluptuous, prompting her opening to him. Despite his arousal he was careful, meticulous, delaying his pleasure to prepare her, to open her with a finger, and then a second.

And then his cock pushed into her, slick and heavy. She cried out a little, more from surprise than pain, although it did hurt; she supposed it could not be helped. He slowed, murmured indecent words about her big tickler and her pretty cunt, touching her there while his cock pushed and opened her. The crudity was unlike March, his usual suave demeanor—it was like being with another man, an avid, wonderful stranger. *Too much*, she thought. *It's too much. I can't. Please stop.* She wanted to say it, but instead she was moaning and crooning back at him to do it, do it to her, fuck her. *Please fuck me, fuck me.* She too transformed into someone crude and lustful. When she came, her orgasm was an unexpected and delightful shock. *How did* that *happen?*

The next morning she was once again the proper governess although still shocked and a little sore from March's attentions. But also, strangely at peace—the ghost of her former lover had somehow been laid to rest by her eroticized confession.

"We're going for a walk," Clarissa said to Celia.

"It's too hot," Celia whined.

"Nonsense."

"I'll get dark. Dey t'ink I'm a negro."

"Certainly everyone will if you speak that way, but your complexion will be perfectly fine if you wear a bonnet and carry a parasol." Clarissa held the aforesaid items out to the girl.

Celia scowled but tied the ribbon of her bonnet beneath her chin.

"I thought we could make some sketches of the plants," Clarissa continued. "Just think, we might discover some new varieties. Wouldn't that be exciting?"

"Ladies don' walk outside de garden," Celia insisted. "I want to get ready for dis evenin'. Dat lazy girl Rissa, 'er disappeared."

"Try again," Clarissa said. She found Celia's accent rather charming, but was obliged to honor March's wish that his daughter learn to speak properly. Grasping her own parasol and the drawing tablet, she led the way out of Celia's room, downstairs, and out of the house into the garden.

It was warm and rather sticky, but Clarissa was certain a brisk walk would be good for Celia. She led the way along an oyster-shell path to the edge of the garden, where deep green foliage and twining vines lined the way, now reduced to a dusty track.

Clarissa halted to look at a red flower the size of her hand. "Isn't that beautiful!"

Celia giggled. "'Dat look like a man's part."

Sure enough the pistil of the flower thrust aggressively from the petals. Clarissa shot the girl a warning look as they resumed walking. "That's not the sort of thing young ladies talk about."

What a hypocrite I am. I've spent most of the night fornicating in her father's bed and now I'm lecturing her on propriety.

"I don't t'ink Papa like us to come down here," Celia said.

Clarissa, after pausing to watch a many-legged insect scuttling away, looked up. "Why's that?"

"De slaves live near here." Celia sniffed and wrinkled her nose.

Clarissa ignored her and walked forward. Behind her, she heard Celia heave a martyred sigh, and the rustle of her muslin gown as she followed. The path wound through the forest—the walk would have been more pleasant if flies did not buzz about them so—and Clarissa made note of some exotic ferns and vines that would be good subjects for sketches. After a few minutes, she saw the gleam of bright sunlight, and the two of them stepped into a clearing.

A dozen or so round huts stood on worn-down, dusty ground. Clarissa had seen ancient thatched cottages rather like these daub-and-wattle huts in the poorest parts of her father's parish. Waste, human and animal, and the rinds and stalks of plants were strewn around as though the occupants lacked the will to clean up. Flies buzzed and a mangy dog, ribs visible, appeared, showed its teeth, and slunk away. Each hut had a small patch of cultivated ground, where some sort of gourds grew and beans climbed up poles. Of course, the slaves would be expected to grow their own food as well as labor in the fields all day.

"I want to go back!" Celia tugged at her arm.

A sound—the whimper of a child—came from one of the huts.

"Wait," Clarissa said. She stepped forward and peered into the opening. The stench nearly made her gag. A baby, tethered by a piece of rope around his waist, sat naked on the floor. Flies crawled around his eyes and mouth. In the shadows, something mumbled. An old woman, her eyes milky and clouded, hands knotted with arthritis, sat behind the child.

The baby picked something from the floor and gnawed on it. Clarissa didn't want to think what it was.

Celia repeated, "I want to go back!"

So this was what happened to those too young or too old to work, or a baby too heavy to be strapped to his mother's back. Clarissa had seen comparative poverty in her father's parish. She'd visited the sick in hovels much like these, but there was a particular misery and hopelessness here that appalled her.

Celia shrieked.

"What's wrong?" Clarissa went to her and shrieked in turn as something struck her sharply on the knee.

" 'Dat devil!" Celia pointed to one of the garden patches.

There, a child—at least, Clarissa thought it was a child—grimaced and flung another handful of missiles at them. The creature scuttled on all fours, cackling, and Clarissa saw he was horribly twisted, one withered leg dragging behind him.

"Stop that!" Clarissa dodged a handful of stones and shit.

"What are you doing here, Miss Onslowe?"

She whirled around. Blight, astride a mule, regarded her with bright, sardonic eyes. "Visiting the poor?"

His statement was so close to the truth, she felt her

face redden. "Can't you provide a better place for them to live? Where do they get their water?"

He shrugged. "A half mile off. They don't mind." He looked at the creature scrabbling in the garden patch, and lifted the whip from the pommel of his saddle. "Twisty Billy, you leave the ladies alone."

Twisty Billy whimpered and scuttled away.

"Lemarchand wouldn't like to know his daughter was here, Miss Onslowe."

"I suppose not." Clarissa held out her hand to Celia, who was in tears, with a large smear of filth on her face and another on her dress. "I'm sorry, Celia. I shouldn't have brought you here."

"Come to our house, Miss Onslowe," Blight said. "Miss Celia can wash and you can take tea with my lady. Here, miss, you may ride on my mule."

Clarissa really couldn't think of a way to refuse. Blight was almost being genial, and she should pay her respects to Mrs. Blight as common courtesy demanded.

Blight tossed Celia into the saddle of the mule, and led them on another path, through the vines and strange trees, to the working part of the estate. There were several outbuildings, a carpenter's shop, and a forge. Blight drew the mule to a halt in front of a small stone house nestled between what looked like barns and a high fence of wooden planks.

"Mrs. Blight," he called, "we have guests." He lifted Celia down from the saddle.

The door opened and a young black man came out of the house. Clarissa noticed how he shrank away from

Blight, but there was something of a swagger in his step. Clarissa knew exactly what a well-satisfied man looked like. She blinked. Surely she was imagining things?

The slave's gait changed to a deferential shuffle and the smirk on his lips died away so that he almost appeared another man.

A maid, little more than a young girl, opened the door, Mrs. Blight behind her. "Miss Celia and Miss Onslowe! How delightful. Do come in. Sally"—addressing the girl—"you put the kettle on directly. Why, Miss Celia, what's happened to you?"

"They visited the slaves' huts." Blight bowed and placed his foot in the stirrup. "I'll leave you to tea and gossip, ladies."

Elizabeth Blight, somewhat pink in the face and disheveled, led the way into a parlor, apologizing for the house's state of disarray. The house appeared to be little more than two rooms separated by a passage leading to a back door. She closed the door to the other room smartly, but Clarissa saw a very rumpled bed. Well, well, so Mrs. Blight took her pleasure with the slaves. Clarissa wondered what Blight thought. He'd had no discernible reaction to the sight of the young man leaving the house.

The parlor was sparsely furnished with whitewashed walls and a stone floor. Mrs. Blight fussed over Celia, scrubbing at her stained clothes, and gently cleaning her face. "Just muck. I don't believe you're bruised."

"Papa will be angry," Celia said.

"Then don't tell him, my dear."

"I shall tell him," Clarissa said.

Mrs. Blight raised her eyebrows knowingly.

"I wouldn't keep an animal in conditions like those," Clarissa continued. "He should know."

"I expect he does know, my dear. It's best not to interfere. More tea, Miss Celia? I hear you are to have some new gowns."

Celia, cheered by a favorite subject, chattered on about what she was to wear that evening, and how her father wanted her to attend an assembly in St. James, the main city of the island, some fifteen miles away. Mrs. Blight countered with a comment on handsome officers, since the city served as a harbor for the Royal Navy.

As the two of them chattered away, Clarissa gazed out of the window. The parlor looked out onto a narrow alley between outbuildings and an open space, which she thought must be some sort of yard. Chickens pecked in the dust.

A sound reached her ears, a low, agonized moan.

"What was that?" Clarissa asked.

Mrs. Blight and Celia stared at her.

"There's someone out there—someone hurt." Clarissa rose to her feet. "Mrs. Blight, is someone in your household ill?"

"No. Miss Onslowe, where are you going?"

Clarissa ran to the back of the house and out the door, looking around for the source. In a small shed nearby, a boy chopped wood. It wasn't him, then. In a lean-to against the house, Sally tended a fire, stirring something savory in a large pot.

"Sally, who was that crying?"

"Dat Rissa, milady."

Nerissa? What had happened to her? Clarissa dashed into the yard. In the center stood a wooden contraption—stocks—a crude cross, with holes for a miscreant's wrists on the cross bar. Rissa hung there, her body drooping, stripped naked. As Clarissa paused in horror, the girl gave another moan and moved her head feebly as though to dispel the flies from around her mouth and eyes.

Her back was striped oddly, and then Clarissa realized the glittering lines were more flies clustered on the open wounds of a beating.

"Miss Onslowe—" Mrs. Blight had followed her out.

"Let her go!" Clarissa said, and then added as Mrs. Blight hesitated, "Now, if you please." She ran to Nerissa's side. "Don't worry. We'll have you down in no time."

Mrs. Blight, her lips in a thin line, unbolted the cross piece of the stocks. "Mr. Blight will not like it."

"And I don't like her being punished so." Clarissa caught Nerissa as she collapsed. "What has she done?"

"Tell Miss Onslowe what you did," Mrs. Blight said.

"Fetch her some water," Clarissa said. "See how parched her lips are. She can't speak."

Mrs. Blight nodded at the two young slaves, who had abandoned their woodcutting and cooking to watch the drama unfold. The girl, Sally, ran up with a cup of water, which Nerissa gulped down.

"Tell her, you wretch," Mrs. Blight said.

"I sorry, milady."

"Tell Miss Onslowe." Mrs. Blight's voice was threatening and cold.

"I stole," the girl sobbed.

"And what did you steal?"

Clarissa bent to comfort the slave but she shrank away.

Mrs. Blight gave a huff of annoyance and picked a cotton gown from a pile of firewood. "Get dressed." She reached into her pocket and handed Clarissa a length of silver-and-red ribbon, now faded and tarnished. "Yours, I believe, Miss Onslowe."

Clarissa looked at her, and then at Nerissa, who struggled to pull her gown over her injured back. "Yes, it is mine. I gave it to Nerissa last night."

"I see." Mrs. Blight looked at her with active dislike. "I would never have given you such an item if I had known you were to hand it over to a dirty black slut."

"It's a lovely ribbon," Clarissa said, "but I'm too old to wear such a thing. It's best suited to a younger woman, such as yourself. And Nerissa seemed to admire it so, and she's done some splendid work repairing my gowns, and working on Miss Celia's. I wanted to reward her."

"I see." Mrs. Blight didn't believe a word Clarissa said; it was quite obvious. "That's what she said." She poked Nerissa contemptuously with her foot. "But she's a lazy, nasty thing, Miss Onslowe, and you'll spoil her. I suppose you'll want to take her away. Blight intended to leave her there for the rest of the day as an example."

"I'm sorry to disappoint you both," Clarissa said. She bent down and took Nerissa's arm. "Can you walk?"

"Yes, milady." Nerissa stumbled to her feet and knuckled her eyes.

"Go to the kitchen of milord's house, Nerissa," Mrs. Blight said, her eyes bright with contempt. "You won't have to act as nursemaid, Miss Onslowe, although I'm sure you'd like to. They'll give her something for her stripes there."

"Thank you for your hospitality, Mrs. Blight," Clarissa returned with icy civility. "I shall take Miss Celia back to the house now."

<hr />

"It is unworthy of you!" She was fairly sure she was red in the face from her time in the sun, as well as from her righteous indignation. She leaned over March's desk—mahogany, highly polished, as beautiful as its owner—and pointed her finger at him. "You—they call you the king of the island. You are in a position to make a difference. I know, you insist that slavery is necessary to your trade, but cannot you go about it in a more decent way? Could you not at least dig them a well closer to their huts? Must you—"

"Clarissa, I do not think this is the concern of my mistress or my daughter's governess. Neither is it appropriate for you, in whichever role you choose, to burst into my study and make wild accusations. We have had some unpleasantness with the slaves, some mutterings of revolt, much sullenness, and poorly done work. Now, more than ever, they need a firm hand. If a slave steals, he or she should be punished. And I leave that to Blight."

"Blight is a monster!"

"On the contrary, he is a useful and hardworking

member of my estate." March, too, was somewhat red in the face. "He knows his place."

"And I don't?"

There was a long pause. "Sit down, Clarissa."

She remained standing.

"Sit down." The words were no longer a request.

She sat.

He did, too.

So few nights they'd had together, she thought in some misery—nights in which she believed she had become close to him; hours in the darkness when she craved for more than his body and his touch. And now it was too late.

"Clarissa, I have run this estate for most of my life, whereas you have been here for only a few weeks. I know our ways may seem uncouth or harsh, but believe me, there is no other way. Many are shocked when first they come out here, but they learn. You will, too."

"I hope not."

"As my mistress, you must and will. Come, Clarissa, you knew when you boarded the *Daphne,* well before you entered my bed, that you were seduced by the wealth of the sugar trade."

Tears pricked her eyes. She swallowed and faced him. "I am aware that I must make some compromises. I hope my conscience allows me to do so. Otherwise . . ."

"Quite."

She continued, again close to tears, not daring to look at his face. "If I were to leave you, I believe I should die. Do not ask how love has happened in so short a time—I believe it happened when first we met. I must tell you this now, for if you wish to send me back to England, I must speak before I go."

"My dear," March said and reached for her hand across the desk. "I—"

She heard footsteps outside the study and hastened to finish what she had to say. "I do not expect you to tell me you love me. I know you do not. It does not matter. Say nothing. I shall speak only of it this once. I . . ."

She looked up to see March stare past her, his face transformed. He looked younger, unsure of himself, full of hope—as though he too could not contain his feelings.

Oh God, do I look like that when I look at March? Am I so vulnerable, so transparent?

Her hand slipped from his as he rose to his feet.

CHAPTER 16

Allen suspected he'd interrupted a rather tense scene in the study. March had been particularly pleased to see him, as though seeking some sort of distraction. Clarissa was merely polite, and that was hardly surprising after the last time she'd seen him, when he made his idiotic proposal. He noticed how she looked at March most of the time, while playing the part of the attentive hostess.

Of course she hadn't broken Allen's heart. He had recovered. And what a relief it was to be with friends—or the closest to friends that he had here—after the days spent with his maudlin father.

Now it appeared he was to entertain Celia, who giggled and insisted he dance with her while one of the slaves played the fiddle. Clarissa occasionally corrected Celia's steps. "Third position, if you please, and keep your head up."

March smiled at his pretty daughter and invited Allen to dine.

Celia and Clarissa left to change their gowns for dinner and Finch, March's valet, escorted Allen upstairs to the room in which he'd previously stayed, and offered him hot water and a clean shirt and neckcloth. When he came downstairs again, he and March were alone for the first time, other than a slave who waved a palm branch to keep the mosquitoes away.

"I'm most glad you came to call," March said.

Allen shrugged. "To tell the truth, it was entirely unexpected. I found myself close by with a lame horse, so I decided I should throw myself on your hospitality. My father went to St. James unexpectedly on business."

March caught his eye in a knowing, man-to-man sort of way. So he knew that the grieving earl had left to seek consolation in the arms of a mistress of many years' standing. Probably the entire island knew. It was a small place, after all. Doubtless it was common knowledge that March had a new mistress.

March continued. "Thank you for taking an interest in my daughter. She's not used to company, as you know."

"She reminds me of my eldest niece."

"I hope to present her in London society when we return to England. It's important she makes a match befitting her wealth."

Allen nodded, wondering if he was being warned off as a suitor.

At that moment Celia entered the room. "Papa, Mr. Pendale, look at my new gown!"

"Very fetching, my dear." March patted his daughter's hand.

"Most stylish," Allen responded. He found himself, to his annoyance, looking around for Clarissa.

She entered the room wearing the gown he had ripped, but now repaired with a piece of the same blue silk that Celia wore; the inserted scrap of color at her bosom drew attention to her pale skin and her breasts. In her ears were the earrings March had given her.

Another civilized dinner in March's dining room, eating with silver cutlery from French china set on the mahogany table, attentive slaves filling Allen's glass again and again. March and Clarissa matched him glass for glass, although Clarissa shook her head after Celia, becoming even more giggly, had consumed her second.

The ladies withdrew. March and Allen, passing a decanter of brandy, made desultory conversation on horses—were they both relieved at the neutrality of the topic? But how neutral was it? Allen remembered March's declaration in the stable, the brush of their mouths, their cocks pushing together through layers of cotton and wool. He stared at March's finely made wrists and hands, not wanting to meet his gaze. *This man desires me. Do I desire him?*

It's a hanging offense, a cautious, lawyerly voice said. *Only if you're caught and admit to it,* answered the voice of another sort of lawyer, the sort he sometimes was.

"We must not keep the ladies waiting," March said. Swaying slightly, he took the brandy decanter in one hand and gripped Allen's shoulder with the other. His touch was neutral and friendly. "I trust you're not too drunk to dance with my daughter again."

"My pleasure."

When they entered the drawing room, however, Clarissa was alone. She sat at the pianoforte, her head bowed, and picked out a few chords. "I'm afraid I shouldn't have let Celia drink that second glass of wine. She sat here and yawned her head off, poor girl, so I sent her to bed." She frowned. "The instrument is out of tune again. I suppose it's the damp." She looked up and smiled at March.

She used to smile at me that way, Allen thought. *That lovely smile, like sunrise over a calm sea.*

Clarissa stood with a swish of muslin skirts. "I'm too drunk to play, sirs. Shall we take a stroll in the garden?"

"You don't fear the light of a full moon?" March offered her his arm.

"Too late. I am already struck by madness. Possibly I am not the only one."

March made no comment to her cryptic remark. It must have been some sort of joke between him and Clarissa. She reached for a couple of cheroots from a slave who stood nearby, a silver platter in his hand. The ease with which she leaned to puff them alight at a candle suggested this was a service she frequently performed for March.

Allen accepted the cheroot, still warm from her lips.

To his surprise she slipped her hand through his arm, and so linked together, they made their way outside onto the portico and onto the lawn. Their shadows stretched long on the silvery grass.

Clarissa bounded ahead of the two men, stretched her arms wide and declaimed:

The moon shines bright: in such a night as this,
When the sweet wind did gently kiss the trees,
And they did make no noise, in such a night,
Troilus methinks mounted the Troyan walls,
And sigh'd his soul toward the Grecian tents,
Where Cressid lay that night.

She whirled around, lost her footing and giggled.

"I've never seen you drunk before," Allen said, emboldened by his own tipsiness to address her directly.

"Not as drunk as this. How very debauched we are." She leaned against March, rubbing her face against his sleeve, and then danced away again. "Which way is the sea, March? I want to see the moonlight on the water."

"Come then." March caught her hand. "Let us take this madwoman to the shore, Pendale. Come, I'll show you the way I discovered through the mangrove trees when I was a boy."

They seemed to disappear into the dense thicket of greenery—shadow and silver by moonlight—that edged the lawn, but Allen, when he followed, found a winding narrow path. The air was thick with honeysuckle. For a fleeting moment, he wished he were back in England on a summer's night.

The path plunged steeply downward into a grove of trees that stood in brackish water. A bird, disturbed by the clumsy humans, gave a harsh call. The oyster shells of the path were long gone. Now it was a matter of finding footholds among twisted tree roots as the scent of salt became more evident. A cool breeze arose, welcome after the humidity of the garden, and the slope flattened out into tall grasses interspersed by palm trees. The sea lay ahead, a glimmering track laid upon its surface by the moon.

Clarissa gave an exclamation of delight and ran forward onto the white sand, toward the creamy fringes of breaking waves.

"She is . . . she is quite remarkable," March murmured.

The remarkable woman, unsteady on one leg like a drunken stork, peeled off her stocking, and then the other, having already kicked her shoes aside. Lifting her skirt to her knees, she ran into the water.

"It's warm!" She splashed in the shallows and waded forward.

"Do you fancy a swim, Pendale?" March asked.

Allen knew that sardonic tone, the challenge in March's voice. "A swim only, my lord."

"Very well." March tossed his cheroot aside and unbuttoned his coat. "I wonder if we can persuade Miss Onslowe to divest herself of her garments, also. It could make for an interesting night."

"Certainly, although I'd say that was her choice." Allen pulled his shirt over his head and turned away to unbutton his breeches. No point in flaunting himself at March, although now he wondered whether March had been merely toying with him, trying to shock him.

March, already stripped, ran past him and plunged into the water, splashing Clarissa, who gave a loud squeal.

Allen raced for the water and, ignoring March and Clarissa, waded in. He dived through breaking waves and out beyond, where the water was smooth and gentle. He'd never swum in water so warm and bouyant, only chilly English rivers and ponds. He turned onto his back to float, drunk and content, gazing up at the stars, arms and legs spread wide.

"Don't fall asleep." March's voice tickled Allen's ear.

"I won't." Allen plunged beneath the water, seeing the moon distorted and wavery, and below waving weed and pale sand. A small shoal of fish passed by as he swam down until pressure in his ears forced him upward again. He rose to the surface, shaking water from his hair, and met March's gaze.

"Damn you, March." His breathing was fast, faster than it should have been after the relatively short dive. "Stop looking at me like that."

"Like what?" March, treading water, regarded Allen gravely.

Allen lunged toward March, not sure of his intent, or the other man's. *Do it. Put an end to the tension. Do something. You cannot let this go further or even stay where it is. Damn him*—his hand closed on March's shoulder, their legs tangled together underwater.

The kiss was clumsy and intimate, unexpected in its ferocity; he tasted sea, tobacco, brandy, and a darkly pungent arousal. He was shocked enough that he forgot to keep himself afloat, and the two of them sank, entwined, below the surface, where they writhed briefly before surfacing, both of them spluttering.

"Do you seek to drown me?" March raised a trembling hand to push his hair back from his face.

"I don't know. It might be simpler." Their mouths collided again with clumsy force. Allen tasted blood—or maybe it was not so, only the taste of seawater.

March's hand cupped Allen's head, adjusting the angle so their tongues slowed to a lazy underwater dance. March groaned into Allen's mouth, as his hand—was it hand or Allen's own?—closed on Allen's cock.

March withdrew his mouth but with his lips still against Allen's. "I have dreamed of this."

"And I have tried not to."

"May I?" March's hand slid and grasped. Up and down. Knowing the rhythm, the pressure, strong and sure.

Allen made no answer but slid his own hand around March's cock. So strange, to have this part that was like and unlike himself to handle, to stroke, while the sea lapped around them in a gentle caress. They drifted together linked by the touch of hand and tongue, while a pressure built, as inexorable as the tide that pushed them back to the shore and the woman who waited there for them.

Now he withdrew his mouth from March's. "I'm going to come," he muttered, embarrassed and thrilled. His arousal was fast enough to shame him, or would have been so with a woman, but March's skillful touch urged him to climax soon, very soon. There was no need for extended play here, not with a partner equally frantic to climax—he detected between his own fingers the texture of March's own excitement.

"Come then," March said. "Now, damn you."

And Allen did—saltwater stinging slightly on the sensitive head of his cock as he spurted in March's hand and his own fluid flowed into the sea.

March groaned, thrust against Allen's hand and released warm and slippery, silk on Allen's fingers. March's head drooped briefly onto Allen's shoulder, his mouth warm against the skin as he took a deep breath and laughed softly.

"You took me entirely by surprise, Pendale."

"I took myself by surprise." Allen felt warm, relaxed. *Safe.* What an extraordinary thing for a grown man to feel, and after an unnatural act. He dropped his arm around March's shoulders.

"I still like women," Allen added, just in case March thought . . . Well, he wasn't quite sure what March thought.

"As do I." March laughed. "Come, I'll race you back." He plunged away from Allen, his body slicing through the water, while Allen followed with his less stylish, powerful stroke.

Clarissa was quite grateful she was drunk. Sober, she might have been shocked or appalled at what she heard, or imagined, or wanted to imagine. The men's voices carried quite clearly over the water, over the gentle break of the surf.

So she was not mistaken. But Allen? A man who was so very . . . well, masculine. A man she thought she knew. March was no surprise, not after that helpless, lost way he'd stared at Allen earlier.

A dreadful pang of jealousy made her fists clench. *Look at me like that, damn you. I'm your* mistress! *You're meant to love me!*

And then she giggled at her own absurdity. There was nothing in that contract about love, and while you could persuade someone to bed, you could not persuade his heart—or your own, for that matter.

March emerged from the sea first, wading naked through the surf, handsome enough to break her heart. He was doing that, certainly.

"Oh," she said. "I know how those silly girls in antiquity felt when a god visited them." She stepped forward to remove a slick of seaweed from his dripping chest, letting her fingers slide downward. "You're so beautiful, March. It really isn't fair."

He laughed and caught her in his arms. His genitals stirred against her damp skirts. "May I strip you here and now, Miss Onslowe?"

"If you wish." She placed her palms on his damp back. "How do you intend to dry yourself?"

"Please, do not let me interrupt anything of import." Allen, strong and dark—a wave of nostalgia washed through her—wandered over to his pile of clothes, and shook his head like a dog. Drops of seawater gleamed like quicksilver.

March grinned. "We'll dry off eventually. Meanwhile you should avert your eyes, my dear."

"Whatever for?" Did he know Allen had been her lover? No matter.

She broke their embrace and took March's hand in hers,

reaching for Allen's with the other. "We must talk, sirs." She giggled a little at the formality she naturally assumed, particularly with what she was about to announce.

Allen dropped the shirt he was about to pull over his head and took her hand.

Miss Clarissa Onslowe, once an almost respectable housekeeper, then a briefly respectable governess, held the hands of two naked men by the light of the full moon. How absurd. She glanced at them both, March, lean and muscled like a greyhound, or some other thoroughbred animal, and Allen, stocky and powerful, each beautiful in their own way. They could represent air and earth, and she the fire that would ignite them here, with water as witness.

"We three are shackled together like March's slaves. I to you, March, Allen to me, and you to Allen. It is such a pity we are each in love with the one who cannot reciprocate."

March stared at her. "Clarissa, I—"

"Do not dare to feel pity for me, March!"

He shook his head. "I was about to say you are the bravest woman I know, to openly state such a thing."

She laughed with a note of hysteria that she did her best to suppress. "Well, it's a pity I don't have a cock, March."

"I'm quite glad you don't," Allen said. His own stirred, very gently as he smiled at her. "And I can only agree with March." Very slowly, he reached out his hand to March, who, with the slightest hesitation, closed his own hand around it.

"So," Allen said, "I'm sorry, March."

"Ah, don't be maudlin. We are all three of us sorry, and what I have to suggest may make us sorrier yet, but I see no alternative." Clarissa smiled at them both. "I think we should all go to bed together."

CHAPTER 17

"Absolutely not!" Allen broke his hands free, backed away, and reached for his clothes. His stride, as he walked away, approximated a drunken attempt to retreat with dignity on uneven sand.

"He has such a lovely arse," Clarissa commented, too much claret and brandy making her feel quite tragic at his retreat.

March cleared his throat. "Indeed. Well, I'm afraid your idea, although extraordinarily arousing, has fallen on deaf ears."

"Possibly we can persuade him otherwise."

She stroked her hand down March's chest and belly. His cock, eager as March might be for another man, lifted slightly.

"Ah . . . the sand . . ." So this wasn't the first time he'd fornicated on a beach.

"We'll use my gown and petticoat."

"You're so practical, my dear." He unbuttoned her gown as he spoke, bending his head to kiss her. He whispered into her mouth, "Can you see him?"

"He's stopped. I think he thinks we can't see him. He's in the shadows."

They made short work of her stays, petticoat, and shift, spreading the cotton garments onto the sand, but remained standing.

She cupped March's cock in the palm of her hand. "He's watching."

"Capital." He weighed her breasts in his hands, his thumbs chafing her swollen nipples. He raised his voice slightly. "If there were another man present, Clarissa, what would you like him to do?"

"I think I'd like him to lick me while you do that."

"Anything else?" March nipped her ear, whispering, "Is he still there?"

"Yes. His cock is hard now."

"And . . . ?"

"He looks a little . . . exasperated. He's scratching his ballocks."

"Turn so I can see." March raised his voice. "So, as I touch you here, you would like it to be another man's tongue? You're exceedingly wet. I think you'd drench his face."

She gave a lustful groan that was not entirely feigned, her hand sliding on March's cock. He had hardened considerably. With her free hand, she took March's hand and slid his fingers, one by one, into her mouth.

From the shadows, she heard a muffled curse.

"Oh, very well." A spray of sand announced Allen's arrival. He flung his clothes onto the sand and scowled at them both.

"A little enthusiasm might be in order," Clarissa commented. "March, please stop laughing. It is not helping."

"Don't think you'll get up my arse," Allen said.

"I wouldn't dream of it. I'm not even sure how I'd do it." She tried to look shocked at his suggestion.

"Not you, you ninny. March." With the expression of a man about to face his execution, he dropped to his knees and groaned. "Open your quim, for the love of God. I want to taste you."

It was March who held her open, whose hand dropped to Allen's head in a brief caress.

Allen's tongue flicked right where she wanted him, causing her to moan aloud and clutch at March's arms for support. March smiled as he stroked and kneaded her breasts, her legs quivering.

"I—I—can't. . . ." Clarissa wanted to say that she could stand no more, that her impending orgasm robbed her of all strength elsewhere, but March scooped her into his arms.

"Now," March said. He laid her on the pile of crumpled linen, spreading her legs wide, and knelt before her. His cock hovered, rubbed against her, pushed inside her, and she clenched on him, hard.

"Take me in your mouth." Allen, his voice rough with lust, knelt over her, facing March. His hands pinched and stroked her nipples.

Clarissa took Allen, choking a little at his eagerness,

the avidity with which he invaded her mouth, his sheer girth and weight, salty from the sea. Wiry hair tickled her nose, his belly close to her face. She wanted to see more; she wanted more of everything: the plunge of March inside her, the urgent thrusts and fierce caresses of both men.

With an effort she disengaged her mouth from Allen. "Kneel by me," she gasped. "I want to see what you do."

Allen obliged, swaying gently on his knees as he stroked his cock into her mouth.

March moved forward, kissing her breasts, her shoulders. "I'll take him."

Allen gasped as his cock slid from her mouth and into March's. Both men's bellies were taut, poised, both of them groaning deep in their throats, and she came, clenching again and again on March's cock, helpless, drowning.

The two men subsided; they must have come, too. How disappointing that she'd missed the moment, caught up in her own.

March lay with his head on Allen's belly. She lifted a languid hand to touch her finger to March's mouth where a smear of semen clung, silver in the moonlight, and touched it to her tongue.

<hr />

"It's . . ." Allen reached a hand out to Clarissa to help her up the steep slope crowded with trees. How they had negotiated it earlier in pitch-darkness and drunkenness, he had no idea. Her face glowed pale beneath him. "It's . . . March. And here. This place. I don't usually . . ."

"Don't be a fool, Pendale," March said from behind

Clarissa. "Am I the only one with sand in his arse? We should bathe."

Out of breath, they stepped onto the oyster-shell path that led back to the house. Allen hoped he did not look quite so debauched as March and Clarissa. In the dim light before dawn, they appeared tired and bedraggled, hair hanging loose, clothes disordered.

Clarissa's petticoat dragged damp beneath her gown, and she clutched her stockings in one hand. She yawned. "I would love a cup of tea. And my bed."

"Not mine?" March slid his arms into the sleeves of his coat and retrieved his neckcloth from a pocket.

"If you wish." She attempted to straighten the collar of March's coat. "Finch will be most upset with you."

They seemed less like a man and his mistress than a married couple, sharing the same sort of comfortable intimacy she and Allen once had. Or so Allen thought. He turned away, struck with sudden weariness, and continued to the house.

March, Allen had to admit, had superb sangfroid. Arriving in his house, with his mistress and another man, debauched, sticky with seawater and sand, stinking of fornication, March quelled his slaves' curious glances and ordered the plunge bath be made ready and fresh clothes prepared.

For all three.

In an English household, Allen knew the servants, after barely hidden amusement, would gather to hoot and cackle at the goings-on upstairs. Here, he wasn't quite sure whether the slaves' impassive silence hid secret contempt or merely represented a complete lack of interest. Yawning, he watched as dark figures flitted in and out of March's luxurious Turkish bathroom, bearing towels, soap, tea for Clarissa, coffee for the two men, armfuls of clothes. Nerissa knelt at the fireplace, building a fire with quick, deft movements

March and Allen, both in their shirtsleeves, shared the same mirror as they shaved. March chatted with Finch about house and estate business, his elbow occasionally brushing Allen's. Clarissa, seated in a nearby chair, yawned as Nerissa brushed her hair, frequently stopping to tug out tangles.

The whole scene reminded Allen of the levee of an absolute monarch, in which private, insignificant acts became public ritual. All they needed was some groveling courtiers.

Finally, the three of them were alone, free to strip off their remaining clothes and step into the luxuriously hot water. Allen dunked his head and rubbed his hands through his hair, which was stiff and gritty with saltwater and sand. Jittery from coffee, sated and physically exhausted from the night's activities, he washed Clarissa's hair, remembering how once she had done the same for him. She murmured her appreciation, then turned to lather his chest, exchanging a kiss over his head with March.

Strange how Allen felt, again, like a beloved child in such indecent circumstances. But even though he could have sworn he would not suffer further attentions, when March soaped his back in slow, lazy circles, he found himself responding. He disentangled himself from them to sit on the tiled ledge that ran around the circumference of the bath and sluice water over his head and chest.

Allen stole a glance at Clarissa. With her wet hair slicked back, she had something of the facial appearance of a handsome boy. Was that why March lusted after her? March leaned to whisper in Clarissa's ear and plant a kiss on her shoulder. And on one breast, round and shiny with soap and water. And the other. No, Allen decided, there was little of the boy about Clarissa.

They—or March, at least—had lured in Allen like this before on the sand. He wouldn't rise to their bait this time—although, glancing down, he was certainly rising, his cock seeking the surface.

March smiled at Clarissa. "I bathed here with Allen once before. He was most put out by my advances."

"I am hardly surprised. You probably did it only to tease him." Clarissa, for all her amorous drowsiness, still retained a touch of her usual waspishness.

Allen wanted her, then, quite sharply, and apart from his physical discomfort. His desire for Clarissa was absolute and distinct, quite different from the turbulent feelings he had for March, which were borne of lust and curiosity. She might have betrayed Allen by becoming March's mistress, but he felt he could trust her. Indeed, as she knew what transpired between him and March, he had no choice but to trust her. And March?

"What are you thinking of, Allen?" March laid his hand on Allen's knee, giving it a gentle shake.

"To be honest, I think that I don't trust you," Allen said.

For a brief moment, pain flashed over March's face before he covered it with an easy laugh. "You fear for your precious arse, you mean." He toyed idly with Clarissa's breast. "Tell him I am not a monster, my dear."

"No, he's not a monster," she said. "Prospero rather than Caliban, if you like."

So she shared with Allen his perception of March as the autocratic ruler of the island.

"You'll stay for a few days more, I trust, Allen," March said. "Your father, when he returns, can send word."

"Thank you. With the greatest of pleasure."

"Oh, I think we can promise you that." March reached to touch Allen's face, then slid his hand down, slowly and with great attention. He paused to circle a nipple, much as he had with Clarissa. Allen, although determined to show no reaction—idiotic, considering the state of his cock—found himself short of breath.

"Why do you pretend indifference to me?" March's whisper was sharp and urgent.

"I've never claimed indifference to you," Allen said. "I can't give you what you want."

"I'd settle for less." March looked bewildered, uncertain.

"Forgive me for saying it, sir, but you hold a winning hand."

Clarissa, who lay in the water, eyes closed, sat bolt upright. "Pardon me, gentlemen. I am not a playing card."

"Not even the queen of hearts?" March teased.

She frowned and stood, scattering drops of water, her nipples hardening. "I think I should dress."

"And leave us here, in this condition?" March gestured toward Allen.

"I am sure neither of you will suffer for long."

"I assure you we shall not." March hoisted himself onto the tiled seat opposite Allen, his legs spread, one hand cupping his balls. "Take him, Clarissa."

She looked uncertain. "You mean I should . . ."

"If you please." March's voice was neutral, almost bored. He might have been asking Clarissa to pour Allen more coffee. March added, "If we are to continue in this way, there will be various . . . arrangements, various roles for us to play. And I ask you to obey me in this."

"And if I refuse?"

March smiled. "But of course you won't. You're my mistress. You serve my pleasure. And my pleasure at this moment is that you should serve Allen."

She scowled at March. Allen bit back a smile. Despite his efforts to teach her how a mistress should behave, she seemed to be incapable of hiding her feelings.

And then she laughed. Standing in the tiled magnificence of March's plunge bath, water lapping gently around her thighs, she reminded Allen of the vibrant creature who had thrown her stockings overboard. She lifted her wet hair to the back of her neck in both hands and squeezed the water out, her breasts lifting.

"It will be my pleasure, my lord Prospero." She waded over to Allen and sat astride his thighs. With one forefinger, slightly damp and wrinkled from the water, she touched his lip. "Let me give you this," she whispered. "You know I cannot give you more."

Allen closed his eyes. He wanted her, but he didn't want her pity. Her finger still rested on his lip and he drew it into his mouth, biting softly. Her breasts rubbed against his chest, soft and springy, their tips hard, while her thighs gripped his.

He did not dare look into her eyes, fearful of what she might see in his, and equally fearful of what he might see in hers—pity, indifference. Touch only, then, the gloriously smooth velvet of her skin, the tickle of fine hairs, and the scent of her, fine lavender soap, the saltiness of her arousal.

Thank God she was aroused, unless it was the presence of March that fired her, or the prospect of performing for him. Or, despite her objections, the submission of her will to his, the abandon of self.

Water lapped. The fire crackled. She breathed soft into Allen's ear.

Allen ran his hands over her back, the tender knobs of vertebrae, the sharpness of her shoulder blades—fine, smooth skin, the flesh riper, with more spring on her buttocks. He slipped a hand around between their bodies, to rub the springy mass of hair, rotate the hard bead of her clitoris.

Clarissa sighed, her lips brushing his. Yes, open for him, take him in, tongue, cock, the perfect fit he never expected to experience again. One hand on her arse, guiding her to his orgasm, the other leading her into her own. Her arms brushed his head. She must have been clutching the tiled surround.

Clarissa moved, Allen hardly at all, her breasts brushing his chest—he knew she liked that, a stolen pleasure. Her thighs tightened against his, her quim changing the way it did before she came, her breathing fast and urgent now.

Behind his eyelids he imagined her face rapt and intent, as she sought release.

She engulfed him, gripped, shivered, whimpered, her mouth sliding to his shoulder.

Behind his eyelids now, flashes of light, a leap into the abyss.

She raised her head to kiss the salt that welled at his eyes.

Allen hoped March had not noticed. But Prospero knew everything that happened on his island.

CHAPTER 18

"Dey say you and my papa . . ." Celia struck a note rather too hard on the pianoforte.

Clarissa winced. After a night of very little sleep, the sound jangled in her aching head. Out of tune again, too. She was not surprised Celia had heard something from gossiping slaves, but she was not sure how to respond.

"That is a matter between Mr. Lemarchand and myself," she said. "You need not concern yourself, and it should certainly not affect your lessons. Try that scale again, please."

Clarissa was not ready for Celia's response. "You better than the others."

"The others? The scale, if you please, with your right hand and then the left hand."

Celia began to play, murmuring to herself, "*One, two, three, thumb under* . . . No, Miss Onslowe, I don' like his other mistresses. Some of them only greedy black girls.

And the white ones, they not much better." She landed triumphantly on the final note. "So I like that he like you."

"You know," Clarissa said with as much delicacy as she could, "in most houses, I would not continue as your governess."

"No!" Celia, her scales abandoned, grabbed Clarissa's hand. "You must stay, Miss Onslowe."

"I shall. I am saying only that this is a most irregular situation, and when we return to England, I shall probably live in a different house. Things are different there."

"I know. Everyt'in' like ice."

"*Everything.*" Clarissa corrected her. She didn't know whether to feel relief or embarrassment that Celia accepted the situation with such equanimity. March, she thought, had been somewhat careless in dragging a succession of mistresses through the house. She hoped that with Allen he would maintain some sort of discretion—if anything more were to happen. Last night seemed like a dream now. They had each slept for a few hours in their own beds, and today the two men had ridden out together.

Clarissa became aware of Celia's expectant look as the girl said, "Three octaves, Miss Onslowe!"

"Very good. Would you like to try both hands together? And then we'll go into the garden for some sketching."

※

"You are killing me," March said. His horse sidled, made restless by her rider's agitation.

"I doubt it," Allen said. He was uncomfortable with

the role he felt March forced him to play, the cruel lover who would not yield. "You cannot force desire—surely you should know that."

"You say it was the one time, then. One night. An aberration. Nothing more?"

"Precisely."

March gave a contemptuous snort. "At least I have the courage to admit to my desire."

Allen reined his horse in. "You accuse me of cowardice?"

"Of course not. As you say, if you do not desire me, then I cannot possibly accuse you of cowardice—only, according to you, a lapse of judgment." March dug his heels into his horse's side. His mare lunged forward, shaking her head.

Damn March. Allen was the lawyer. He was the one supposed to entangle others with their words, to tempt them into verbal traps. He shouldn't be the one feeling foolish, dishonest and, what was worse, unkind.

The sunshine, the spectacular view of the island— March and he had ridden up onto the range of blue mountains you could see from March's house—were spoiled. Allen sighed. It was a pity Clarissa was not here; she would have enjoyed the view: the textures and colors of forests and cultivated land, smudges of smoke marking estates, and the larger, darker haze on the coastline, only just visible, that was St. James. St. James where his father was; and doubtless the earl would return any day.

And then Allen would have to go back to his father's house, which he both feared and anticipated. He would get away from March, but leave things unresolved—and he would leave Clarissa, too. Allen clicked his tongue and urged his horse forward to catch up with March.

What could he do? Apologize. March was his host, after all.

Allen drew his gelding level with March's mare, which was at a sedate walk. March stared straight ahead, his lips tight.

Allen's leg bumped against March's. "I beg your pardon, sir. I do not mean to cause you injury."

March laid a hand on Allen's knee. "I know you do not. I hate myself that I am sunk so low. I fear I am wretched company."

"You're not."

March did not reply but slumped in the saddle—uncharacteristic for such a skillful horseman. His hand slid from Allen's knee—and kept sliding.

"March!" Allen grabbed the other man's reins and drew both horses to a halt as March sagged into his arms. March's hat tipped forward and rolled onto the ground.

"Get me down," March said.

Allen swung his leg over his horse's withers, dropped to the ground, and helped March dismount. With both sets of reins looped over his arms, Allen fumbled for the flask of water at his saddle.

"Sit down, sir." Allen helped March to a rock near the shade of some scrubby thorn trees and offered him the flask.

"Thank you. A sudden dizziness, that is all."

"I can ride back for help, if you—"

"Ah, don't be a fool." March closed his eyes and leaned against the rock.

Allen tipped water onto his handkerchief and pressed it to March's forehead. March looked ill—there was no denying it—with a blue tinge to his lips, the shadows beneath his eyes accentuated.

March raised his hand to hold the handkerchief to his forehead. "I'll rest awhile. See to the horses, if you will."

The horses were still close by, taking advantage of the pause to crop sparse tufts of grass. Allen tethered them, loosened their girths, and returned to sit by March's side.

"How do you feel?"

"Better." March took another sip of water. "I feel a fool. To have lived here so long, yet to still succumb to the climate."

The men sat in silence for a while, the only sounds the chirps of crickets, the chomp of the horses tearing at grass, and the buzz of an occasional flying insect.

"Generally," March continued, "I feel a fool these days. To have taken on a new mistress, and after so many adventures in love, to know the one I love is the one I cannot have. It is most humbling."

"I know." Oh yes, it was certainly humbling.

"Well," March said with the glimmer of a smile, "we have that in common, at least."

Allen leaned his head back against the rock, thinking how easy it would be to sleep. And how difficult it would be to submit to March—or, now, in this languid afternoon heat, how easy it would be.

March's hand closed on his knee again. "Of course,

you suspect I feign illness to take advantage of your some-what sullied innocence."

"Of course," Allen agreed with the same sort of ironic humor. Yes, there was something about March he liked, that spoke to him, even as he mistrusted him. "And have you consulted a physician recently?"

"Yes, yes." March's fingers moved, a gentle caress. "You deny me, but you deny yourself, too. Will you look back on this moment when you lie dying and regret that you never let me love you?"

Allen opened his eyes, somewhat alarmed at March's tone. "March, how ill are you?"

"I'm perfectly healthy. As I said, this is a momentary weakness—the effect of heat and exercise. I'm somewhat more advanced in years than you, and besides, the island weakens the constitution."

Allen nodded and closed his eyes again, lulled by the sultry afternoon air, and reassured by the strength return-ing to March's voice.

March's hand still lay on Allen's knee, warm and still. "Look at me."

Allen opened his eyes, blinking slightly in the sun-light that filtered through the thornbush. March's face was close to his.

"I never thought to say the words 'I love you' to someone so damnably stubborn and arrogant," March said. "Someone who fights as though he would kill me, and almost drowns me when he deigns to offer one kiss. A man who almost certainly fights inside himself the truth of his nature—"

"Go to the devil, March!" Allen sprang to his feet. "I have told you a thousand times that I prefer women. You jump to extraordinary conclusions—"

"I beg your pardon. You came in my hand, in my mouth, Allen. I've tasted your seed. Or have you forgotten those insignificant details?" March rose to his feet. "You say you're not a coward. You deny all, any, feelings for me, but I cannot forget that moment, and, I think, neither can you."

They faced each other, both breathing heavily.

"Think about it, Allen."

March turned away to the tethered horses, and jerked the mare's girth tight. Gathering the reins in his hand, he said, "I challenge, you, Allen. Come to my bedchamber tonight."

The door creaked closed behind Clarissa. She took a step forward into the darkness of March's bedchamber, smooth wood beneath her bare feet. The shutters were closed and the room perfectly silent.

"March?"

No reply. She shouldn't have spoken. Darkness and silence were to be the order of the night, apparently.

She concentrated. The room held the faintest scent March's familiar bergamot. But of course she wore perfume, and it rose around her like a fine mist, masking other scents. Outside, far away, a night bird called.

She took another tentative step. Another one—so— and if she stretched out her hand, she'd find a bedpost.

Warmth spread down her back, the awareness that someone—March—was close behind her. Silk lapped against her calves—as he had commanded, she wore only a shift—and against her arms. His fingers closed on her wrists. He let out his breath in a long sigh. Had he held his breath ever since she had entered the room?

Now she felt the brush of his loosened hair against her shoulder. March's hands tugged at her shift and she raised her arms to help him slide it over her head. There was a slight puff of perfumed air as it floated down and landed on the floor, glimmering pale in the darkness. He drew her hands behind her into the small of her back.

Clarissa moved her fingers against March, tickling the hard muscles of his abdomen.

March let out a hiss of annoyance. Something swished in the air and a line of fire imprinted itself on her backside.

She yelped.

He made a slight tsk-tsking sound, more warning than indulgence, but this time she understood. If she made a noise, she would be punished. And what else, what other transgressions might she commit? She was sure she would, excited and fearful.

Something slithery and smooth encircled her crossed wrists and pulled tight.

So she was bound. At his mercy. Just in time she stifled a small nervous giggle.

A familiar part of him bumped up against her stinging buttocks, pushing her forward—and a hand at her shoulders guided her. Onto the bed. On her knees, arse in the air—she'd overbalanced, but somehow had the impression that was what he wanted—her face in the sheets. Well, this was something new. She was totally, gloriously helpless and in a most undignified position.

March walked away—she heard the swish of silk, the pad of his bare feet—and the bedroom door opened, letting in a flood of golden light. For one moment she feared that slaves would enter, but March took the lights from Finch or whoever it was who waited outside. She heard the metallic taps of a candelabra placed on furniture, as light filled the room.

March paused behind Clarissa as though admiring the view. Well, he probably was. That was why he'd arranged her like that.

"Turn your head." March spoke for the first time.

Clarissa found herself staring at her reflection in the cheval glass, her eyes wide, her hair tumbling around her face. March himself stood in the shadows. She could only just make him out.

"These are the rules," he said. "Any sound you make, until I tell you otherwise, will be grounds for punishment." He stepped forward into the light, a small black whip in his hand—almost a toylike version of the sort of whip March's overseers carried. "And sounds of both pain and pleasure will warrant—this."

The whip flicked out again and she bit the sheet. Only just in time. Of course, she was sure he would trick her into making some sort of sound, or response.

"Do you understand, Miss Onslowe?"

She hesitated. Was she meant to respond?

The lash descended again. "Yes. Yes, sir, I understand."

"Good." March drew the leather through his fingers, his eyes fixed on her exposed parts. She imagined how she looked there, plumped and shining with moisture—shamefully, she wished the reflection could somehow reveal that, too. And how embarrassing that she could feel how wet she was. How ready for him, how eager, despite the indignity of her position.

March's hand dropped to the fastening of his silk dressing gown, and revealed his nakedness and his rampant cock. He bent forward and kissed her arse, where the skin still stung—she could see a red stripe in the mirror—and she found herself wriggling with expectation.

He straightened up, his expression stern. "I don't believe I gave you permission to move."

Clarissa hesitated. Was she meant to apologize? "I beg your pardon, sir. I didn't realize I should not."

March bent his head in acknowledgment. Apparently she had made the correct response. His hands planted firmly on her hips, he buried his face between her buttocks—how wonderfully indecent—kissing his way down to her quim, wetly luxuriant, pausing to plunge his tongue inside. She let out a long breath—almost a sound, not quite, and tensed in anticipation. He paused as though considering the matter himself, before resuming his attentions with a twisting coil of his tongue around her swollen clitoris.

Clarissa cried out in surprise and delight.

March trailed the whip over her arse. "You forget yourself, Miss Onslowe."

"Yes, sir. I am most sorry." Her voice shook. She didn't know whether from fear or excitement.

"Remind me, Miss Onslowe, what happens if you misbehave."

"You will beat me, sir."

"I regret it is so."

He raised his arm and the lash landed with a loud snap and—*Oh God*—that hurt. She did not expect it to hurt so much. Tears sprang to her eyes and ran into her hair and the sheet.

"Very good." He knelt on the bed behind her, reaching beneath her to caress a breast. "I trust that will not occur again, Miss Onslowe."

A pause.

"Will it, Miss Onslowe?"

"No, Mr. Lemarchand."

"Very well. We shall proceed." And proceed he did, plunging his cock deep inside her so she had to bury her face into the bed to suppress the sounds she longed to make, racked by astonishing pleasure.

After a while, he withdrew—his cock shone wet and red in the reflection—and arranged her on her side, one leg raised.

Clarissa could see her quim now, the hair darkened by her pleasure and his mouth, red and swollen, her clitoris prominent. March positioned himself behind her again and guided himself into her. She saw his cock divide and penetrate her, sliding between the folds, dark against her pinker flesh.

"See how I fuck you?" March murmured into her ear.

As usual, when he lapsed into vulgarity, the indecency ignited Clarissa's excitement. "Feel how your quim takes me inside you, welcomes me, sucks me inside. Shall I rub your tickler?"

"Yes, if you please," she gasped.

His hand reached for her clitoris, fingers spread, not needing to rub her because the movement of their hips provided enough friction.

His other hand appeared at her breasts, toying with her nipples, touching her in exactly the right way. She began the climb to another orgasm, fearing that her inevitable cry of pleasure would earn her further punishment, then not caring—watching herself, seeing her face soften, her mouth fall open, March's cock thrust into her faster and faster, her body contract.

And, yes, she cried out, an incoherent gasp of sound she could not help. March, too, she saw in the mirror, lost control—his movements spasmodic, his teeth bared in a grimace that looked almost like pain, before a final deep thrust.

"So," he whispered in her ear, "do you think I should beat you again, Clarissa?"

"If you wish," she murmured.

"No. I'll spare you." March withdrew from her in a gush of fluid and tugged at her bound wrists. "Well done, my dear."

Her arms fell apart, still behind her back. Sated and drowsy, she lacked the energy to move. March rubbed her wrists and rearranged her, rolling her onto her belly.

"Surely . . . not again, so soon." She started as something cool, smelling of herbs and tallow, spread onto her damaged backside.

"I didn't realize quite how hard I hit you," March said. "While I admit I find the marks somewhat arousing, I should like you to be able to sit down tomorrow."

"Thank you." She turned, with some care, to face him, and stroked the lock of white hair back over his shoulder. "I wish . . ."

"Ah, Clarissa." March touched his mouth to hers.

She pulled him in closer, deepened the kiss, loving his taste and smell, the touch of his gentle hands, the squash of her breasts against his hard chest.

"What a charmingly amorous scene."

Allen Pendale, wearing only a pair of thin cotton drawers, stood in the bedchamber doorway.

CHAPTER 19

"Pendale," March drawled. "My dear fellow, how delightful to see you. Come in, do. I believe we have some brandy somewhere. Clarissa, will you not offer Allen some refreshment?"

Clarissa, from surprise more than anything else, had grabbed March's dressing gown as soon as she realized they were no longer alone. Now she wrapped it around herself, tying the belt, and fetched Allen a glass. She glanced at him; he stood awkwardly a few steps inside the bedchamber, his feet planted squarely on the floor.

March appeared to be enjoying his discomfort.

"Will you sit down?" Clarissa asked, as though speaking to a guest in a drawing room. She only just suppressed a giggle that she was sure would have turned into a loud, vulgar snort.

"No, thank you. I won't be staying long. I came only to say . . ." Allen took the glass.

Clarissa tried not to smile. He was wearing his draw-ers, for God's sake, and it was the middle of the night. Surely he must realize that they could not be fooled into thinking this some sort of bizarre social call. She shot a look at March, who sprawled naked on the bed, his cock still wet and leaving a trail of semen on his thigh. Surely he should be the one trying to put Allen at his ease? She seemed to be incapable of normal behavior—whatever that might constitute—all too ready to burst into loud in-appropriate laughter at any time.

Allen took a sip of brandy. He placed the glass on a cabinet and squared his shoulders, as though making some sort of decision. To Clarissa's delight he cocked a hip forward and hooked one thumb into the waist of his drawers, posing. The thin fabric slid down a little onto his hips. "So, who wants me first?"

Clarissa burst into loud laughter and heard March's guffaws.

Allen gave a rueful grin. "I beg your pardon. I've no idea how to go about this. Maybe I should leave. . . ."

"Wait," Clarissa said. She grasped Allen's hand. "Please, don't go. We are dreadfully rude. I am so very sorry but . . . you took us by surprise." She clamped her mouth shut before she said anything she'd regret, over-joyed at the thought of Allen offering himself up like the next delicious course in a meal.

She didn't dare try to meet March's gaze, afraid they would both lapse into helpless laughter again. Instead, she tugged at Allen's hand. "Come and sit with us. We're both quite tired—you must be, too. I don't even know if we'll . . ."

March covered himself with the sheet—*About time,* Clarissa thought, *shame on you for flaunting yourself at Allen*—and moved over on the bed. "You are most welcome, Allen."

Allen nodded and climbed onto the bed, keeping some distance between March and himself.

As unobtrusively as she could, Clarissa retrieved the whip from the floor and placed it inside the cabinet where March kept his indecent toys, including the ivory phallus. There was no point in intimidating Allen, who veered between nervousness and flirtatious bravado. She sat on the other side of the bed, near the foot, placing a pillow against the bedpost, and waited to see what would happen.

She had expected to feel jealousy, possibly even revulsion. Lust under the stars, fueled by a great deal of brandy, was one thing—but this? She had a wild curiosity about what the two men might do together, as well as a fear that they might ask, or tell, her to leave. After all, March and Allen had had a good part of the day alone. Maybe they had already . . . She remembered March swooping down to take Allen's climax in his mouth, and her nipples peaked against the silk of the dressing gown.

March murmured, low and intimate, to Allen, ". . . your choice alone. As Clarissa said, we're all somewhat fatigued. I should be honored if you choose to stay." He glanced at Clarissa. "My dear, maybe you could, ah, help Allen."

Help Allen? From the stirring in the thin linen drawers, she could tell that very little help was needed.

Allen shifted, cupped the bulk of his genitals, and

muttered something polite and, she suspected, untruthful, about being tired himself.

Clarissa crawled across the bed and loosened the fastening of the drawers. Allen's cock spilled out, half erect; she knew without a doubt that a pinch, a gentle slap, would bring it to its full hardness. Her hand or March's?

She looked at Allen. His lips were slightly parted, and his dark eyes held a pleading expression. She leaned to plant a kiss on his cock. He grew firm beneath her lips.

"Surely we don't need all these candles," Clarissa said. An easy remark, but one she resented having to make. March wanted Allen, not her; she wasn't sure what Allen wanted, but he was here, after all, of his own free will. To please March, she must make herself unobtrusive, a bystander to his desires. She slipped off the bed and busied herself with blowing out candles, pinching the smoking wicks between her dampened thumb and forefinger. After a leisurely circuit of the room, and when only the candles by the bed still burned, she crossed to the window and opened the shutters a little to let in starlight.

Only then did she turn to the bed to see what the two men did.

Her breath caught with something—jealousy? What she saw between Allen and March surprised her as much as it excited her. There was gentleness, as well as a sort of intimate brutality. They moved together like a pair of wrestlers, playfulness mixed with lust. They were kissing each other, March lying on his side, one arm beneath Allen's head, and the other hand roaming over his body. March's hand and arm were pale against Allen's dark skin as March stroked the other man's chest and belly, dipping occasionally to clasp Allen's even darker cock, now fully erect, protruding from the cotton drawers.

Clarissa stepped a little closer.

Allen groped a hand toward March, reaching for his cock.

March captured his hand, bringing it to his mouth to kiss—a gesture that Allen need not attend to his pleasure, perhaps? He slid his mouth briefly to Allen's nipples before returning to his lips again.

Clarissa squeezed her legs together, wanting to be part of them, to feel what March did to Allen, to join in their caresses.

March saw her and smiled, granting her permission.

She climbed onto the bed on the other side of Allen and dropped her mouth to his chest. Now she was close enough to hear the low sounds both men made—growls of tenderness, lust, surprise. Allen's skin tasted of sweat and soap. She joined her hand with March's on his cock, tickling the scrotum with her fingernails, letting him slide, slow and delicious, in her palm. March's hand closed hot and slick around hers, sliding, pumping.

March raised his mouth from Allen's and gave her a quick kiss on the lips.

Allen opened his eyes, drugged with pleasure, his mouth loose and swollen, eyes dark.

And March looked at Allen the way he would never look at Clarissa—dazed, imploring. March, offering himself, with no trace of his usual amused reserve—his mask was gone. He was a man disarmed by desire. *Humbled, too,* she thought, as Allen turned toward her, and she saw the disappointment on March's face.

"Clarissa," he murmured, breaking free of March's embrace, "how much pleasure can you take from the two of us?"

So March would pleasure her because it was Allen's desire. They scrambled together briefly on the bed, with the clumsiness of eager but underrehearsed actors finding their places. March sat with his back against the wall, she on his lap, his cock sliding home, while Allen knelt before her.

Allen's mouth moved over her breasts and belly, down between her parted legs. March groaned loudly in her ear. He must be aware of Allen's chin and tongue, so close to the root of his cock, his balls. Lost in the pleasure of Allen's lapping tongue, she grasped his head, digging her fingers into his thick curls. She knew how badly March craved his attention—didn't she feel that way about March himself? But right now, she wanted March's cock to stay exactly where it was and Allen's tongue and lips, his fingers on her breasts, to continue their astoundingly wicked play.

Both men urged her toward orgasm—must everything between men be a contest?—March's steady thrusts upward providing a solid foundation on which Allen embellished and decorated. Ripples ran up her body, her thighs tensed and spread, and she came in a tumult of pleasure, her body lifting and thrumming. March bit into her shoulder, his sweat dripped onto her already wet skin, and he groaned, thrusting hard inside her.

"Now you'll have me." Allen pulled Clarissa onto

him, onto his cock. March's semen trickled from her down her thighs and onto Allen's belly as she shuddered and came, again and again. She was dimly aware of March's kiss on her mouth, March's hand reaching behind her to cup Allen's balls and caress her buttocks, his thighs. One flesh, the three of them.

A brief rest—Allen actually fell asleep after that first orgasm—to wake to a hand on his cock. To his disappointment the hand was not Clarissa's, and the look on March's face made Allen feel both guilty and ashamed. He should reciprocate this time, he decided, although he was far more interested in Clarissa, who stroked and sucked both men with equal abandon. Clarissa's splayed legs and flushed bosom, her wet and swollen mouth, tempted him far more. She seemed to have reached some sort of plateau of sensuality where orgasms came to her with rapid ease.

But after several (he'd lost count), she took Allen's hand from her quim. "Touch him. I want to see you do it together."

March raised his eyebrows. For a moment March looked like himself, sardonic, in control, cynical. "We'd best obey the lady, Allen."

See you do it together? What the devil did she mean? Allen opened his mouth to negotiate—*My hand only, your mouth if you wish, and definitely not my arse and I've no desire for yours*—but Clarissa sprawled beside him naked, her hands idly running across her breasts. March's plaintive gaze made Allen feel guilty and uncomfortable.

"My dear . . ." March said.

Allen grunted, hoping he sounded lustful and not merely ungracious. At least he had an erection, which was hardly surprising after he had caressed Clarissa with assiduous attention, and received the intermittent attention of her tongue and lips.

"I grow impatient, gentlemen." She took Allen's hand and placed it on March's cock. "Kneel facing each other."

"Yes, ma'am," Allen said, thrilled by the idea of Clarissa telling him what to do, if not by what she requested. He rose to his knees, his cock waving in front of him.

"And you, March," Clarissa said.

Allen took March's cock in his hand. Much like his own, of course. And the obvious advantage of having another man fondle you was that men knew where and when to be rough, where to apply pressure and how much. And unlike caressing a woman, there was a blessed directness about the whole business—none of that dabbling for a subtle splinter of flesh among slippery folds while its owner wriggled in silence or snapped out directions. Unless the woman was like Clarissa, whose clitoris was obvious and ready—from the very first time he had homed into hers like a bee diving into a flower. She caressed herself now, watching the two men, one hand at her breast, the other between her legs, her face flushed.

"Will you come together?" she asked in a bright if breathless tone.

"We'll try," Allen said, grinning.

March cursed, grasped Allen by the back of his neck,

and pulled him close, March's kiss a frantic invasion of teeth and tongue, a demand that Allen concentrate on the pleasure at hand. March groaned deep into Allen's throat, shuddered against him, and splashed warm onto his belly and hand. His head dropped onto Allen's shoulder. "Come for me," he whispered. "Please, my love."

Allen turned his head to look at Clarissa. Her hand moved fast now, her legs splayed wide, her pretty quim gleaming ripe and red. Oh yes, she would come soon. Very soon. *Look at me, Clarissa. Help me.* Her gaze met his, and they were the two who came together—not something he usually strove for while fucking, far better to take turns, to see and hear and feel the other. . . . He groaned and gasped and spurted messily over himself and March.

Sated finally, they settled to sleep. He was afraid March would dismiss him, exercising his rights as Clarissa's protector—and damn it, he wished March would stop looking at him like that. Lustful glances, he could have laughed off, but March's plaintive yearning unsettled him. Allen made sure Clarissa lay between March and him—she was almost drunk with pleasure and exhaustion, her limbs flopping like a rag doll's. After drawing the sheet over her and smoothing her sticky hair from her face, he tucked himself behind her, one arm circling her.

March took his hand and Allen let him, too tired for embarrassment. *Poor sod, let him have this small scrap of affection.*

With a satisfied sigh, Clarissa softened into an embrace

as innocent as that of children sharing a bed, brothers and their sister, tired after a long day, intimate and at ease.

Allen kissed Clarissa's shoulder—the nearest part he could reach without moving. This was the first time they'd actually shared a bed to sleep, but unfortunately, someone else was there.

CHAPTER 20

"Can't we go and watch the gentlemen fight?" Celia threw her French lesson book down.

"No. Not until you have memorized your list of words."

"Dey be finish den." She gave Clarissa a challenging, sideways glance.

Clarissa, who knew by now that Celia could speak perfectly well when she chose, ignored her.

Outside, through the large glass doors, open to let in a breeze, March and Allen fenced. Clarissa heard the rattle of foils, the occasional laugh or gasp of effort. When she glanced out, she saw a crowd of slaves had gathered to watch.

Celia clasped her book to her chest, shut her eyes tight in concentration, and gabbled some French to herself.

"Are you ready?" Clarissa asked.

"*Le chien*, dog; *le cheval*, horse; *le cochon*, pig; *l'oiseau*, bird; *le boeuf,* cow; *la chat,* cat; *le mouton,* sheep," Celia chanted, a female Noah taking inventory of her ark.

"Very good. And what about the word for chicken?"

"I said the word for bird," Celia pointed out.

"You did. And the chicken?"

"Oh . . ." Celia's brow creased. *"La poule!"* she cried in triumph and ran outside.

Clarissa bent to pick the French primer from the floor, where it had tumbled as Celia made her escape. As she straightened, she heard Celia's scream.

"Papa! Papa!"

Clarissa's first thought was that Allen had killed him when she ran outside and saw both Allen, his foil still in his hand, and Celia crouching over March's slumped body.

"March!" So much for discretion in front of his daughter. March looked ill, with blue lips, and he scarcely seemed to be breathing. He was more like a corpse than a living man. "Oh God, Allen, what's happened to him?"

"I don't know. We were fencing and he swooned." Allen pushed gently at Celia. "Let him have some air, girl. Fan him if you want to be useful." He unbuttoned March's cuffs as he spoke.

Finch, impassive as ever, arrived. "Let me see to Mr. Lemarchand, sir," he said to Allen. He directed some of the slaves to carry their master indoors, and the rest of them followed.

Clarissa put her arm around Celia, who was crying uncontrollably. "We must send for a physician, Finch."

"I've done so, Miss Onslowe, as soon as I heard the master was taken badly again."

"Again?" Allen looked furious. He tossed his foil onto the table, where it landed on Celia's French book and rolled onto the floor. "This happened yesterday, too, and he assured me he was perfectly well." He turned to the milling, excited slaves. "Don't you have work to do? Get out of here."

On the sofa, March sighed. "Allen, please do stop shouting."

"Damn you, March, you told me yesterday you had consulted your physician!"

"It is nothing," March said, his voice feeble. "Pray do not create such a commotion."

Finch intervened. "Brandy, sir."

A little color returned to March's face after he drank. He smiled at his daughter and Clarissa. "Celia, I am perfectly well. Don't cry."

"I thought you were dead, Papa!" Celia flung herself onto her knees and sobbed on his shoulder.

"You can see I'm not. I shall retire upstairs and rest, and I'll be perfectly well in a little while." March patted her arm. He looked at Clarissa, a mute appeal in his eyes—*Take her out of here, please.*

"Come, Celia," Clarissa said. "Your papa needs to rest. Let's fetch our bonnets and go into the garden with our sketchbooks."

Allen waited outside the bedchamber while the physician conferred with March. He had offered to stay, but March shook his head, and after a while Finch emerged and escorted Allen downstairs to cool his heels. He paced around, getting in the way of slaves who swept and dusted—a lot of them, working with little energy, and he wondered if they were concerned about their master.

After a while a rather seedy-looking fellow dressed in dusty black arrived and in a strong Irish accent introduced himself as Father O'Brien. Allen stared at the slightly ridiculous figure ascending the staircase. A priest. March had sent for a priest, which could mean only one thing— he believed he was dying.

From the drawing room came the sound of hesitant scales on the pianoforte—the women must have come back inside. Allen went to join them, and found Celia, her face streaked with tears, hunched over the pianoforte. Clarissa sat close to her, silent. She looked up with hope as Allen entered.

"You have news?" Clarissa asked.

"I regret not."

"You said the same happened yesterday."

"Yes, March blamed it on the heat."

But March had recovered enough to ride home. This time March had made no effort to stand or to disguise his weakness.

Clarissa subsided and took Celia's hand.

"You should eat something," Allen said. He had been aware of clocks striking as time passed, but taken little notice of them. Surely it must be afternoon now, by the heat and stuffiness of the house.

Both women shook their heads.

"I'm hungry. I'd be obliged if you keep me company.

Your father will not get better if you make yourself ill, Miss Celia." Allen called out to the nearest footman and told him to serve some food—no, he did not care, whatever the cook had at hand, something cold would be preferable— cold meat and fruit and bread. He wasn't hungry either, but it gave them something to do while they waited.

And waited.

Allen didn't tell Clarissa and Celia about the priest.

Finch emerged, finally, and announced that Celia should see her father alone, upstairs, in his bedchamber.

"Do you think I should return to my father's house?" Allen asked Clarissa.

"No." She grasped his hand. "No. Please, stay. He will want you here."

Allen released her hand. "Very well."

As though having her hands occupied might somehow help, Clarissa sank down into a chair and took up a piece of abandoned embroidery that Celia worked on from time to time. After a few minutes, she tossed the needlework to one side and rose to pace up and down, much as Allen had before. "I cannot bear it, Allen."

He longed to take her into his arms and comfort her, but she seemed stern, remote.

Finch entered the room. His expression was exactly the same as always: a blank slate. "Miss Celia will dine with Mr. Lemarchand upstairs and stay with him until her bedtime." He paused. "Mr. Lemarchand has requested the pleasure of your company later tonight, Miss Onslowe. And yours, Mr. Pendale."

"He must be well, then," Clarissa said after Finch had

left. She clutched Allen's sleeve with the intensity of a drowning woman. "He has to be. If he wants us both."

"Of course," Allen said. He decided, again, it was best not to mention the priest's visit.

Clarissa dressed with care for the night. First, she had new stays—ones that required someone to lace her into them and were lined with silk, for she was to be naked beneath them. Nerissa stepped forward to assist her, eyes downcast.

March had made his wishes plain when the dressmaker and stay maker called to dress Mr. Lemarchand's mistress. He wanted her breasts exposed, pushed high above her stays; he wanted her jeweled and perfumed; and so others might not gaze upon his property, she should wear a thin muslin scarf tucked inside her bodice. When they were alone, she would expose her jeweled breasts to him.

Behind Clarissa, Nerissa threaded the lace of the stays tight. Clarissa stared at herself in the mirror. *Indecent*— that was the word that sprang to mind. The stays ended at her hips, leaving her quim exposed for March's pleasure.

She clipped the strand of jewels to her nipples and dabbed perfume in the hollow between her breasts. Her new gown slipped over her head, weightless, a whisper of fabric, with an underskirt that almost hid her. Almost. In certain lights, and certainly for anyone looking closely enough, you could see the shadow between her thighs, the hint of dark garters above her knee.

Clarissa dismissed Nerissa and waited for Finch's tap at the door.

As usual the valet led her through the house and stood back for her to enter March's bedchamber.

Allen, casual in shirtsleeves and breeches, lounged on the bed, chatting easily with March. She caught a few words before Allen rose to bow—Allen seemed to be arguing for the introduction of crops that would not require such a concentration of labor as sugar.

"Yes, but this is not good soil. It's too heavy, and requires much manure to make it productive," Lemarchand was saying. He smiled at her. "Clarissa, my dear. How charming you look. What do you think, Allen?"

Allen stared at her, anger in his eyes. Oh yes, he remembered that particular piece of jewelry. But his gaze was hot with lust, too, taking her in, her lifted breasts, the translucent gown. "She looks like an object of pleasure," he said after a pause.

She flushed. Her nipples tightened and stung.

"Now, Allen." March patted his hand. "Wouldn't you say she looks like an object to be pleasured? Come here, my dear." He beckoned Clarissa to his side and took her hand.

She bent to kiss him. "Are you well, sir?"

"I am trying to persuade myself that a bleeding and the prospect of a lowering diet have made me so," he said with a grimace. "No brandy, I fear, although I am allowed a little wine. Pour us some, Clarissa, and now you are here, I can tell you of my condition."

She handed glasses of wine to the two men and sat beside March, uneasy. His voice had an ironic inflection on the word *condition,* and he did not look well, his face almost colorless against the creamy white of the pillows, contrasting sharply with the dark hair that fell to his shoulders.

He smiled at them. "My physician tells me"—he swirled the wine in his glass, staring at the deep ruby liquid—"that I must rest tonight, and I admit to being somewhat fatigued. So, my dears, now you are both here, oblige me." March nodded toward Clarissa's bosom.

She understood; she took the piece of gauze from her bodice, revealing her nipples and the strand of jewels that constrained them.

Allen swallowed.

"Wait." March's hand landed on hers, unfolded her fingers from the fabric and tossed it aside. "This at least I can do." He lifted her breasts in his hand and kissed the hard nipples through the transparent fabric. "Allen, are you willing?"

Allen frowned. "To do what, exactly?"

March laid a hand on his thigh. "I wish to watch you and Clarissa."

"You've seen me fuck her," Allen replied.

"To be honest, Allen, I should like to see a little more finesse, a little more flair. Besides, I do not believe you would deny the wishes of an ill man."

"You know, I think you are taking advantage of us." Clarissa said.

"Quite likely." March leaned back against his pillows. "I am feeling somewhat fatigued. I trust you will obey me. You are my mistress, after all."

"I, however, have no financial arrangement with you," Allen said.

"Very true." March, a wicked gleam in his eyes, addressed Clarissa. "You may proceed alone, my dear. The ivory item, I think, will be most stimulating—for us all."

"I shall need some help undressing," Clarissa said.

"I am sure Allen will oblige."

Allen, muttering under his breath, undid the hooks of her gown. Behind her, he drew in his breath as the gown floated to the floor like a piece of gossamer.

She turned to face both men from the foot of the bed, wearing now only the playfully indecent stays and stockings and garters

"On second thought," March said, "I believe that is all the undressing you need to do. What do you think, Allen?"

"Christ." He shifted in a way that indicated to Clarissa that he had an inconvenient erection.

March gazed at the front flap of Allen's breeches and smiled. "I trust you're not uncomfortable, Allen."

Clarissa strolled away from the two men to the tall japanned cabinet where March kept his curios, erotic and otherwise—shells, the skull of a small animal, some tiny, intricately carved statues of jade, and the inlaid box that held the phallus. As she bent to retrieve the box, she heard the sharp hiss of Allen's breath.

She sauntered back to them, offering the box to Allen. "I believe you may find this interesting."

He examined the erotic decoration of the box, undid

the catch, pulled away the silk wrapping, and became absolutely still.

Clarissa ran her finger down the smooth ivory surface. "It's very hard. Quite large, too."

Allen looked up at her, eyes twinkling, his equilibrium apparently recovered. "Oh, I'm sure you'll manage."

She gave a sigh of mock dismay. "Well, it seems there is nothing else on offer, so I shall have to make the best of it." She lifted the phallus from its silken nest.

Both men watched as she slid the ivory between her breasts. "It is best not to deal with the item when it is cool," she explained in a helpful tone.

She settled on the bed between the two men, her shoulders on March's knees, forcing Allen to move farther down the bed. She placed one foot on his leg, casually allowing her thighs to fall open. March tugged gently at the strand of jewels between her breasts, and shocks of pain and delight thrummed through her, down to thighs and belly and quim. He bent to kiss her.

Allen's hand landed on her ankle, moved up her leg, tickled the soft skin inside her thigh.

March lifted his head. "Tell me what her quim looks like, Allen."

Allen cleared his throat. "Wet and plump. Her lips there are parted."

Clarissa lowered the phallus between her thighs and rubbed the smooth head against her tickler.

March plucked at the jewels again. "See how the clips engorge her nipples. Pretty, is it not?"

Allen stared at her, at the phallus moving between her thighs. "Put it in," he said, his voice rough.

He stood to pull his shirt over his head. His cock was erect, pushing against the fall of his breeches.

As she slid the phallus inside her, she heard the thud of his boots falling to the floor. His breeches and drawers were down in a second. He knelt between her outstretched thighs and placed his hand over hers, watching the slide—she imagined the stark white of the phallus sinking into her own wet, pink folds—what he could see. His cock jutted dark and hard, a drop of moisture hanging on the tip.

Allen leaned to briefly kiss March's mouth, then lowered his head to hers. His kiss was long, slow, ardent—as intimate as though they were alone and not on display. For a moment the warmth of the Caribbean night and the richness of March's bedchamber swirled away, and they were alone in the darkness of a rocking ship.

"Finesse," March murmured, bringing her back to the present—her head rested on his thigh still, his hands toyed with her captured breasts.

Allen bent his head to lick March's fingers and then turned his attention to Clarissa's engorged nipples. She cried out at the pressure and heat of his mouth, twisting beneath him. Her next cry was of disappointment as the phallus slid from her, and Allen lifted and turned her, arranging her for March's benefit, her legs parted wide, one foot on his own shoulder.

Allen's penetration slowed time, as though they could pause the shift of a clock's hand or the wheel of stars in the heavens, making all subject to the beat of their pulses, the slow trickle of sweat between her breasts. In this place beyond time, she was wild and greedy, straining to reach her climax while Allen held back, checked her.

"You're so close," Allen murmured. "You grip my cock like death, like love."

Allen slid from Clarissa, licking down her belly and into her quim while she squirmed and clutched his hair, cursing him to get back—*Now, Allen, now.*

March laughed. He reached for Allen's cock.

"Damn you, he's mine!" Clarissa shouted. She drew her legs up, almost kneeing Allen's chin, and knocked him off balance, onto his back.

"Take me, then!" Allen shouted back. He looked mad with lust, sweat darkening the hair on his chest, his teeth bared in a grimace.

She took Allen, ravished him. Scrambled astride him, his wrists captured in her hands while he cursed and thrust beneath her, inside her, and strained against her, fighting for his orgasm as she fought for hers.

Damn finesse. Clarissa collapsed onto Allen's chest, both of them sucking in air as though they had nearly drowned. His heart thudded madly against her, their bodies stuck together with sweat—there was a strange sort of comfort, a peace in their sprawled embrace. She pressed her face into Allen's neck and inhaled his familiar scent. In a moment, just a moment, she should disentangle herself from him—his cock was still hard inside her, and she moved a little to capture a faint flutter of her pleasure.

Allen groaned and clamped one hand onto her arse. She wasn't sure if it was complaint or encouragement.

Allen's breathing slowed. He turned his head to plant a kiss on her forehead and she felt, rather than heard, a slow rumble of laughter, her signal to disengage.

March had not said a word, nor made a sound—possibly she would not have even noticed if he had, so intent had she been on Allen and their mutual release. Now she turned her face to March's, seeking his approval at their performance.

March sat as still as any statue, his face gaunt and pale. He held out a hand to Clarissa. "I'm dying."

CHAPTER 21

"Dying?" Beside Clarissa, Allen pushed himself up onto one elbow.

She felt a terrible shame at her nakedness, at her absorption with her own pleasure, and struggled to cover herself with the sheets.

Allen retrieved and refilled their wineglasses. "What the devil do you mean, March?"

March continued. "The problem, apparently, is my heart—a flaw in its construction, something that hitherto has not inconvenienced me at all, until now. My physician orders me a lowering diet and forbids me any sort of exertion if I wish to live."

A drop of red wine fell from Clarissa's glass to the sheet. Stupidly she watched the red bloom and spread among the interlaced fibers. Someone—she thought it must have been Allen—took the glass from her hand. She heard the small click as the glass was placed on a solid surface.

March continued. "I wish I could say I was sufficiently heroic to laugh in the face of death and continue as I live now. Unfortunately, that is not my choice. I have a child for whom I am responsible, and for her sake, I must keep alive. I must try, although my physician tells me that even with the most valiant of efforts, death could take me at any time. Today that almost happened."

March's voice became gentle. "Clarissa? You say nothing. I am most sorry to have brought this upon you."

"You have nothing to apologize for. How absurd . . . Does Celia know . . . ?" His face blurred in her vision.

"That I am under sentence of death? No, only that I am ill and that we shall seek passage home from the Earl of Frensham when his next ship is laden."

Someone, Allen, pushed a piece of fabric in her hand. Linen, strong, soft with wear. A handkerchief to blot the tears streaming down her face.

March continued. "So I must live as a monk. No riding, fencing, swimming. I must keep mostly to my bed, but there is to be no carnal excitement, to use the physician's quaint expression." He handed his wineglass to Allen and took their hands in his. "It is a great regret to me. And a great puzzle to me, too. I suppose the physician believes my body will oblige; I assure you it does not. My illness makes an impotence of my potency."

Allen looked angry, quite ludicrously so for a man completely naked and with a half-erect cock. "You use Clarissa and me as your playthings and then toy with us further by announcing your impending demise? How do we even know you speak the truth?" He laughed. "Oh,

I suppose it's true. After all you confessed your sins to the priest today. You'd better send for him again after tonight."

"You sent for your priest?" If Clarissa had had any doubts, now she knew it to be true—March believed he would die soon. Tears flooded her eyes again. "I'm sorry."

"Don't cry, my dear." March reached gently for her breasts and unclipped the jewels. "Allen, try not to be so angry with me, I beg you."

Allen shook his head, muttering. He reached for his drawers and pulled them on. "Are you—the physician, that is—absolutely sure?"

"There is no doubt. Death could come at any time, although I pray it will not be too inconvenient."

"Are your affairs in order?" Allen asked. "If I may offer my professional assistance . . ."

"Thank you. I believe they are, although I should be grateful if you could go over a few items for me." March smiled and held out a hand to Allen. "May I further beg your indulgence by asking for some time alone with Clarissa?"

"Of course. I'll bid you good night."

When Allen had left, Clarissa reached for her gown. March's hand on her wrist stilled her. "You misunderstand. The physician did not forbid me the use of my eyes. I would not see you shamed."

She waited to see what he required of her. He said nothing. "Sir, do you feel ill?"

He shook his head and took a deep breath.

She saw, to her horror, that this proud, reserved man was about to weep. With no words she took his head onto her breast and held him while he cried.

Allen returned to his father's house the next day. To his surprise, he hadn't wanted to leave March; he certainly didn't want to leave Clarissa. She, however, was teaching Celia, and he had no opportunity to speak alone with her. Besides, his father was now home, and Allen had to play the role of the dutiful son.

"You're looking much better, sir," he said, with a noble effort to keep any sense of irony or disgust from his voice as they visited his father's fields. They rode along side by side beneath the blazing blue of the sky, the horses' shadows sharp and black against the sparse golden grass. A flock of birds flew from a thorn tree as they approached.

"Ah, well, a change of air, you know . . ." The earl nodded to his overseers, who doffed their hats. "I'm thinking of clearing the trees there for another field. What do you think?"

Allen chatted of agricultural matters with his father and waited for a pause in the conversation. "Sir," he said finally, interrupting his father's speculation on future sugar and ginger prices, "there is a matter much on my mind. Who is my father?"

"Why . . . I am, for God's sake." Frensham jerked at the reins, his face reddening, and kicked his mare around. "We should return for dinner."

Allen kicked his own horse forward to draw level with

his father. He grasped the mare's bridle so his father could not ride on. The two horses danced and sidled together. "I mean no disrespect to you or my mother, but I must know, purely for my own peace of mind. It takes little to discern that you and my brothers and sisters are of a different breed."

"A different breed!" His father gave a harsh laugh. "I suggest you drop the subject."

"I cannot." Allen released his hold on the mare's bridle, but anger and apprehension made him tighten his grip on the reins of his own mount. "I know there is more to the matter than you wish to tell me. I found some troubling evidence—what it means I am not sure, but I must hear your side of it."

"What evidence?"

"A letter from my mother's sister, written when I was two years of age."

His father clicked his tongue and the mare moved forward. "We should walk the horses to cool them off. There is one thing only, Allen. If I speak of this, I must have your word that you will return to England as soon as possible."

"I thought you had already arranged that, sir."

"So I did." His father flushed. "I assure you it was for your well-being. But you must agree to leave as I ask."

They rode back to the house in silence and met in Frensham's office. Allen had never seen the earl so ill at ease.

"Sit," his father barked.

"Only if you will, sir." Allen used the calm voice that was so effective in putting a client at ease.

The earl glared at him and continued to pace.

"Very well, sir." Allen handed him the letter and watched carefully as his father read. He knew the section by heart, slipped in between accounts of domestic activities and news of acquaintances long forgotten.

I am glad to hear the child settles in well, but am surprised, indeed, that Frensham acknowledges him as of his blood, and further that you choose to name him after our dear papa. If as you say he is not too dark, then all will be well and certainly we shall never speak of his origins.

His father folded the letter and shook his head. "I wish to God . . ."

"In addition," Allen said, "my sister told me that she did not remember my birth, but only that I appeared suddenly, at the age of two or thereabouts, and creating much trouble, breaking her dolls, and babbling in a language only I understood."

"Some things are best left undisturbed," his father said. "This is one of them." He slumped into the chair behind the desk looking older and somehow defeated.

"I regret it is too late. You must tell me, sir."

"Some twenty-five years ago," his father said, "your mother—Lady Frensham, that is—lost a child. She was much cast down, as I was when I received the news in a letter from England. Her physician had told her she must bear no more children, and although she loved her surviving children, she suffered greatly. I made plans to return to England when I received the news, and took with me one of my natural children. I thought—"

"A moment, sir. What does this have to do with me?" What was his father saying?

"You were that child, Allen."

Allen's mind struggled to make sense of his father's words. "You brought me from here—from the island?"

"Yes. This is why you must return to England—"

"Wait." Allen sat opposite his father. "You are saying that I am—I am the child of—"

Allen's father met his gaze. "Yes. Your mother was a slave." He added, in a shamed rush, "She was the daughter of one of my overseers, and her own mother had a fair amount of English blood. I assure you there was very little of Africa in her, or in you, for that matter, but you do see now why I—"

"Why you lied to me?" Despite the stuffy warmth of the office, Allen felt cold, chilled with disgust and rage. He remembered black pages owned by wealthy women in England—tiny boys decked out in jeweled, feathered turbans and silk livery. "So you took me to your wife as some sort of plaything—you thought she should have a negro lapdog to console her?"

"I assure you, she came to love you as her own child—"

"And my own mother? What of her? Does she live still?" Allen doubted it. Slaves did not live long here. She—the woman who had given birth to him—must be long dead.

"Her name was Jenny. She gave birth to you when she was fifteen." His father stared straight ahead. "I trust you will do nothing foolish. I believe my overseer sold her shortly after our departure."

"You realize, sir, my position here is somewhat precarious. I may be now someone else's property—yours at any rate. No wonder you are so eager to get me off the island, to spare yourself embarrassment. And to whom did you sell my mother?"

"I'm not sure," his father said. He cleared his throat and gazed at his locked hands. "A number of transactions took place then. I—"

"No matter," Allen said. "I'm familiar enough with your accounts that I can find the truth out for myself. And I shall do so." He stood, shaking with rage. "Do you not realize what you did? That there is a part of me that is a terrified two-year-old child who seeks his mother still? I have dreamed of that voyage to England all my life, not understanding until now why."

Allen pulled down ancient ledgers from the shelves. They landed on the desk in a shower of dust, knocking papers onto the floor.

"Allen, I beg you—"

"Leave me."

It took less than an hour to find the record of Allen's mother's sale, leafing through the pages of the account book from twenty-six years ago. An insect of some sort had attacked the book, drilling a neat hole through the pages and leather cover, so that when Allen opened it, a cloud of fine dust arose. Allen stared at the entry in shock.

Amos, Jenny, Hiram, Peter, Grace, and their children.

No other details, nothing of age or gender, not even a specification of whose children they actually were. It didn't matter. Children were not expected to live, but if they did . . . Was this some act of clemency on his father's part, to keep children with their parents? And now his father's mercy was about to rebound on his youngest child. You didn't have to be a lawyer to untangle the vagueness of that description.

And their children. Among whom was a man who had grown up to be Allen Pendale, Esquire, lawyer and would-be country gentleman.

The second shock was the name of their new owner. Lemarchand.

Allen was black, a slave—now he could see it in the tint of his skin, his dark eyes. No longer an English gentleman. Not here. On the island he was a slave, a chattel, a possession. No wonder his father was nervous on his son's account; it was no surprise that Allen, alone among his brothers, had never been invited to the island estate.

The full enormity, the shame of his discovery, washed over him in a great tide of pain and loneliness. Everything he had ever believed in, everything had thought to be the truth, everything he knew of himself—it was false or altered beyond repair.

He dropped his face into his hands and wept.

When he stopped weeping, the light had changed—the study was in darkness. He wiped his face with his shirtsleeves, stood, and unbolted the study door. He pushed it open to find Reuben, his father's majordomo, standing there.

"His lordship, 'im want to know if you need anything, sah."

Reuben thought I was a negro when I arrived unexpectedly at dusk that day.

"Some beer, if you please." Allen's voice still sounded the same, if a trifle hoarse. The voice of an educated English gentleman.

"Yes, sah."

"Wait. Reuben, did you know Jenny—a slave who was sold some twenty-five years ago?"

Reuben looked away. "Dat a long time, sah. Lots of girls sold."

Reuben knew. Surely he knew. Allen reached into his pocket. He pulled out a shilling and showed it to Reuben. "Does this refresh your memory?"

"No, sah. I fetch de beer, sah." Reuben backed away, and Allen wondered if his father had told him not to answer any questions.

Allen rode out again the next day and watched the slaves toiling in the fields. A veil had been lifted from his eyes; he noted the variations of skin color, from deep ebony to the color of creamy coffee. So much was clear now: the anomaly of a dark child among slender, fair-haired siblings; his surprise, when he traveled in Italy, at how he was taken for a native of that country, where curling dark hair and bronzed skin were the norm. He considered that his father might have other bastards, and his mother, too. How many of these men and women he looked down on from the horse's back, and who would not meet his white man's gaze, was he related to?

The anger and shame of his origins burned, a wound as permanent as any slave's brand.

⁂

For three days he rode up and down Lemarchand's lands, asking, always asking, *Did you know a woman named Jenny? Do you know if she lives still?* His questions were met with sullen silence or cowed shakes of the head. He saw Blight occasionally from a distance; the fellow touched his hat as was proper, but now Allen saw a sinister mockery in the gesture.

Allen returned each evening to his father's house, where they dined together, stiffly formal. Allen tried to ignore the pleading expression he occasionally saw on his father's face.

Finally it occurred to Allen that his mother might well be named something else now, and his questioning was in vain. He knew word must have reached March that Allen Pendale rode his fields, questioning his slaves. Sooner or later he should call at the house and explain.

The most extraordinary thing, March. I need to buy one of your slaves. Seems she's my mother and I'm your property.

⁂

Allen was weary, the sun beginning its precipitous drop to the horizon while color flamed in the sky, and he decided to call on March there and then. Under normal circumstances of course he would have called sooner, to visit a dying friend. He thought March was his friend, at any rate. Whether March would be his friend in the future was another matter. But of course he would—hadn't March expressed his love for Allen?

Allen approached the house from the fields, winding through the scattered outbuildings and houses that made up March's enterprise. Ahead was the kitchen, attached to the house by a covered wooden walkway, the air thick with the scents of cooking and woodsmoke. He was weary, thirsty, and sweaty after being in the saddle all day. Surely the kitchen could provide him with some beer and a basin of water to wash his face and hands. He pulled his horse to a halt, dismounted, and tethered the animal to a small tree.

From the inside of the kitchen came voices, mainly female, and laughter. He knew as soon as they saw him the laughter and intimacy would cease, and he would be regarded as an intruder come to spoil what little amusement they had in their lives.

He stepped onto the wooden walkway and pushed open the kitchen door. As he expected, silence fell, followed by some scuffles as people who probably shouldn't be there headed for the far door.

Others became busy with chopping, mincing, sieving, doing various tasks, apparently absorbed in their work. All except for one woman who stood staring at him, a pottery bowl in the crook of one elbow, a whisk in her other hand. The whisk fell to the floor with a clatter, rolled, and was still. The pottery bowl slid against the woman's apron; she made a halfhearted attempt to grasp it, and that too slid down, spilling a froth of something pale and fluffy—eggs, it must have been eggs—onto the floor.

The bowl rolled to his feet, miraculously unbroken.

"I t'ought my pappy walk again." Her voice was deep and rich—his voice, in female form—or it would have been if she spoke in anything greater than a whisper.

"I—" He stepped forward.

She shrank away. "Who you, sah?"

"Who are *you*?" He countered, but he knew.

Behind her the other slaves had gathered into a knot, whispering and rustling together, their work abandoned.

"Leave us," Allen said to them. They didn't move. "Go!" he shouted at them—something he regretted because he sounded like an overseer—and they rushed for the far door.

The woman still stared at Allen in terror—a handsome woman, with high cheekbones like his own beneath a turban of white linen, skin the color his would be if he stayed out in the sun all day (he'd been that dark in Italy), but now with a grayish cast from shock.

He took a step forward.

Eyes wide, she held up her hands, in supplication or to stop him, he wasn't sure which.

He spread his own hands, broad, long-fingered like hers. *Look, we are alike.*

She gripped her linen apron with both hands.

"I'm Allen." He stepped into the kitchen, not wanting to alarm her further, and pushed a three-legged stool toward her. "You'd best sit down."

She looked at him now as if he were mad. A white man offering a slave a seat?

"Sit," he said. It came out like an order. He winced. "If you please," he added.

She sat.

Something hissed at the fire, a pot boiling over, and she jumped to her feet, moved pot hooks to adjust heat, stirred a couple of things with a large spoon, and, wiping her hands on her apron, faced him. She looked him over without shyness or fear as though attending to familiar tasks had restored her, and gave a quick, approving nod.

Fifteen when she gave birth to him—so that made her three and forty or thereabouts, a handsome woman, quick on her feet. Not young, but tough and strong. His mother.

"I don't remember you," Allen said. He'd hoped that seeing her might force some memory to the surface.

She shrugged. "You too little when 'im take you 'way. It don' matter. I 'member. Now you look jus' like my pappy." She stepped forward and touched his coat. " 'Im made you a gentleman."

"Yes. Yes, I'm a lawyer."

She nodded, pleased, although he wasn't sure she knew what a lawyer was. "You a clever baby," she said. "Dat's why 'im favor you so."

She meant his father, Allen supposed. "I'll buy your freedom."

She raised her chin with a flash of defiance. "I save for dat."

"Then I'll add to what you have."

"And den what?"

"Whatever you like. You could come to England. I have a farm—much smaller than this, quite different. There are no slaves. I need a housekeeper, someone to look after the place."

"Why you no got a wife?" She touched his wrist very lightly. "You handsome enough."

"The last woman I asked refused me."

"Ah. Dat Miss Onslowe."

"How did you know?"

She smiled. "We know everyt'in'."

He hoped not. "I'll talk to Mr. Lemarchand about your freedom. I'm sure he'll understand."

She looked uneasy for a moment, then touched his hand. "I glad 'im took you 'way even though I cry and cry. Better'n stayin' here." Something caught her attention at the fireplace, and she darted back to rake fresh coals under a pot on a trivet. She padded over to a cask and drew him a mug of beer as though sensing his thirst, but whether it was a maternal instinct or merely the act of a well-trained domestic, he couldn't tell. "You seen me. Now you go."

"But—"

"Go. I got work to do, and I need dem other slaves back, or dinner be late and de master get angry."

"When may I see you again?"

She looked at him, her dark eyes somber. "Tomorrow. I got to t'ink what to do. I don' know. . . . You gone too long. You a man now." She repeated, "You go and come back tomorrow."

Allen's throat tightened. "What should I call you?"

She took the empty mug from his hand and smiled. "Dey call me Ceres."

CHAPTER 22

"My dear fellow!" March gestured in typical lordly fashion from a chaise longue set in his study. Papers cascaded from his lap to the floor. "Come in, do. You are a welcome distraction from tedious business affairs. Forgive me if I do not rise."

He looked, Allen thought, more like a pasha or some sort of Oriental king than usual, draped in a silk dressing gown, black silk embroidered with red-and-gold dragons, and a loose shirt and trousers.

"How are you, sir?" As usual, Allen found himself responding to March's warm affection. He clasped the other man's hand in his.

March grimaced. "I find the nights somewhat difficult—no, not for the reason you imagine, sir—merely that sometimes I have trouble breathing. I fear I wear Clarissa out. But how are you? Is there something that troubles you?"

"Yes, sir, there is." Allen delayed the unpleasant task by pouring them both wine—watered wine, rather, for March could only drink it that way—and sat on one of the chairs. March didn't look well, his slenderness turning to gauntness, eyes shadowed.

Allen took a sip of his wine. "I'm come on business, sir."

"Ah, it's good of you to help Frensham. Of course—what can I do for you?"

Allen reached into his coat for the bank draft he had persuaded his father to write. "I wish to buy the freedom of one of your slaves."

March's eyebrows raised. "Not Nerissa? My dear fellow, you can have her anytime you want, with my blessing. I assure you there is no need to go to the trouble of buying her."

"No. Not Nerissa." Had March offered his mother to his guests in such casual fashion?

"Which one, then?"

"Ceres."

"My cook?" March grinned. "Oh, good heavens, Allen, I couldn't stand to lose my cook. And she's a little long in the tooth for you, I would have thought—"

God only knew what sort of expression Allen had on his face. March stared at him until Allen, realizing he loomed over the sick man, fists clenched, stepped back.

"I beg your pardon, Allen," March said. "I seem to have offended you. Please tell what it is that upsets you so."

"She's my mother."

"Your mother?" March's voice and demeanor changed. He pulled the silk dressing gown to himself as though for protection. "You'd best tell me."

As Allen told the story, he found himself standing, pacing. He poured more wine, tapped spilled papers on the desk into shape, gazed out of the window.

He ended with an attempt at humor. "And so, you see, I'm technically your property, as far as I can tell from the wording of the sale, now I am returned to the island. Of course, you know me as the Earl of Frensham's son and an English gentleman, but you must understand, I have concern for my mother, to whom my family must make amends."

Only then did Allen dare look at March. In the dim light March's eyes were deep shadows. Allen heard March take a long, shuddering breath.

"Are you well, March?" Alarmed, Allen stepped toward him, his hand outstretched.

March flinched. "Don't touch me!" He gazed at Allen with a terrible coldness. "I am under no obligation to sell any of my slaves, for any reason. You expect me to grant you this favor after you have denied me my heart's desire?"

"Sir, I have told you I cannot force love where there is none. I can and do offer friendship—"

"Friendship!" March spat the word back at him. "You presume too much, Allen. After all, you are my property, as you say."

There was a short silence. Then Allen said, "Perhaps I should return with my father. I have taken the liberty of preparing a manumission for Ceres and a bank draft for you, sir."

March looked at Allen as though he offered excrement. Allen lowered his arm and laid the papers on March's desk.

"As you wish. Call for lights, if you please. And ask them to send Finch." March's voice was remote and formal.

When a lamp had been brought into the room, March, leaning on Finch's arm, made his way to the desk, where he told Finch to sharpen a pen, and wrote a brief note.

Allen offered March his arm to return to the couch, but March ignored him and accepted Finch's help before sending off the valet with the note.

"It's a devilishly awkward situation," Allen said. "I'm sorry to have . . . I see you're tired, sir. I'll call on Miss Celia and Clarissa if I may and then return to my father's house."

"No!" Again, a sudden, violent reaction. "Neither Miss Lemarchand nor Miss Onslowe is receiving visitors."

"I'll leave you then, sir." Allen bowed. "My father and I will call on you tomorrow."

"Yes, yes." March turned his face away.

"May I send for someone, sir? You don't look well."

"Go."

Alarmed that he had shocked March with his news, Allen left. Telling his story had not proved as cathartic as he hoped; maybe he should have told Clarissa first. She would have been able to break the news tactfully to March and persuade him to agree to Allen's request.

Or would she, too, have been repulsed? Was that what he'd seen in March's expression, and not been able to comprehend it at the time?

The sky was a hushed violet, the first stars appearing as Allen wandered outside and headed for the stable, where he had left his horse. The scent of tobacco floated toward him.

"Pendale!"

Allen turned in surprise. "Good evening to you, Blight."

Blight strolled forward. He carried his whip, coiled lightly over one arm, a cheroot clamped between his teeth. "Your choice, Pendale—you may accompany me quietly, or these gentlemen will persuade you to be docile."

A clanking sound came from the shadows. Two large, man-shaped shadows separated themselves from the darkness and moved toward Allen. He saw the gleam of their eyes and teeth, the gleam of metal. Castor and Pollux, Blight's muscle-bound assistants, carried shackles and ropes.

"What the devil are you up to?" Allen demanded. A terrible, cold fear gripped him.

One of them—he couldn't tell Castor or Pollux from each other—laid a large hand on his arm.

Allen stepped back, outraged. "Take your hands off me!"

"Chain him up, boys," Blight said in a casual sort of tone.

"The devil you will!" Allen dodged away, and kicked his assailant hard on the kneecap. The man staggered back, cursing. "You'll have the Earl of Frensham to answer to for this."

Blight laughed. "Indeed?"

Something lashed out, like the flight of a bird through the air, a bird that clawed the side of his face and eyebrow. Allen clutched in terror at his face, fearing blindness. As he shook the blood off and prepared to defend himself, Castor and Pollux advanced on him, fists like dark lumps of meat.

Blight removed his cheroot from his mouth. "Your choice, Pendale."

"I'll see you in hell!"

Blight nodded to Castor and Pollux.

Darkness. A pain in Allen's shoulders, something hard and gritty beneath him, and the taste of dried blood in his mouth. He couldn't move—not his arms, at any rate. Was he dead? Or blind? Probably not dead. He could smell the stink of human waste and hear the whine of a mosquito and the chitter and scratch of rats.

He stretched out his legs cautiously. Grit and sharp things that were probably stones—and he could feel them so distinctly because he was stark naked. Other hurts began to make themselves known, tender areas on his face and ribs, and the devil of a headache.

Castor and Pollux had done a thorough job.

Now he remembered. March had betrayed him. March, who had once begged for Allen's love, whom Allen had come to care for in a way he didn't quite understand.

Allen moved his head and shoulders and was rewarded with a burst of nausea that left him weak and sweating. Something clanked. His arms were manacled behind his back, the iron already rubbing his wrists raw, a small and humiliating pain. Something scrabbled in the dirt behind his back, and he lunged out of the way—of course, the rats could smell his blood—and crashed into what felt like a stone wall.

Now he knew where he was—the slave dungeon on March's estate, where disobedient slaves were held captive for days at a time. No one would hear Allen if he shouted—or come to help even if he did. No one would think of looking here for Allen Pendale, Esquire, son of the Earl of Pendale.

He could die in this place of thirst and despair, a nameless slave.

Think, he urged. *Keep alive. Keep those damned rats away. Don't sleep or they'll eat you alive. Don't think about the cramps in your shoulders, or all the bruises and cuts you've doubtless suffered, and particularly don't think about how thirsty you are.*

Cool beer in a pewter mug, handed to you by a woman in a smoky kitchen, a woman with your hands and eyes. The purl and bubble of a small brownish stream edged with marshwillow and sedge and meadow rue in the English countryside. Red wine shared mouth to mouth with Clarissa, licked from her breasts and belly.

None of that. You're not thirsty. Keep awake.

A narrow bar of gray appeared at the floor, grew brighter, and glowed gold, illuminating an inch or so of dirt and stones—daylight at the crack beneath the door. Because Allen felt he must, he crawled over to the door and thudded his shoulder against solid wood, which did not yield. He counted his heartbeats and tried to calculate minutes and hours.

With infinite, delicate slowness, the light beneath the door faded back to gray and left him in total darkness again. He had endured one night and one day.

You're not thirsty. Keep awake.

If he slept, something that happened fairly frequently now, the rats were kind enough to wake him with their teeth.

Hear my prayer, O Lord, and let my cry come unto thee.

Hide not thy face from me in the day when I am in trouble; incline thine ear unto me; in the day when I call answer me speedily.

He was dying, or would die soon in the stifling, cruel heat.

My heart is smitten, and withered like grass.

When the gap beneath the door turned to gray next, he heard the thump of hoofbeats outside and for a moment thought rescue had come, before he recognized Blight's voice.

The harsh metallic sound of the bolt being drawn back filled Allen with unreasonable hope.

Blight, whip in hand, bent down from the mule's back and regarded him with a sneer. He reached for the cropper of the saddle and tossed something toward Allen.

Water. Allen caught the scent of it, the sweetest smell

in the world, and saw an arc of precious silver in the air before the leather bottle landed and spilled its contents into the dirt. Allen flung himself at the bottle, getting a precious mouthful before it soaked away. Not enough to quench his thirst, but certainly enough to moisten his mouth and rasp a stream of obscenities at Blight.

The door slammed shut, the sound of the bolt shoved home terrifyingly loud.

The bar of light brightened and began to dim again.

"Not so much of a gentleman, now, are you?" Blight said.

Allen blinked at the light. A lantern.

"Fuck you, Blight," he said, or tried to say. His mouth was too dry, his lips cracked and bleeding, to say anything.

Either Castor or Pollux hauled Allen to his feet. His knees buckled and he fell down, but outside, thank God, where he could see the last flare of the setting sun. He lay on coarse clumps of grass, wondering what Blight had in store for him next, but not caring. Not anymore, now that he'd seen the sky.

A crack and a line of fire across his ribs roused him.

"On your feet!" Blight's voice. "Damn your eyes. Give him some water."

Water cascaded onto Allen's face and into his open mouth, running into his hair—what a waste—but this surely had to be the best moment of his life, even though someone kicked him quite hard in the ribs and forced him onto his belly. One of the two slaves fumbled behind Allen and undid the shackles, causing instant pain as his arms fell free.

Weak and stupid he stumbled to his feet with a vague idea of running, but was manhandled efficiently by Castor and Pollux, who shackled his arms in the front, fastened a rope to the iron, and tossed the other end to Blight.

Blight mounted his mule and tied the rope to the pommel of his saddle. "Run, boy."

He kicked the mule into a trot and Allen followed. He had no choice but to stumble, weak and sick, behind Blight. More pain as his feet were cut on stones, and his strained shoulders cramped in agony.

But he was alive. "Fuck you, Blight," he whispered, "and may you burn in hell, Lemarchand."

How ironic that now that Clarissa and March were no longer lovers, she slept even less. He frequently demanded her presence in the night, and often during the day, too, as though she alone stood between him and annihilation. She hated to see March, once so cool and arrogant, helpless and afraid.

"Miss, Mr. Finch, 'im say you come." Nerissa, yawning, held a candlestick over Clarissa's bed.

"Does he live?" She was afraid, so afraid. She wondered that she had slept at all.

Nerissa held a wrapper out. " 'Im not well."

"Give me the candlestick!" Clarissa snatched it from Nerissa's hand and set out at a run for March's room, one hand shielding the flame. Her shadow bobbed along, huge and ungainly, her feet pounding on the wooden boards.

Finch waited at March's door for her.

"Have you sent for the physician?" she asked.

Finch shook his head. "He said not to, but he asked for Father O'Brien. He's in there with him now."

Clarissa shook her head in exasperation.

The door opened. "Miss Onslowe, Mr. Lemarchand would like you to come in, if you would," the priest said in his soft brogue.

It was the sight she dreaded above all: March propped up against his pillows gasping for breath, the air of the bedchamber thick with the smoke of burning pastilles. The punkah rose and fell, swirling scented smoke around the room.

"March!" She clutched his hand. "We must send for the physician."

March shook his head. His fingers closed on hers. "Nothing he can do." His voice was hoarse, breathing labored.

"Please, don't die."

He smiled a little at that. "Not . . . not my choice."

She raised his hand to her cheek and kissed his fingers. "I would do anything to have you well once more."

"Must talk." He gestured over his shoulder.

She understood and plumped the pillows, her arm supporting him. Was it her imagination, or did he feel frailer?

He took her hand again and spoke in a hoarse, wheezy voice, pausing frequently to gasp in air. "I fear for Celia.

I may not live long enough to travel to England. She'll be alone."

"But you have family. She has godparents, does she not?"

"Not the same. They don't know her. She'll be in a strange place. Need friends." He coughed, and Clarissa offered him a sip of watered wine.

"She needs you."

"If I accompany her as her governess, which I shall do, then—"

"No!" His fingers tightened, dug into her wrist. "No . . . no status. No say in how her life shall be. My family can't . . ."

"March, what do you want me to do to help? I can write letters for you. I can . . ."

He shook his head. "Not . . . not good enough. Not enough. Not what I need, what she needs."

"You're exhausted," she said. "I'll stay with you until the morning, and when you're rested, we can talk more of this."

He raised himself, a flash of the old arrogance and charm showing. "All very well, if I have until morning. I may not see the sun rise again." He sank back, and pity and love brought tears to her eyes. "Help me and my child, Clarissa. Marry me."

CHAPTER 23

Run, boy.

Allen would kill Blight—he swore it. Meanwhile he had to keep alive, and that meant running, putting one foot down in front of the other, breathing, keeping going, like climbing the rigging. Never mind the pain. Keep alive. Keep running. Allen fixed his eyes on the rope at his wrists, looking ahead at the ground, trying to spare his feet on the rutted track. He wasn't even sure where they were going. Wherever it was could not be good, but anything would be better than being entombed alive. There might even be some water—no, he couldn't think that. Even if he felt he could abase himself, sell his very soul for a mouthful of water, he would not weaken.

Meanwhile one foot in front of the other, dust and blood, the smell of the mule, the smell of himself, the thud of the mule's hooves, the rattle of an occasional dislodged stone. Pain in his side, his head, everywhere. The clatter of hooves on cobbles then, and he slowed to a walk, the rope slackening, and fell facedown in the muck of a cobbled yard, not that it made any difference.

The fanged bird whistled and tore fire across his back.

"Get up!" Blight shouted.

Black spots floated in front of his eyes as he staggered to his feet. The whip caught him again as he was shoved into another place, a beaten-earth floor beneath his battered feet, and he tumbled down, retching and sick.

Someone kicked him in the ribs and tugged at his manacles. He wondered if he were to be freed, but the steel scraped across his wrists, and he heard another metallic sound, that of chains. He really didn't care. The blissful relief of lying down was enough. He would examine his surroundings later.

A door slammed.

He slept.

Allen awoke in a gray light that he thought was probably dawn, swiping wildly at rats, except there were none in this place. He was chained to the wall of a small room with a window, high up; there was a bucket in one corner. It looked like a storage room, a place to store goods; and that was what he was now. In another corner, a jug and a bowl stood. He lunged for the jug, manacles and chains dragging and clanking, and drank. It was some sort of thin beer; he swallowed it all in greedy, desperate gulps. The bowl held porridge, or something equally tasteless and sticky, and he gobbled it up, eating with his fingers.

He was becoming an animal. That was what people said about slaves, wasn't it? Had he thought that, too, even if he'd never actually said it aloud?

He went back to sleep.

"Mr. Pendale!"

Allen woke with a great jangling of chains and clapped his hands over his genitals. "Mrs. Blight. Forgive me if I don't get up."

She stood in the doorway, bright sunlight streaming in, and for one single, idiotic moment, he thought she looked like an angel.

No, he reminded himself, she was a former whore.

"This is dreadful, dreadful," she continued. "What can Blight be thinking of? What shall I do, Mr. Pendale?"

He'd found her feminine flutter attractive before; now it was only an irritation. "Unlock these chains, if you please, ma'am, and have word sent to my father."

"Oh dear. I regret Blight carries the keys and he is out in the fields. I could send one of the slaves, but . . ."

Best to keep Blight out of things. "Send word to the Earl of Frensham, then."

She nodded. "You must be thirsty."

She snapped her fingers and a female slave scuttled into the room, picked up the jug and bowl, and ran out with them. The slave's demeanor suggested Mrs. Blight was not a kind mistress.

"I'll send a boy to the earl's house, and perhaps you should . . ." Murmuring about hot water, she left, closing the door behind her.

Mrs. Blight expected Allen to wash, with his hands chained together? And of course shaving would be out of the question; he could feel the bristles itchy on his face. On the other hand, he didn't want to face his father looking like a slave even if, technically, he was one—a filthy, dirt-encrusted one.

The female slave returned with more beer and a large hunk of bread for Allen. He wolfed them down while she looked at him with large, scared eyes, and then she ran off with the empty utensils. Perhaps she'd never seen an Englishman naked, dirty, and in shackles before. Or perhaps living in fear was normal for the slaves in this household.

Allen stood, the chains dragging on the floor and the manacles rubbing against his wrists, and took inventory. Every bit of him ached, throbbed, or stung. He hobbled like an old man to use the bucket in the corner, and then investigated the ring to which the chains were locked. Although the ironwork looked too solid and well constructed for him to be able to damage, he tried swinging his manacles at the ring and gained more bruises on his wrists as a reward.

Like it or not, he was going to have to rely on Elizabeth Blight's goodwill, and he wasn't sure that he trusted her.

He heard the door swing open again, accompanied by a rumbling sound, which turned out to be a large wooden tub rolled in by two slave women. Mrs. Blight followed, carrying a large basket from which she took a length of cotton. She unfolded the fabric to line the tub, and snapped out orders at slaves bearing large buckets of steaming water. Two more dragged in a pallet. How long did she expect Allen to stay here?

He meanwhile stood aside, manacled hands crossed over his genitals, and hoped his humiliation was not too obvious. The two women who had brought in the tub remained with Mrs. Blight while the rest of them trooped out.

"Molly and Jane will help you wash," Mrs. Blight said. She handed one of the women a lump of soap, and dabbled her hand in the water as though inviting a reluctant child.

"Thank you, ma'am." He shuffled over to the tub and lowered his aching body into the water. For one long, glorious moment, his pain and embarrassment faded away.

The women washed him, one starting at his head, the other at his feet, and he wondered vaguely what would happen when they met, and then really didn't care anymore. He lay back, eyes closed, wondering at his return to infancy.

"If you please, sah . . ." One of the women tapped his shoulder.

He understood. He leaned forward, head on his knees, as she washed his back and shoulders, scrubbing with a kind efficiency.

As Allen sank back into the water, he heard a rustle of skirts and another pair of hands, smaller and softer, patted his feet dry and applied salve to them—he could smell the tallow and some sort of pungent herb.

"You are in such a state, Mr. Pendale," Mrs. Blight cooed.

He was indeed, although not as she meant, and he hoped the water, opaque with grime, hid his condition. The warmth and comfort, as well as the touch of female hands, had given him a monstrous erection. He was half dead, exhausted and aching, covered in bruises and scrapes, but his prick was alive and well and begging for attention.

"Thank you, Mrs. Blight," he murmured. "You're very kind."

"Can you stand, Mr. Pendale?" She held out a linen towel, her eyes modestly averted.

He stepped out onto another towel she had laid on the floor; then he grasped the linen in front of him. As he did so, the two slaves dragged the tub out of the room, and he heard the splash of water emptied onto the ground outside. Then the door closed, leaving him alone with Elizabeth Blight.

"We haven't washed everything," she murmured, pulling a bucket of water toward her.

The slut, he thought, appalled and lustful. "I don't think . . ." His attempt at polite demurral was pitiful. Once again he was letting his prick make the decisions.

"If I may, Mr. Pendale . . ." But she wasn't asking for permission. She was behind him, soaping his arse, running her fingers between his buttocks to nudge his ballocks, stroking the inside of his thighs. Her intention was absolutely clear. He found himself, to his alarm, spreading his feet apart a little to allow her better access.

"My, you have a big one, Mr. Pendale." Her hand

appeared at the base of his cock—of course he lifted his bound wrists so he could see. The words of a practiced whore, uttered with breathy gentility, almost made him laugh aloud.

She resumed soaping his arse and thighs, rinsed, and then, with a lewd trail of her hand across his buttocks, stood in front of him. She actually licked her lips.

"And now, I must wash this big fellow," she simpered, grasping Allen with a wet, soapy hand.

Allen didn't protest. Far from it. He pushed into her hand, bringing his manacled wrists over her head so her bosom tickled his chest while she pinched and squeezed with a bright, professional air. He was alive, damn it. He had not been eaten by rats or died of thirst—he would become Allen Pendale, English gentleman, again, and if this woman wanted to take advantage of him, well, it was something in the nature of a celebration. A fleshly feast. He would thwart Blight by fucking his wife, a fine revenge, particularly as she was the one instigating the act.

"May I reciprocate, ma'am?" Damn these manacles.

"If you would be so kind, Mr. Pendale." Mrs. Blight turned, presenting her back to him so he could unbutton her gown and unlace her stays.

Allen hoisted up her shift and observed her round white arse. Very nice. Fleshy. If he'd had a hand free, he would slap her to see the skin turn pink. As it was, with his wrists encumbered, he couldn't get a good swing at her.

He admired the sway of her large, pink-tipped breasts, the slight wobble of thighs and bum above blue garters and cream stockings, as she arranged herself on the pallet.

Her hand wandered idly to the burst of dark blond hair between her thighs, touching the pink, wet flesh within, parting herself, exposing her sex to him. It was crude and vulgar and just what he wanted. Oh yes, Elizabeth Blight was skilled at her profession.

With a jangle of chains, he limped over to her and thudded to his knees before her. Above her, manacled wrists over her head, yes, biting her mouth and neck and those big breasts. Like an animal. He plunged inside her, growling, while she emitted small shrieks and cries in that silly genteel way, while her hips pumped as vigorously as his own, heels locked behind his back.

She had an orgasm—at least, he thought that was what happened when she stiffened, arched, and clutched his arms—but he didn't care if it was real or not. This was for his pleasure, his release, his future liberty. *Yes.*

He collapsed on her and she pushed him off with an annoyed grunt and stood. He heard the scrape of wicker on the floor and imagined she fetched something, some sort of feminine device maybe, to rid herself of his semen. If she'd asked him, he would have withdrawn; he was a gentleman. Or possibly he wouldn't have. Let Blight have a cuckoo in his nest. A coal black cuckoo, maybe? Allen's thoughts drifted to litters of puppies and kittens. You rarely knew how they would turn out, whatever their dams and sires looked like. He listened to the rustles, the pop of a cork released from a bottle, and caught the scent of rum.

Then he heard the rattle and creak of the door opening.

"Why, Mr. Blight, Mr. Pendale and I are most gratified that you have been able to join us."

Clarissa sat with Celia in a shady spot in the garden. A footman waved a palm branch to create a breeze; another stood by with lemonade in case either of the ladies was thirsty. If Clarissa turned a little, away from the house and the manicured lawn, she saw sinuous vines and bright blooms, the island trying to take back its own. Every day a gardener had to cut the vegetation back.

She and Celia had books on their laps. Clarissa turned the pages, unable to absorb a word. Celia had fallen asleep, lulled by the heat.

A woman, a slave, marched purposefully toward them. Clarissa stiffened, wondering whether she came with bad news about March, and then relaxed as she realized the slave did not approach from the house. The woman stopped to talk with a gardener, and gave a low, rich chuckle. Clarissa started. For a moment she was reminded vividly of Allen and found herself looking round for him, before acknowledging that worry and interrupted sleep made her imagine things. If she were not so tired, she would feel bitterly disappointed that he had not come to visit March. As it was, Allen's neglect was only another layer of sadness. March had not mentioned his name once since they had last seen him.

The footman with the palm branch now walked over to the slave woman, and after a brief conversation with her, he came back to Clarissa.

"Ceres, she want to talk to you, Miss Onslowe."

"Who is she?"

"She de cook."

Did the slaves know that Clarissa was Mrs. Lemarchand and expect to take orders from her? She was certain Finch would not breathe a word of the marriage last night, as they had agreed. She nodded and waited for the woman to approach, which she did with a familiar, loose stride. Even more familiar was her stance, feet planted slightly apart, chin raised.

Clarissa really was sick from lack of sleep. She was seeing Allen everywhere.

"Miss Onslowe," the woman said, "I come to you 'bout Allen Pendale."

Clarissa glanced cautiously at Celia, whose book had tumbled to the ground, her breathing slow and deep. "What of him?"

"Where he gone?"

"He's at Lord Frensham's house, I believe." What trouble was Allen in now? "Why do you want to know?"

CHAPTER 24

When Clarissa knocked at the door of the Blights' house, a sullen-looking female slave answered.

"Dey not home, missus."

"Not even Mrs. Blight?"

The girl shook her head.

Clarissa didn't believe her. Where would Elizabeth Blight have gone, anyway? "I hear she has a new slave. A man, light-skinned, who is proving difficult."

The words made Clarissa sick, although not as sick as the way Ceres had described Mrs. Blight's activities. *She like to play wid de slaves, missus, like a cat play wid de mouse. De men slaves.* Just as Clarissa had suspected. What she hadn't expected was to discover the secret of Allen's parentage.

The girl hesitated.

Clarissa reached to unhook one of her earrings, a simple pearl bob. "I'll give you these if you tell me where they are."

The slave looked around as though expecting one of the Blights to leap from out of nowhere. Now Clarissa saw, on the dark skin around one bloodshot eye, a purple swelling.

The girl grabbed the earring, and held out her hand for the other. "Round de back. In de yard." The earrings clutched in her fist, she slammed the door in Clarissa's face.

Clarissa made her way round to the yard, where Rissa had been whipped, hoping she would not see Allen hung in the burning sun, his back bloodied. No one was there except for a cat sunning itself on the cobbles. At Clarissa's approach it stood, stretched, and sauntered away.

Then Clarissa heard the sound of a whip cracking through the air and a grunt of pain. A door hung ajar—it looked like the door to a storeroom or some such—and she ran toward it, flinging it open.

Blight turned to her, whip in hand.

"Just in time for a bit of sport, Miss Onslowe. What do you think of your lover now?"

"What do you mean?" Clarissa demanded.

A slave stood against the wall, shackled upright by his wrists, blood oozing from stripes across his back. A fair-skinned man. Darker than her, of course. She knew that skin, that back, that body. Knew it with every fiber and breath of her own.

"Not so proud now, is he?" Mrs. Blight, whom Clarissa had barely noticed, stepped forward. Her hair was disordered, her gown askew and rumpled. She held a rum bottle in one hand. With the other she reached for the whip. "Would you care for a turn, Miss Onslowe?"

Clarissa held out her hand. Her fingers closed on the whip handle, smooth leather, darkened and slick with sweat. She whirled and swung the whip at Blight.

"Let him go, damn you!"

"Have a care, Miss Onslowe." Blight looked amused at her efforts. "It's on the master's orders."

She swung the whip again, heard the rush and crack as it flew through the air, and had the gratification of seeing Blight drop to his knees, one hand clutched to his face. Mrs. Blight gave a gasp of dismay and rushed to his side.

"And I speak for the master. Release him."

"You've no authority." Blight, blood streaming down his face, staggered to his feet. "Give me the whip, Miss Onslowe."

"Address me correctly, if you please." She tossed the whip away and reached into the pocket of her gown—a large, old-fashioned pocket that could hold, for instance, a loaded pistol. She raised the pistol and cocked it, an elegant, deadly thing of tooled silverwork and gleaming wood. Some days ago Finch had shown her and Celia how to load and fire the weapon, in case, as he said, the slaves should make trouble.

The Blights stared at her.

"The question is," Clarissa continued, "which of you I'll shoot. Who do you think, Mr. Blight? You or your bride?"

"Miss Onslowe, I beg of you—do nothing rash," Mrs. Blight whimpered.

"That is no longer my name, ma'am, and I tire of your obtuseness. Release him, Blight."

"You're a madwoman," Blight said in disgust.

She shifted the pistol and aimed it at Elizabeth Blight. "Enough of your insolence, Blight. You'll release Pendale now. Otherwise I fear you will be a widower sooner than you anticipated, instead of merely a cuckold."

"I beg of you—" Blight swallowed. "Spare her."

So her intuition was correct—love had made a fool of Blight, too. "Unlock his shackles now!"

Clarissa kept the pistol trained on Elizabeth Blight, who wept softly in between taking swigs from the rum bottle. Clarissa hoped Allen was not so badly injured that he could not move. She had seen blood ooze from his feet, the bruising and cuts over most of his body as he hung limp in the chains.

As he unlocked the shackles, Blight muttered, "Lemarchand won't like it. You'll lose your position for sure when he hears of this."

Allen slumped to the floor, scrambled to his feet, and to her relief, limped out of the room into the courtyard.

"I am Mrs. Lemarchand, a position only God shall remove, Blight, and you're a fool." For good measure, and to distract them as much as anything, she lifted the pistol and fired it above the Blights' heads, then whirled, ran out into the yard, and threw the bolt on the door.

Her fingers stung from the recoil of the pistol, her ears rang from the shot, and she felt sick at what she had become in that small space of time.

"My felicitations, Mrs. Lemarchand." Allen's voice was raspy and tight with pain. He sank to the cobbles, his shoulder propped against a wall.

"My thanks. And you fucked Elizabeth Blight."

Allen looked at her with a coldness that made her feel as though she was the one who was naked. "Why did you marry him?"

"Because he's dying and I—I love him."

"He arranged—this." He gestured at the storeroom door. "He wanted me to die. I would have disappeared, just another light-skinned slave, no great loss. Are you sure you can love a man like that?"

She stared at Allen in horror. "I don't believe you."

"He owns me, Clarissa. He handed me over to Blight."

"No." She shook her head, raised a hand to her mouth. Tears ran down her face. "I don't believe you," she repeated. "He would never—"

"He did. I was imprisoned in his slave dungeon. I thought I'd die there. And you married him. I wish you joy, ma'am."

Things happened fast after that, in a sort of blur. Allen could barely walk on his injured feet, but Clarissa fetched him some clothes from somewhere—Blight's, Allen guessed—and he sat in the sunlight, chilled and aching, wondering why the heat had so little effect on him. Clarissa, white-faced and holding herself very straight, sent a slave to his father's house. She handed Allen a mug of beer, guessing how thirsty he was, and he thanked her.

Certainly they were civil enough, but there was nothing more to say.

Allen set the beer mug down, closed his eyes, wondering when he would ever feel warm again, and fell into a restless doze, dreaming of uneasy dark places and people who wanted to do terrible things to him.

A clatter of hooves woke him—his father's trap, pulling up so violently that sparks flew from the horses' feet. His father dropped the reins and scrambled out, furious and undignified, and burst into tears.

Allen rose with some difficulty and was grasped in a painful hug while his father ranted in between sobs. "That bastard Lemarchand—I'll kill him, I swear. I'll call him out. How dare he. My boy, my boy, what have they done to you? Death's too good for him. I'll make him pay. Can we sue him? At the very least I'll refuse him passage home on the *Amaryllis*."

"Calm yourself, Papa." Allen hadn't called him that in years. He extricated himself from his father's embrace as the earl's angry words slowed to a halt. Better to let him rave like a madman here than at the actual negotiations. "I'm afraid, Papa, you will be paying Lemarchand."

"The despicable whoreson!"

Allen patted his father's arm. "Forty pieces of silver, sir."

"How the devil can you jest about it, Allen!"

Allen didn't have the energy to explain to his father that jesting was preferable to dwelling on what had happened—the hours in the slave dungeon, the scrape of manacles on his wrists and ankles, the awful despair.

"Sir, may I introduce Mrs. Lemarchand. It is thanks to her that we sent for you."

"Ma'am," his father said, bowing, the automatic re-action of a gentleman. He didn't seem at all put out that minutes before he had been heartily cursing her husband.

And so they now sat in March's library, where other deli-cate business—a contract for a mistress, for instance—had been conducted. Allen realized it was up to him to run the proceedings. His father was too flustered, still liable to burst into angry tears.

March sat at one end of the table, looking gaunt and ill, his face set. He did not look at Allen, who sat at the other end of the table, his father to his right.

Allen asked Finch to send for Ceres. She padded into the library barefoot, and Allen was the only man to stand, although after an awkward pause, his father did, too, and offered her a chair on Allen's left.

Ceres looked at Allen. "What dey do to you, boy?"

"I'm well enough," he said.

She shook her head. "You not." She looked at March. "I buy my freedom, sah." She placed a leather bag of coins on the table.

Allen turned to March. He could hardly bear to look at this man who had first loved him and then betrayed him. "The Earl of Frensham underwrites this endeavor, sir—the price of freedom for myself and Ceres. I suggest you discuss exact terms with him."

March's eyes were as cold as ice. He nodded.

Allen's father rose and went to the far end of the table to confer with March.

Ceres put her hand on Allen's wrist. "You too hot. You got de fever."

"No, I'm well enough. Tell me, how did you find out where I was?"

"We know everyt'in'."

That was what she'd said before. She proceeded to tell Allen how there was a rumor among the slaves that Blight, with the help of his wife, had a new slave to break, a light-skinned man. When Allen had not come to see her the day after their meeting, Ceres became concerned enough to seek out Clarissa. He sensed in her terse words the disappointment of a woman who had learned not to hope. Why Clarissa? She shrugged and repeated that the slaves knew everything.

The Earl of Frensham rose from his seat and rejoined his son, indicating that the negotiations were over.

Allen drew a fresh piece of paper toward him, sharpened a pen, and wrote out a manumission, the official document declaring that Ceres was now a freed woman.

And then Allen's. His hand shook as he wrote; how many other slaves had been privileged to write their own manumissions?

> ... a negro man slave, named Allen Jonathan Robert Pendale, shall and may become free, have manumitted, emancipated, enfranchised, and set free, the aforesaid negro man slave, named Allen Jonathan Robert Pendale, for ever; hereby giving, granting, and releasing unto him, the said Allen Jonathan Robert Pendale, all

*right, title, dominion, sovereignty, and property,
which, as lord and master over the aforesaid
Allen Jonathan Robert Pendale, I have had, or
which I now have, or by any means whatsoever
I may or can hereafter possibly have over him
the aforesaid Negro, for ever.*

March looked Allen in the eye for the first time that day and signed with Finch as witness, and it was done.

Allen stood, a free man once more. The library rocked around him, and he thought for a moment he was aboard a ship. The pen rolled from his fingers and left a trail of ink on the table.

Allen read the document again, his eyes dwelling on the words *for ever*. An eternity, a void, like the one whose edge he tottered on, sick and dizzy. He was free to fall, to let go, away from the sudden clamor of voices and the clatter of a chair tipped onto the floor.

CHAPTER 25

"I really don't think your visit is a good idea, Mrs. Lemarchand," the Earl of Frensham said. "He's been ill for a week, and his fever has only just broken."

"Sir," Clarissa said, "I understand that you feel you have nearly lost your son not once, but twice, with this illness. I beg of you to have pity on me. I am like to lose my own husband, and—" She couldn't continue.

"I'm sorry, Mrs. Lemarchand." The earl stood and opened the drawing room door. "May I suggest you leave my son alone?"

"I know you leave for England soon—"

"As soon as the cargo is loaded, yes, ma'am. I trust this is not a ploy to appeal to my better nature and take passage with us, for I must tell you that I shall not have that man on my ship—"

"Good day to you." Clarissa walked past the earl as

though leaving his house in indignation, but once she was out of the room, she dashed for the staircase.

By a stroke of luck, she found Allen's bedchamber quite easily. Of course he was not alone and, to her regret, fast asleep.

Ceres sat at his bedside, knitting. She looked at Clarissa with deep distrust. "Dis no place for you, Mrs. Lemarchand."

"I—I had to see him. To explain . . ."

Clarissa walked over to the bed and gazed down at Allen. The strong, sturdy man she knew now had a fragility that shocked her, his cheekbones sharper than ever, deep shadows beneath his eyes. Was he fading away like March?

" 'Im strong," Ceres said. " 'Im get better." Her needles clicked.

Allen turned over, sat up, and scratched his head. He blinked at Clarissa and rubbed his face. "What are you doing here, Mrs. Lemarchand?"

"Don't call me that."

Ceres gathered her knitting and left the room.

Clarissa couldn't look at him. She twisted her hands together. "I came to tell you how sorry I am. About everything. I should have—"

Allen's hand clasped hers. She stared at his hand, at the healing cuts and fading bruises, the marks of the shackles on his skin.

"Stop. What's done is done."

"I know you must feel—"

"You know nothing!" He released her hand. "Don't

dare to presume to tell me anything. You cannot know, and I hope you never do, what it is like to find your whole life, the person you thought yourself to be, is a fabrication. Neither do you know what it is to be betrayed by those you love, or who profess to love you."

"I'm sorry." Clarissa kept her head lowered so he did not see the tears in her eyes. "I suppose there is no possibility of forgiveness."

"None. Please leave." Allen lay down and turned away, ending the conversation.

Two weeks later they boarded the Earl of Frensham's ship, the *Amaryllis,* with its hold full of sugar. Allen had heard nothing further from March or Clarissa; as far as he knew, March still lived, but had not yet left for England. Allen gazed back at the shore of the island, where his life had changed forever, watching the gentle sway of the palm trees and the gleam of the white sands. His hand crept into the pocket where his manumission lay: Allen Pendale, freedman.

"How are you feeling, Allen? We'll sail with the evening tide, in a couple of hours," his father said.

"I'm quite well, sir." *And I know when the tide is.* He was becoming tired of his father's solicitude, of being treated like a child, and then felt guilty about his irritation.

His mother, Ceres—or Mrs. Silcombe, as he should think of her now—came to his side and they stood together in silence. She had chosen to name herself after Allen's farm, with the married form of address as a courtesy he insisted on—slaves did not marry. She had mentioned, with her usual stoicism, four other children she had lost as babies, to Allen's dismay and sadness. She volunteered no information on who fathered them.

"Look." She pointed to a smudge of smoke inland that blossomed into a dark column. "Dat Lemarchand's boiling house."

Others joined them at the rail, talking excitedly of the conflagration, the damage that would be caused by such a catastrophic fire. As they watched, another column of smoke arose.

"By God, the slaves must have done it!" Frensham trained a telescope on the shore.

"A slave uprising?" Allen asked.

Frensham lowered the telescope. "Oh yes. It happens from time to time, and God knows, we all warned Lemarchand of his excessive cruelty to his slaves. Yet he insists on keeping such vermin as Blight in his employ. . . . Well, I trust Lemarchand has got out in time."

Allen stared at the columns of smoke. What if March had not escaped? And what of Clarissa and Celia? He turned to his father. "I must make sure Mrs. Lemarchand is safe."

"Allen, I beg of you—don't go!"

"I'll do nothing rash."

His father thumped one fist onto the rail. "You don't need to do anything rash to be in danger. You don't understand. The slaves will kill indiscriminately, without reason or pity. They—"

"They're like animals. Yes, I understand. Remember you talk to a man who carries his manumission in his pocket." He walked away from his father and addressed the captain. "Sir, if you please, lower the longboat. I need to go ashore."

"There's not much time before the tide turns, sir."

"Allen!" His father was almost in tears, and Allen could understand his fear that he was about to risk losing his son again.

"Let 'im go." Mrs. Silcombe touched the earl's sleeve. It was the first time Allen had seen either of them break the wary silence they maintained.

His father nodded.

"Good-bye, Papa." He embraced his father and then, for the first time, his mother before swinging overboard on a loop of rope into the longboat.

Allen told the sailors who rowed him to the jetty to wait for him until the tide turned and then walked up the beach through pristine white sand, hoping he'd be able to recognize the opening in the mangroves that led to March's house. Yes, there it was—he recognized the fantastically bent and knobbled tree under which he'd loitered, watching March and Clarissa caress each other.

The air was moist and thick with insects intent on flying up his nose and into his mouth and eyes. He wished he had a cheroot to ward them off. He removed his coat, waistcoat, and neckcloth, his shirt becoming drenched with sweat, and the scent of burning, overlaid with the acrid stink of burning sugar, became stronger as he started up the slope to the house, making his way along the oyster-shell path that wound through sinuous vines. He could hear voices now—yelling and shouting, and an insistent heavy thudding.

As Allen came to the edge of the wilderness, he heard the sound of a horse tearing at grass. A horse harnessed to a trap, presumably for the Lemarchands' escape, had wandered onto the lawn and was contentedly grazing. So they must still be there. Allen captured the horse's reins and tethered it to a nearby branch.

Something that looked like a crumpled heap of cloth lay a little way off. Still keeping in the shade of the tropical greenery, he moved to investigate. As he drew nearer, he heard flies buzzing, and the heap of cloth became a human shape, and one he knew. Finch. Finch with his throat slashed, blood soaking into his clothes and into the green of the lawn, his eyes staring blank at the sky.

A group of slaves using a huge timber as a battering ram attacked the front door of the house. Every window was shuttered and presumably bolted from inside, although several panes of glass were broken.

Allen tossed his outer clothes into the trap and ran toward the house. He hoped that his initial impression, of a dark man in shirtsleeves, would be enough to make him blend in for as long as he needed—until the slaves saw he was wearing shoes and heard him speak, of course. Then he'd have to rely on his own wits.

Allen got as far as the steps before someone recognized him and let out an angry shout. A young boy—he could only have been about twelve—ran up to Allen, waving a machete, dark eyes wide with fear and excitement.

Allen stood still, his hands spread to show he was un-armed, and then, because the lad didn't stop, sidestepped, grasped the boy's wrist, and disarmed him. Allen tossed down the machete, then ran to the top of the steps and turned to face the slaves. He'd seen riots before; he knew how a crowd could be swayed, cowed, or enraged. He knew he could not stop them, nor could he condemn them.

This crowd, faced with a man they knew to be a white master who was yet something else, slowed, muttering.

Allen looked down at them, at men maddened be-yond endurance, machetes glinting in the sunlight, and knew this might be the last thing he ever saw. Within seconds he could be dead meat like Finch, a butchered thing.

"I'm Allen Pendale," he said in the relative silence, "and I have been abused as you have been, but only for a few days, not my entire life. You know my story. You know I'm lucky enough that I had family to help me and I can go to England. And when I'm there, I swear I'll do all I can to end the misery of slavery. I'll offer safe passage to any of you who wants to come with me and take your chances there. You'll still have to work hard, but no one will own you. You can't be a slave in England.

"I'm only one man, and although the white master in me wants to stop you from taking the house, I know I can't. But I have a quarrel with Lemarchand, as you well know. Leave him and his family to me."

There was some hesitation. One of the men—Allen

recognized him as a groom in Lemarchand's stable—held out a strangely shaped object to Allen. He took it with some hesitation before he realized it was a goatskin filled with sour beer, which he took and drank from, spilling some down his shirt.

Another man, whom Allen didn't recognize, nodded. "You take de master den."

"And his wife and daughter."

They nodded and grinned at Allen.

Allen passed the goatskin to the boy he'd disarmed, stepped back, and let the assault on the front door continue.

The solid mahogany shuddered, splintered, and caved in, and the slaves poured into the house. A large china vase that stood on a plinth in the entrance hall flew against the wall and smashed into pieces on the floor. Allen winced, thinking of china shards like glass under bare feet, but the men rampaged into the house in a wave of anger.

Let them. He couldn't stop them. He glanced up the stairs and saw someone move on the landing—a whisk of skirts. "Clarissa!" he shouted. "Celia! It's I, Allen." He ran up the stairs, in the direction he'd seen the fleeing figure take.

"Stop!" Celia stood outside her father's bedchamber, a pistol in her hands. She was shaking, but the muzzle of the pistol wavered up and down at his chest level. He had no doubt it was loaded.

"Put the pistol down, Miss Celia, if you please." This was a far more troublesome situation than a wildly excited young lad with a machete.

"No! You're one of them. I'll shoot you."

"I'm Allen Pendale. I'm the man who treads on your feet when we dance."

"Stay away!"

"I can crack Brazil nuts and keep the kernel whole, remember?" Allen walked toward her slowly, his voice calm and soothing, hoping she wouldn't panic and pull the trigger. "Give me the pistol."

"No," Celia wailed, then burst into tears.

He gripped her wrist, pointed the pistol away from them both, and uncocked it. Then he took her in his arms.

"All is well," he crooned into her ear. "You're a brave girl."

"I couldn't shoot you." She sobbed messily on his shoulder.

March's bedchamber door opened, revealing Clarissa. Like Celia, she was dressed for traveling in a bonnet and long cloak. "Where's Finch?"

"Finch?" Allen asked.

"He went to fetch the trap. What's happening? What are you doing here, Allen? And . . ." She'd obviously heard the sounds from downstairs.

"You have a mob of slaves breaking up the house," Allen said. "Come with me and I'll get you out of here. I imagine fairly soon they'll set the house on fire. You must leave with me now."

"I can't. Not without March."

"He may go to the devil."

"He is my husband, Allen."

He stared at her in disbelief. "After what he's done,

you're still besotted with him? You're a fool, Clarissa. Leave him."

"I can't. I'm sorry, Allen. I can't. I loved him once."

"Mr. Allen!" Nerissa ran toward them. "I want to come to England wid you."

"Oh, thank God, they don't all hate us," Celia cried.

Nerissa avoided her embrace. "I want to be free like 'im said downstairs, 'cause you a silly, spoiled girl, Miss Celia. I want to work and be paid."

"Excellent," Allen said. "You can start earning right now by helping me carry Mr. Lemarchand and his belongings outside."

Allen pushed past Clarissa and into the bedchamber.

March stood at the window, watching the smoke swirl outside. "The roof of the boiling house has just fallen in," he remarked. "The smithy and the dairy are both gone, too."

"Your house is next, sir. If you wish to perish in it, you may do so, or you may accept my assistance in helping you leave."

"Your assistance, Pendale?"

"Yes, mine. Pray make up your mind. I don't care greatly one way or the other, but Clarissa will not budge unless you do."

"I see." March turned, and Allen saw he leaned heavily on a cane. "I had to do it, Pendale. If she had come to you with your story, I should have lost her to you."

"What makes you think you have her now?" Allen offered his arm. "May I suggest less philosophy and a little more speed, sir?"

March drew on his gloves and laid his fingertips on Allen's arm as though he were afraid of contagion. "I do not generally let Negroes touch me."

"Unless you're fucking them," Allen returned. "I do not generally ransack houses, sir, although I can see now why the compulsion should strike."

Allen turned March over to Clarissa and Celia, and he and Nerissa dragged the large trunk of belongings, which, apart from smaller bags the women carried, seemed to be all that they had had time to pack.

The smell of burning wafted up from downstairs, although the sound of the voices and some drunken singing suggested the slaves had broached March's cellars.

The descent of the staircase took longer than Allen would have liked. March was frail enough that he needed to rest every few steps, and the smoke in the house, now quite thick, made all of them cough. As they crossed the entry hall, a ceiling beam came down in a burst of flames in one of the flanking rooms. Allen wondered how long the house could last—and how long it would be before one of the slaves saw them leave and reconsidered the tenuous bargain they had struck.

There was also the slight matter of catching the tide.

Trying not to let his impatience show, Allen fetched the trap and helped everyone climb in, then whipped the horse into a fast trot—best not to make it seem as if they were in too much of a hurry to leave. The horse was skittish of the flames and smoke coming from the house, and Allen had to concentrate on keeping the pace steady.

Behind Allen, Celia screamed, and he heard the angry yells of the slaves. Something crashed into the trap—one of March's bottles of claret, splashing them with red, and scattering splinters of glass—and Allen whipped the horse to a gallop across the lawn and along the road that led to the sea.

One month later, aboard the Amaryllis

"Get some air, my dear." The words were little more than a whisper. Clarissa had to lean close to March to hear them.

"Later," she said. She didn't like to go on deck during the day, when the others might be there.

"You need daylight."

His hand uncurled from hers. Every day, it seemed, his bones became more prominent, his skin waxier and yellowish, and he retreated further into a place where she could not follow. The light of the lamp overhead made a death mask of his face.

Don't watch the lamp sway, she reminded herself.

"If you're sure . . ." She snatched her cloak, trying not to appear too hurried, as the nausea threatened to return. She bolted out of the cabin and onto the deck, breathing cold, salty air through her nose. Above, the sails roared like wind through tall trees—how she longed for England, for the gentle misty green of lawns and trees and hedges. But every day they sailed closer to home was a day closer to March's death.

On deck, a familiar scene played itself out. Allen and

his mother strolled together, deep in conversation, her hand on his arm. Now and again she turned her head to his and smiled. Lord Frensham, tall and silver-haired, hovered about them—there was no other way to put it— occasionally staggering with the movement of the ship, looking mostly at the son he had nearly lost, but occasionally at the woman who had borne Allen.

The three of them saw Clarissa, and she was actually glad that at that moment the nausea returned, and instead of an awkward confrontation, she had to lurch for the side of the ship.

Someone put a hand on her shoulder. Even in her wretchedness, she knew whose it was—a large, square hand, clad in a leather glove.

"I've lost a guinea on you." Allen Pendale pushed a cup of steaming liquid into her hand.

"Thank you." Tears rose to her eyes, not so much from gratitude for the ginger tea, but that he had enough regard still to include her in the seasickness stakes. At the same time, she scolded herself for how a small scrap of kindness could undo her so thoroughly.

Allen stood next to her at the rail, swaying easily with the rhythm of the ship. "Take small sips." He sighed and handed Clarissa a handkerchief. "Don't cry."

"May I remind you I have quite a lot to cry about?"

"Well, let's see. You're about to be rid of a murderous blackguard of a husband and inherit a great deal of money— Ah, don't Clarissa. I'm sorry."

She blew her nose into his handkerchief, noting with a certain sour pleasure that it would not be of much use to him now and took stock of her belly; would the tea stay there?

He rested his elbows on the side, hands linked, and stared out at the wilderness of shifting gray-green waves. "How is he?"

"Oh . . . weaker every day." She stared into the bottom of the cup, twisting it between her hands. A few specks of grated ginger clung to the bottom.

"Does he ever speak of me?" Allen's voice was so quiet and raw with pain she barely made out the words.

Clarissa laid a hand on his arm. "No. He's dying, Allen, and he barely speaks to me now. It's as though he sets out on his own voyage. Do you wish to forgive him?"

Allen shrugged. "I suppose, for my own sanity, I must, whether he hears it or not. Regretfully, I do not believe he will ever forgive me—for not loving him, and for being who and what I am."

"I'm sorry." She didn't want to start saying she was sorry; there was so much to be sorry for, she was afraid she would never stop. "What is Celia doing? Maybe I should send her to sit with him, although he is probably asleep."

"She's below, probably fighting with Nerissa. They're at it like cats and dogs, according to Mrs. Silcombe." Allen paused. "I'm curious about something—the circumstances of your marriage."

Clarissa turned to him, surprised, and somewhat suspicious. "Well, we were married in the middle of the night by Father O'Brien. March thought he was dying, so . . ."

"And that was it? A marriage by the rites of the Catholic Church?"

"Yes." She had the nasty feeling she was on trial, being needled by a clever lawyer.

He threw back his head and laughed. "You're not married, Clarissa. There is nothing remotely legal about such a marriage, whatever March may have told you. There's no way now to even make it legal under the law. The bastard."

Tears rose to her eyes. "I made a vow, Allen."

"Ah, don't cry any more, Clarissa." He placed an arm around her shoulders. "Whose child is it, my love?"

So he'd guessed. "I don't know. I'm sorry. I don't even know if you want it to be yours."

He grinned. "Well, to put it delicately, there was rather a lot of spunk flying around."

She snorted. "*Delicately,* Mr. Pendale?" She leaned her head against his shoulder. "I am so sorry, Allen. So sorry for what happened."

"I, too."

"I have always liked you above any man I ever knew."

"Well, I'd hoped for a more passionate declaration," he said, but held her closer.

Clarissa broke away. "I am pregnant, sad, and either vomiting or on the brink of doing so all the time, Allen, and you can hardly expect more from me at the moment. And I am a fool."

Allen grinned and caught her hand. "No more than I am, my love."

"What will you do when we return?"

"Ah. I, too, made a vow of sorts, to March's slaves.

I've sat too long on the fence, but a spell in irons in a slave dungeon can be very persuasive. I plan to be quite busy and troublesome. I believe the abolitionists could use a competent lawyer." He took the cup from her and shook the last drops of liquid overboard. "My father wishes to free his slaves as an example to other plantation owners, and to form some sort of utopian community. While I applaud the idea, I can't help but think he's finally entering his dotage. And Mrs. Silcombe thinks I should marry. So I shall, I expect, when I'm not quite so busy."

"Of course."

"My bride should be a capable, practical sort of woman who knows how to run a household, and can get along with Mrs. Silcombe, and who can give me a son to inherit my farm. I'd have no objection to a daughter, though. Would you know such a woman? She doesn't have to be particularly young, but she should be quite lecherous."

"I believe I do, although the woman in question has to give up lechery for sleeping and vomiting."

"It won't be forever. Do you remember when we first met aboard the *Daphne*? You thought me an utter fool."

"You were."

"I told you then I had not met a woman worth marrying or worth dying for. Do you remember?"

"Oh, yes. I remember. I remember also that you had a certain weakness for other men's wives."

"And other men's abandoned, pregnant mistresses— one of whom, I'm happy to say, is worth marrying or dying for." Allen let go of Clarissa's hand and stripped off his glove, turning back the sleeve of his coat. New pink skin marked where the manacles had torn his flesh. "I carry other scars. I can't deny the circumstances of my birth, but I'm not yet sure who I am or what I can be. What we can be, you and I, Clarissa."

She took his hand, running her fingertips over the familiar bones and skin.

Allen wrapped his cloak around them both. For the moment, it was enough—a moment of sweetness on this great ship full of sugar as the winds blew them toward familiar shores.

ABOUT THE AUTHOR

Jane Lockwood is the pseudonym of a writer whose award-winning debut was released by Penguin in 2005. Before becoming a writer, she worked as an archaeologist, draftsperson, classical music radio announcer, arts publicist, and editorial assistant at a small press. She lives near Washington, D.C. Find out more about Jane at www.janetmullany.com/janelockwood.htm.